MW01031379

AGENTS OF MAYHEM

AGENTS OF MAYHEM

FEDERAL AGENTS OF MAGIC™ BOOK TWO

TR CAMERON   MARTHA CARR   MICHAEL ANDERLE

DISRUPTIVE IMAGINATION

This book is a work of fiction.

All of the characters, organizations, and events portrayed in this novel
are either products of the author's imagination or are used fictitiously.
Sometimes both.

Copyright © 2019 TR Cameron, Martha Carr and Michael Anderle
Cover Art by Jake @ J Caleb Design
http://jcalebdesign.com / jcalebdesign@gmail.com
Cover copyright © LMBPN Publishing
A Michael Anderle Production

LMBPN Publishing supports the right to free expression and the value of
copyright. The purpose of copyright is to encourage writers and artists
to produce the creative works that enrich our culture.

The distribution of this book without permission is a theft of the
author's intellectual property. If you would like permission to use
material from the book (other than for review purposes), please contact
support@lmbpn.com. Thank you for your support of the author's rights.

LMBPN Publishing
PMB 196, 2540 South Maryland Pkwy
Las Vegas, NV 89109

First US edition, April 2019
Version 1.03, July 2019
Print ISBN: 978-1-64202-231-5

The Oriceran Universe (and what happens within / characters /
situations / worlds) are Copyright © 2017-19 by Martha Carr and
LMBPN Publishing.

AGENTS OF MAYHEM TEAM

Thanks to our beta reading team
Mary Morris, Nicole Emens, John Ashmore, Larry Omans,
and Kelly O'Donnell

Thanks to the JIT Readers

Micky Cocker
Diane L. Smith
Misty Roa

If we've missed anyone, please let us know!

Editor
The Skyhunter Editing Team

DEDICATIONS

From Martha

To everyone who still believes in magic
and all the possibilities that holds.
To all the readers who make this
entire ride so much fun.
And to my son, Louie and so many wonderful friends who
remind me all the time of what
really matters and how wonderful
life can be in any given moment.

From Michael

To Family, Friends and
Those Who Love
To Read.
May We All Enjoy Grace
To Live The Life We Are
Called.

CHAPTER ONE

D iana reveled in the sight of the giant Kilomea bound, shackled, and hunched in the interrogation chair. Despite the seriousness of the situation, her grin was both broad and smug as she watched him through the one-way mirror. "Well, at least that ambushing bastard is right where he deserves to be."

Her two colleagues laughed appreciatively beside her. Bryant's was low and familiar. Warden Murphy's rose into the middle ranges but sounded hard-edged and brittle. Everything about the prison's overseer was sharp, from the body that seemed to consume itself for fuel to drive her quick movements to her hard face with its narrow cheek-bones and bladed nose. *This is a woman with whom you do not fuck,* she thought.

"So, he's totally secure? I wouldn't want to have to beat him down again and get your pure white room bloody."

The warden laughed. "That chair was designed to hold a full-sized troll on amphetamines. He won't break out of it anytime soon."

"Excellent." Diana's grin widened.

Murphy matched the smile with a thinner one. "You'll need to leave your weapons outside, though. Standard policy." She gestured at a locker beside the entrance. The agent nodded, drew her pistol and spare magazines from the holster hidden under the back of her leather jacket, and stowed them in the thick metal box. She was about to close it when the warden coughed. "*All* your weapons."

Diana shrugged as if to say, "I had to try, right?" She removed the Ruger from her ankle-high black spy boots, which perfectly matched the shade of the dark slacks she wore.

The name is Bond. Diana Bond.

Kayleigh Dornan had given the shoes to her before Diana had departed DC, and they held a number of surprises should she find herself in need. So far, she'd put the backup gun to good use but none of the hidden blades. She felt the weight of the warden's gaze on her after she deposited the revolver and sighed inwardly.

Well, at least their security is strong.

She withdrew the stiletto blade from her right boot and the throwing knives from the left and stowed them, then closed the locker and pressed her palm against it to activate the biometric lock.

Murphy nodded. "Very good." Despite her serious expression, the woman's eyes crinkled at the edges with humor. She led the agent to the small hallway connecting the observation room to the interrogation cell and entered a code into the keypad beside the door. The lock released with a mechanical whir. "We'll be watching. If you need us to intervene, use the word *sphere*."

Diana gave a thumbs-up and pushed through the door. It swung behind her, and heavy bars slammed home with a muted *thunk*. The walls shone with a dull plastic sheen. The only surface that didn't seem to be made from the material was the massive two-way mirror installed to divide the chamber from the observation room. She grinned at the hairy alien as he glowered at her from his security chair. Then, he groaned.

"It had to be you, didn't it? The luckiest tiny human on the planet."

She sauntered in front of him, slipped her hands into her front pockets, and rocked on her heels. "Little old me? Lucky? Hardly. I busted your ass fair and square, big guy. And if we had the chance for round three, you'd hit the mat again. Only this time, you'd be in the hospital for a long stretch, not prison."

He bared his huge teeth at her. "How about right now? You're tough when your enemy is restrained, aren't you?"

"Seriously, Sasquatch, no one is that stupid." She rolled her eyes. "If we didn't want you alive, we'd simply kill you, not give you the chance to go out fighting. So, is there anything you want to tell me?"

He gave as much of a shrug as his restraints would allow. They had locked his forearms and biceps to the arms of the chair and bound his chest to the back, while his thighs were strapped to the seat. The chain that connected the shackles on his feet was attached to a hardpoint in the floor.

"The food's okay but the company's lousy. It's not quite a fancy hotel, but it's fairly cushy. You must feel special, having brought in the toughest guy in the place."

Diana laughed and patted him on the head. The convict strained to reach her with his teeth. "You're merely an average everyday thug, buddy. Don't worry, though. I'll do my best to send you friends who are *actual* threats. Maybe you can learn something before you get out of here." She snapped her fingers. "Oh, wait. That's right. You'll never get out of here. Once we had your information, digging into back cases showed what a bad boy you've been."

His grin was both vicious and unrepentant. "I have had a...colorful life. All self-defense, though."

She stared pointedly at his bulging muscles and vented a prolonged sigh. "Right. That's what it was."

He laughed again, and Diana had to smile. He was a scumbag, but she'd met worse. His offenses were all against other criminals, as far as the techs could tell, which was a point in his favor. Still, she wasn't ready to release the personal grudge he'd earned when he'd thrown her into her car and dented it.

She folded her arms. "So, how about you tell me about your boss and whatever he was doing? Why go after the ambassador? What was the plan?"

He blinked and donned an innocent expression. She imagined that if his hands weren't bound, they'd be clutched over his chest in a gesture of feigned incomprehension. "You mean the owner at the Twisted Lizard, right? I was the bouncer there. He was a nice man and paid me well. Plus, the work was easy. It came with free drinks, too. I wouldn't mind going back there." Much to her surprise, he actually managed to sound wistful.

In the next moment, the surprise gave way to the sheer lunacy of the statement. She laughed, unable to restrain her reaction. He soon joined in. She wiped at the corner of an eye and said, "You're good, Cresnan. But I'm afraid you won't be able to resume that prior life. Your boss is dead, and your alleged place of employment coincidentally burned down shortly after you failed to abduct the ambassador. Did you make someone angry at you?"

The Kilomea shrugged, seemingly unfazed by the information. "Oh, well. I'm sure I'll find something entertaining to do when I get out of here. Maybe I'll pay you and your little family a visit."

Diana suppressed the instinctual growl that rose in her throat and shook her head. "We were getting along so well, and you had to ruin it. Remember what happened the last time you threatened my family? It didn't go so well for you, did it?" She raised her index finger and a jolt of electricity surged through the chair, drawing an angry curse from the prisoner. "That shock is only level one. Imagine if we took it to ten. And ours is special. It goes to *eleven*. Do you think you're tough enough to handle it? Would you like to give it a shot?"

The giant was far more annoyed than hurt. He hissed through clenched teeth. "Bring it, bitch."

She sighed. "I knew you wouldn't be reasonable about this, but we all thought it was worth a try." Her voice adopted a singsong tone. "Oh, Bryant?"

The sound of the door unlatching echoed through the spartan room and her boss entered. He looked serious and official in a tie and suit that hugged his frame. The man was the very picture of a government agent on the rise. His brown hair had been carefully combed to the side to reveal more of his narrow face. If she'd met him now for the first time, she might even have believed he *wasn't* the chuckle-head she knew him to be.

He crossed the intervening space to stand beside her and gestured at the Kilomea. "Is this one being an idiot?"

She nodded. "I told you he would be. I gave him a little shock, too, but it doesn't seem to have triggered any sense of self-preservation. Did you get word?"

"We did." He turned to the bound prisoner with a half-smile. "It is my distinct pleasure to inform you that the Oriceran consulate has agreed that your extensive list of crimes is substantial enough to warrant imprisonment in Trevilsom Prison."

The effect was more profound than Diana had thought it could be. All the color washed from Cresnan's face, and he gave a single visible shudder before a clear effort brought it under control. He licked his lips as if they'd suddenly gone dry.

She grinned. "What was that about the Cube being a cushy gig? You're not quite so tough now, are you, Sasquatch?"

His voice was more subdued than she'd imagined it could be. "You can't send me to Trevilsom. That's for the worst of the worst. I'm not in that league." She had heard of the prison, of course. It was located in the middle of an Oriceran ocean. Prisoners kept there were slowly driven to madness by the excess magical forces that permeated the place—without exception. It was a death sentence, but one preceded by extended torture measured by the heartbeats of those imprisoned.

Diana imagined that the brute before her would last a long time and had no doubt that he was aware of it, too.

"Do you want to stay here? Then talk. And don't lie." She gestured at the two-way. "We have an empath back there." They didn't, of course, but Cresnan wouldn't know that.

He spoke in a flat, emotionless tone. "Kergar was the leader of our group. We were only muscle. None of us were on the inside. Only him and maybe the bartender."

She checked the case notes on her smartwatch. "Enthan?"

The Kilomea nodded. "Yeah, that's the guy. Anyway, we only took orders. We weren't in on the big picture."

Bryant turned to her. "That's not enough to make it worth keeping him here. Life in the Cube is expensive. We have to provide clothes, food… The courts even think they should have full access to books. Before long, we'll have Oriceran convict scumbags with law degrees."

She smothered a grin and turned back to Cresnan. "You heard the man. Last chance. Give us something useful, or we're out of here and you blow your only shot to avoid being sent home."

Given his current options, the outcome was obvious. "Okay," the prisoner said hastily. "But you have to keep me away from any members of the Remembrance who come here. I want guaranteed protection."

She forced her face to stillness. "We don't know very much about the Remembrance."

Understatement. We've never heard of it.

"Tell us more. And you better be sure it doesn't conflict with the information we've already gathered from the others."

He nodded. "All I'm sure of is that there's a group of shady assholes at the top who follow Rhazdon's ideas. They sweep up those who still believe and band them together in her name. They communicate with these fancy coins. Kergar was very excited when he finally got his."

Diana shot a look at Bryant. Taggart's suspicions were right on the mark. They hadn't found a way to activate the coins yet, though, and weren't willing to tip their hand by pairing one with the statue they'd discovered for fear that it would alert whoever was on the other end.

I guess that was a good call. Go you, Taggart.

She turned back to Cresnan. "How many people?"

"I don't know."

"Who's in charge of it all?"

He shook his head. "I don't know."

"Okay, who's above Kergar?"

The Kilomea barked a laugh filled with mockery. "I saw him once, the bastard, when the boss was drunk and forgot to ward the door. He used that little crystal thing he had, and a small glowy version of the dude hovered over the top of it." Cresnan looked at the ceiling and sighed as if remembering hurt. "He wore a robe and some sort of hood. I can't tell you anything about him other than he's male and has an accent. He sounded like an elf, but who knows?"

"What *kind* of elf?" Bryant asked.

He shrugged. "One elf sounds the same as another. Weak, pretentious."

Bryant turned to her. "Do you have enough?"

Diana tapped her chin and felt the prisoner's eyes on her. She let her face fall as if she was about to say no, and the Kilomea blurted out, "There's a branch here, too."

Both of their heads snapped around. Bryant asked, "Here in the Cube?"

He waved a hand as far as he could, given the restraints. "No, idiot. Here in this town."

Diana fought down the desire to chuckle at her partner. "We already knew that. Thanks for nothing. But since you came clean, we'll keep you here—well, for at least a while longer."

Here, too. Damn.

The two agents moved toward the door. The brute behind them barked a hopeless laugh. "How about round three, Sheen?"

She didn't turn to face him. "I told you. We want you alive. When that changes, you'll see me again." They exited the room and the door clanged shut.

The warden frowned as they rejoined her behind the mirror. "That's concerning."

Bryant nodded grimly. "To say the least. Remember, you can always call on Diana and her team if you need to."

Murphy nodded, then smiled at her. "Agent Sheen, I hope you'll come back soon for a real tour. It would be good for you to learn the ins and outs of the place, just in case."

Diana extended a hand and they shook. For such a lean and sharp-looking woman, her grip was surprisingly warm. "Count on it. Together, we're gonna clean up this town."

CHAPTER TWO

B ryant swung the SUV into an underground parking garage after a short drive over one of the many bridges that spanned the river from the north side of Pittsburgh. They descended to the bottom floor and parked across two spots in the mostly empty lot. He waved an arm as they walked toward an unmarked door. "There are always open spaces on this level. The office building nearby doesn't have the same demand it used to."

Diana nodded and looked ahead. She was eager to memorize every section of her new home, from the cracks in the pavement to the chips in the walls. They reached a door that featured a hefty lock above a long handle. She tested it for kicks and smiled at the stout resistance it offered.

Bryant grinned. "I was the same way when we opened the office in DC." He waved his smartwatch at an unmarked portion of the door frame and a soft *click* sounded. A fire alarm on the wall was no longer flush, and he swung it aside to reveal one of ARES' ubiquitous keypads. "The code is the same as the model year of your car." She grinned and typed in *2018*. The sound of the barrier unlocking echoed through the vacant level. He glanced around, presumably to be sure they were alone, then pulled it open and gestured her inside. "Of course, you'll want to change it."

She rolled her eyes. "Duh."

He swung the door shut behind them and laughed. Motors rumbled as they extended a set of heavy metal bars into place.

Diana nodded in satisfaction. "Not skimping on security, eh?"

"Not a bit." He shook his head. "Your location in such a public place here in the downtown proper of Pittsburgh carries a little more risk than our comfortable home in the DC cookie-cutter office park."

She followed him down a long corridor. Her internal compass was fairly sure it ran at an angle toward the city's other river, but she made a mental note to study the layout in more detail and fix it in her head. The hallway was dim but clean and freshly painted, and the construction was new.

The lights are probably motion-sensor-controlled and still warming up.

Bryant paused while she observed the structure a little more closely. "As far as anyone outside ARES knows, the garage doesn't connect to your building. We've run construction on this alongside other hidden infrastructure over the last few months."

"The city didn't complain?"

He raised his palm, turned it over, and flipped it back

up again. "This is one of those need-to-know things. The Council determined that local government did *not* need to know, so they've run interference with the bureaucracy. There's a legitimate Army Corps of Engineers project going on nearby, which has provided good cover. They're upgrading the underground portion of the city's light rail to cope with flooding issues. At the same time, they'll add a few special features for us."

Diana shook her head in wonder. "It's amazing what you can accomplish when you don't have to tell anyone what you're up to."

"Right?" They resumed their trek and soon arrived at another heavy door. Bryant typed in the same code. It released, and they entered the new base of the Anti-magic Response and Enforcement Service, affectionately known as Black-ops Agents of Magic.

She frowned. At first glance, in the minimal glow of hanging work lights, it resembled a dump. A second and closer look confirmed it. "So, this is what—a storage floor?"

Bryant chuckled. "Hardly. This is your main site." He slapped a palm against a button to his right and fluorescent bulbs buzzed to life throughout the cavernous space. Support pillars dotted the structure at regular intervals, and a staircase and elevator entrance were both visible on the distant wall.

She scuffed the sole of her boot along the dirt on the cement floor. "I know you said it was a startup, but this is, uh…less started up than I expected."

He laughed at her obvious distaste. "Construction teams will be on site before long. We want to use our own people for this part of the job, and they're currently on assignment elsewhere." He escorted her forward and pointed to several stacks of military-style crates. "Your version of the core is in those boxes. It will go here." He gestured at the area in which they stood, which was roughly the center of the room. "We've beefed up the signal security in every direction and run dedicated fiber into the space from the local hub. The cable company for the city has no idea, of course. The cord itself is shielded and monitored for issues. No one will hack into your stuff that way."

They walked toward the staircase and he pointed at the elevator doors. "That's a private elevator and goes between here and the top floor, nowhere else. The building's main elevators don't come down here, and they're locked out of the top floor without one of our watches." He led her up the stairs to the next level. This area was also empty, but the tape on the ground marked the likely placement of walls and various other pieces of equipment.

"I assume these will be offices?" Diana asked.

Bryant nodded. "Offices in one half, space for labs and medical in the other. The armory will be downstairs near the core."

She folded her arms. "I always assumed that ARES was deeply committed to this location but mentioning medical right off the bat suggests that you're more serious than I thought."

"We are. Your proximity to the Cube would be enough to justify this level of concern on its own. But data shows us that this is a particular hotspot, even without the prison. And the Kemana nearby adds any number of potential wrinkles to the situation." He gestured to another staircase and led her up it. "You won't be a DC level of importance, at least not at the start, but you'll be as vital as any of our other locations, and more so than most."

Diana nodded. "Okay. I can work with that."

They emerged into a lobby where sunlight streamed in through the many windows. The warm glow illuminated a seating area with several couches and chairs, a small desk with a security guard, and a local-brand coffee shop on the opposite side. A sign announced *Thirty-Four Coworking* in bright gold letters on a black background.

She raised a skeptical brow at Bryant. "The street address? That's the best you could come up with for a business name?"

He shot her a long-suffering frown. "Dammit, Diana. I'm an agent, not a marketer."

The Star Trek reference deserved a small laugh, at least. Seconds later, he introduced her to the guard. "Larry, this is Diana. She's from Thirty-Four Corporate and will be around from time to time to check on things."

Larry nodded. The man was the size of a college linebacker and didn't appear to have much fat on his large frame. His sharp blue uniform, short buzz-cut black hair, and professional, stoic expression combined to suggest a heavy level of commitment. His voice was deep but smooth. "Welcome to Pittsburgh, ma'am."

Diana smiled. "Thanks, Larry. Please, call me Diana. What do you think of this place?" She gestured around.

He scratched the back of his neck and sighed. "Well, first let me say that I like working for Thirty-Four—good company and treats me right. But some of these people you rent to…they're plenty strange."

Both agents laughed and Bryant replied, "As long as they have the money, who are we to judge? Am I right?"

The guard nodded but still frowned disapprovingly. Bryant gestured toward the elevators, and Diana gave the guard a wave. "See you around, Larry." He grunted what sounded like an affirmation, then turned to deal with a person who'd rolled up to the desk on a skateboard.

A short negotiation of various electronic devices and an elevator ride later, they stepped onto the fifth and final floor of the building. It was well-appointed, with an unmanned reception counter, several offices with sizes and furnishings appropriate to upper-level management, and a giant conference room with windows that faced the river and the mountain beyond it. Diana sighed an appreciative, "Ah," at the reflection of the bright sunlight on the water, even though it was still frigid outside. "Now this, I could get used to."

"Don't." Bryant stepped beside her to gaze at a barge going past. "This is your public face when required. If you need to bring someone in who's not cleared for the base below, this is where they come. With enough notice, one of our managers below will come up and handle reception. If needed, we can always put bodies in the offices to make it look more legit. We have staff on floors two, three, and four and we're close to breaking even, too. The place is catching on."

"You really have thought of everything." She tapped on the window. "I presume these are bulletproof?"

"Up to a fifty-cal, they say. But if you see a missile

coming in, get to one of the offices. They have go-bags and reinforced walls."

"Roof access?"

He led her back to the offices and pointed to a small closet. When she opened it, she found a shallow area only slightly larger than the ladder inside that led to a trapdoor above. "Nice."

Bryant nodded. "It has full security, of course. No one will get in that way unless they're one of us. We had hoped to reinforce the structure so we could land a helicopter on top of it, but no dice. If you want to leave by air, you'll have to climb up to the bird or dangle."

She'd already anticipated that and ran her fingers through the black straps on the climbing harness attached to the wall. "It seems like everything a team of agents could need. You even gave us a coffee bar."

He laughed. "Uh, no. We'll get you an espresso machine. You should rarely be seen in the cover business."

Diana backhanded him on his abdomen. "I'm not an idiot."

"But you do have a fierce coffee addiction."

"Touché."

Bryant grinned. "Let's go see the other location." They emerged onto the parking level again and he pressed a button on his watch. A nearby sedan beeped, and its headlights flashed to acknowledge receipt of the command signal. They entered the vehicle and it started with another tap of his watch. He opened his mouth to speak, but she interrupted.

"Let me guess. We own a limousine service or car rental agency."

"Right on target, Agent Sheen." He laughed easily. "The cars should change on a fairly regular basis, but there will always be one for each of the agents on the team parked here, gassed up and ready to go."

She shook her head as they emerged from the parking garage and drove the short distance to the city's strip district, where wholesale vendors of every variety competed for business. As the GPS led them through the turns, Bryant cleared his throat. "So, we have a good second-in-command candidate for you."

"I'll be the judge of that. Tell me more."

"Cara Binot. Total ball-buster. Former army, I think. Now, she's a US Marshal and has a solid blend of skills and potential." He took the street closest to the river past a long warehouse along the left and a series of restaurants and nightclubs housed in converted warehouses on the right.

"Magic?" Diana liked the sound of her already.

"Unknown, actually, but she's so good that even if she doesn't have it, she's still worth a look." He pulled in at the end of the row, and they jogged up the short flight of stairs to the cement loading dock that extended the full length of the front of the long building.

She studied the area and noticed several restaurants that seemed worthy of her patronage. "When do I get to meet her?"

"She'll fly in tomorrow." He fumbled in his pocket for his keys.

Diana clapped briskly. "Excellent. The faster, the better."

He withdrew a key from his pocket and unlocked the

very ordinary-looking door. They walked inside, and she whistled, then smiled as the echoes of their footsteps bounced around the room. The space was at least two stories high at the lowest part of the angled roof. The cement floor was broken only by a tiled area at the entrance. None of the flooring was fresh, but it clearly wasn't original, either. The material gave a satisfying click against her boot heels.

Bryant spread his arms wide. "Voila. The home of your brand spanking new security consulting and bounty hunting division."

She spun in circles to admire the high ceilings and the tall, narrow windows that covered most of the second story to admit the sunlight. The way the dirty panes filtered the light lent the location an old-time feel. "It's fantastic, actually." She turned to him and smirked. "Someone with taste must have chosen this location, which leaves you out."

"True enough." His laugh was genuine and perhaps a little sheepish. "We worked through a local real estate agent." He gestured at a space that included the tile plus a dozen feet in each direction. "This front area can be the office. That will leave you the remainder of the building to outfit for training as we discussed."

"Perfect. Now, all I lack is the money to do it. Give me your credit card."

Bryant took a step back and swiveled the pocket that likely held his wallet away from her. "You have access to the startup funds you need. Keep it reasonable, and there shouldn't be any problem. But if you want true financial independence, get your security side up and running."

Diana folded her arms and narrowed her gaze. "But, naturally, don't slack on the main job while I do it."

"Of course."

"There won't be much time to have a life with this gig, will there?"

He shrugged and immediately dropped the playful grin in favor of a grim stare. "You're in charge, now. Those decisions are yours. You need to do what's essential in the short-term and what's best for the long-term. Burning yourself or your people out is not a good plan."

"That's...actually pretty heavy." She frowned. "Speaking of agents, assuming Cara works out, I still need someone who knows investigation and the town to make the security side work."

"Agreed."

"Any thoughts on that?"

"No idea. You're the boss now. Figure it out." He shrugged and smirked.

CHAPTER THREE

"**M**ax. Go."
The main door of the house Diana had rented in the Oakland area east of downtown was far easier to open than the one in their other home had been. It had only a single bolt lock, with none on the handle. Rath waved at the small camera on the wide covered porch before he and his Borzoi mount descended the stairs to the street.

It was a strange neighborhood, quite unlike the other. Maple and white oak trees lined the hill where their house stood, and families with children lived all around instead of the many men and women in suits and dresses.

"Must protect," Rath said and patted Max on the back. The dog barked joyfully and paused to check scents every few feet. He was clearly as committed as the troll to this vital matter of protecting his neighbors.

As they followed the sidewalk down the slope, the residential section melted away to be replaced by wide streets filled with cars and lined with businesses. A constant stream of bodies moved in all directions—many more than where they used to live. Diana called the place a university, but Rath hadn't really grasped what that meant until he saw it for himself.

It was *fantastic*. People of every description walked and socialized everywhere, some together and some alone. He imagined what it would be like when the weather warmed and grinned. "Many adventures. Must train."

Ahead, a towering form resembled an over-tall castle keep. It reminded him of Oriceran, and he tapped to steer the dog toward it through the currents of people. Grass surrounded the building on three sides, and they circled it to be sure they had identified all the access points. Finally, they came to a stop in front of the main entrance, where a set of broad stairs rose to meet a series of rotating doors that Rath didn't trust.

He patted Max, who immediately sat in response. "We wait. Patience is key to all things."

The troll had spent the previous day watching the kung fu channel, which he was excited to find in the new house. With the assistance of that and various other movies, he had learned many wise life lessons that he looked forward to applying in combat.

After a short delay, the self-opening normal doors at street level parted to allow a woman with a cane to emerge. Max dashed into the building, careful not to interfere with her progress.

Rath called, "Thank you," and received a hesitant wave in return.

An open staircase located immediately on the duo's right

led up to the main floor. It was gray stone all over, and very high in its construction—it stood at least fifteen Maxes high. The Borzoi mount padded quietly through the space and took care not to disturb the people who sat at the many tables with the open books strewn about them. A strange combination of happiness and despair hung in the air. A woman suddenly threw her hands up with a small moan and dropped her face into the book in front of her with a *clunk*. Rath was ready to ask her what was wrong when someone spoke from nearby.

The voice was calm, warm, and patient.

She must watch the kung fu channel, too.

"They're studying for midterms. It makes them miserable. Not like in my day." He gazed to his left to discover a woman in a large skirt and button-down shirt grinning down at him. She wore a pretty silver necklace with an oval pendant, and her straight blonde hair that cascaded down her back was restrained by a thin elastic band. She patted the table in invitation.

Rath dashed to the end of the Borzoi's long nose. "Gentle, Max. Launch." The dog flicked his head, and the troll performed a single somersault on the way up to land on the table beside her books. The woman clapped, which startled students nearby and sent echoes around the common room. "Very nice moves, my friend. What's your name?"

"Rath."

She nodded as if he'd confirmed a thought. "One of the deadly sins. I imagine you're no end of trouble." She laughed—at herself, he assumed, as he was most certainly not a laughing matter. "Mine is Charlotte Stanford. I'm a professor here. I study Oriceran history and it's given me some insight into what troublemakers trolls can be."

He grinned. "Good to meet you."

"Same to you." She leaned forward and lowered her voice a little. He caught a scent that made his nose twitch.

Spicy perfume. Nice.

"I haven't seen you around before. I'm sure I would've noticed."

He nodded. "New here. House on hill."

Charlotte smiled. "Well, welcome to the University of Pittsburgh, then. Call it Pitt. We all do. What are you and your friend up to?" She gestured at the dog, who had shifted out of the path of shuffling students to lie beneath her chair. Rath scowled at him, and Max stretched and sighed contentedly under the accusing glare.

"Recon. Max must train."

She gave a single decisive nod. Clearly, she understood the importance of training.

Definitely watches the kung fu channel.

"He seems more interested in napping at the moment."

Rath nodded sadly. "Max needs energy."

The professor laughed and fumbled in her bag. "It just so happens that I didn't finish my lunch today. I have two pierogies left. Would you each like one?"

The troll tilted his head, a little dubious despite his excitement at the thought of food. "Pi-roe-gee?"

"It's pasta with potato and cheese inside. Well, sometimes, there's other stuff, but I'm a purist."

"Mmm. Cheese."

She took that for the affirmative it was and handed him the treat. It was about two-thirds his size, so he nibbled at the edge. He actually enjoyed the chewy texture of the outer shell and once he reached the filling, it was even better.

"Thank you. Max can have?"

Charlotte passed the other down to the dog. He gulped it greedily in a single bite and gave her a grateful lick on the hand as a reward. Or, possibly, to get any residue off her fingers, but she didn't seem to mind.

Rath was only a quarter through his but didn't want to give his partner time to fall asleep again. "Can keep for later?"

She nodded and laughed. "Of course. Here." She used the waxy paper she had taken the food from and helped him to cover what remained. Her gaze flicked to the large clock at the apex of a stone arch. "I have to go teach my class, Rath. I'd love to talk with you again, though. I'm on the eleventh floor if you want to visit me sometime." She gestured at the bank of elevators across the room.

"Will. Thank you."

He looked down and shook his head. His partner now sprawled in a manner that indicated his intention to sleep. "Max. Let's go." The Borzoi stood slowly, stretched, and moved to the side of the table. Rath jumped and his balance was off due to the large treat he carried under his arm, but he recovered quickly. The woman laughed as they renewed their exploration.

The troll patted his trusty steed's neck. "Max. Good dog. Continue recon."

Rambo would never get distracted by food. Food is for later. Now is for training.

Diana waited impatiently in the sunny lobby of the Coworking building. A different guard now sat at the desk. Keith seemed like Larry in most respects. Apparently, five guards in total took shifts to cover the twenty-four-seven access the company provided to its clients—another useful piece of subterfuge, Bryant had pointed out. Diana wasn't buying it.

This hiding out in the open could easily come back to bite us.

She caught motion in her peripheral vision as a tough-looking woman navigated the revolving door. Diana focused on her and blinked decisively. Her AR glasses responded to the command immediately and snapped an image to check against the woman's file. **Positive match** flashed on the far right of her display.

At least the data encoder and wireless are working.

Not much else was. At least, not yet. She knew her frustration was a symptom of her enthusiasm to get moving, but that didn't make it any easier.

Cara Binot's scrutiny worked systematically from right to left to analyze her surroundings. The signs of rigid training and discipline were easily recognizable. It had taken Diana a long time to break that habit after she entered the FBI. It was too big a tell for targets who knew what to look for.

She was taller than Diana—naturally. Everyone was taller than her. The woman made no hurried movement and simply took time to categorize everything and everyone as threat or non-threat. When the candidate finished her assessment, Diana stepped forward and extended a hand. "Cara? I'm Diana."

The woman smiled and took the offered hand in a strong grip. Her long black hair fell in unkempt waves over her shoulders, and dark eye makeup set off the thin nose and pale pink lips below. A burst of laughter immediately followed from both women as each sought to refrain from indulging their reflexive instincts. Diana gestured at the elevator bank. "Let's head upstairs."

The black espresso machine on the credenza burbled and saturated the air with the smell of dark roast as the pair took in the view. Diana filled two mugs that featured the cover company's logo, left both free of sugar and cream, and handed one to her guest. She chose a chair on the far side of the table, and Cara took the seat on the end nearest her.

The woman perched on the edge of her chair with the rigidity only a soldier could master. Diana straightened her spine to match. "So, Cara, thank you for coming. I've heard a few things about you, but how about you help fill in the blanks for me?"

Cara nodded, took a sip of her coffee, and set it on the table. "Basic background, I'm Army. I completed basic training and advanced individual training in infantry at Fort Benning." She hesitated as if waiting for a response, then continued. "Did airborne school, then joined the Marshals. Along the way, I grabbed an online degree in sociology from Central Florida."

"Sociology? I would've guessed criminal justice, or maybe military history."

Cara grinned. "My mother would say it's because I hate

being predictable." She shrugged and her eyes gleamed with what could have been a private joke. "Mainly, I thought it would be useful to study why groups of people do the things they do and interact in specific manners. Psychology was a possibility, but I found it was too individually focused."

Diana nodded. "What's your day-to-day like with the Marshals?"

"I'm in the special operations group. We apprehend or eliminate fugitives in addition to standard investigations."

It confirmed what she'd seen in the file. The fact that she didn't emphasize exactly how good she was—*very* good, by all accounts—was a point in her favor. "Have you faced any magic?"

Cara laughed. "It's hard to avoid in this day and age, isn't it? Sometimes, our targets have magical support. At other times, we're invited to take on bounties when there's no one else around to handle it."

Diana perked up. "Give me an example."

The candidate took another sip and eased her posture in the chair to make herself a little more comfortable. "Okay, this jerk wizard down in South Carolina had set himself up in a dilapidated old plantation building and ran a fight club out of it. Ordinarily, that would've been fine." She shook her head and corrected herself. "Well, not fine, obviously, but not squarely in the Marshals' purview. The fact that he actively recruited people on our wanted list made it ours to deal with. Even then, it might not have risen to an immediate priority, except he cheated. Once someone had won through the brackets and expected their reward, he tossed in the little wrinkle that they had to battle him to be paid, with no rest and directly after their winning bout. He killed three of them with fire before we got word."

She nodded, took a sip of her brew, and waited for the applicant to continue.

Cara shrugged. "Anyway, we went in for a capture, but he fought and burned the building to ash around us. We were forced to take him out."

"We?" Diana pressed.

"Okay, *I* was forced to take him out. The bastard would've killed us otherwise. We were lucky to be in range of his protective runes. The downside of that meant we were in range of all his other spells, too. It was only the anti-magic rounds that saved me."

Diana nodded as she recalled her own previous encounters with stubborn mages.

If ARES can't find a supplier soon, I'll need to go out of house for those. Someone is intercepting our deliveries. But who's the traitor? She shook her head. *I can't think about that now.*

"What level was he?"

"Three. He probably should have been a four, considering how well he trapped his home against unwanted intrusion. Taking on a bad guy in his stronghold always sucks."

Diana grinned. "Sociology?"

Cara shook her head. "Military history."

The two shared another laugh at the brief exchange before Diana stood and refilled their mugs. "So, you've had the brief about ARES and what we're up to, yes?"

"Mostly. Basically, you deal with magical threats wherever they pop up."

She returned the coffee pot and sat again, then slid the extra cup to her guest. "That's generally right. Although we'll aim for the higher end of the danger spectrum and leave the lowest ones for independent bounty hunters."

The other woman nodded.

"Do you still want in?"

Cara sipped the brew, then lowered her mug to look her in the eye. "First, I have a couple of questions for you. Since you're the one in charge, what's important to you? Why are you—*personally*—doing this?"

The earnestness in her voice suggested it wasn't a throwaway inquiry, so Diana took her time to carefully consider the answer. "It's a mix of all the normal things, I guess. Patriotism, responsibility, a desire to make a change. All that stuff is real and important." She paused and looked out the window. "But at the heart of it? I despise bullies." She turned back to her companion. "And all the assholes we've faced so far are classic condescending, better-than-thou, card-carrying, bullying trash. They need to be taught a lesson, and ARES is open to tutor them."

The candidate grinned. "All right. You've sold me. What's next?"

"How about a test?" Diana's grin was now a little feral. "There's a level two bounty who's popped up on the radar over the last couple of days. Breaking and entering, destruction of property—normal criminal stuff. How about we teach him the error of his ways?"

Cara slapped her palms on the table. "Absolutely. There's no time like the present."

CHAPTER FOUR

She took Cara through the basement levels and out to the garage. *There's not much risk, even if she decides not to join us.* A tap on her watch activated a current-model sedan, and they circled to the trunk. She popped it with another touch to reveal a pair of cases inside. "While we're still spinning up, our armory's mobile."

Her companion nodded her understanding.

Diana heaved the containers out and set them on the car. The longer box opened to display two Colt M4 carbines with collapsed stocks. She handed one to Cara and was satisfied to see the woman check the rifle carefully, verify that the magazine was full, and extend a hand for a spare. She slapped it into her palm and laughed. "Standard load. Depending on where we find him, they might be too much bang, but let's at least have them ready."

Cara nodded. "There are usually civilians present when the Marshals have to confront someone, too. It seems like a deliberate defense mechanism."

"It hasn't been a problem in many of my BAM missions yet, but I'm sure that's the exception, rather than the rule."

"BAM?"

"Only the suits call it ARES. We prefer Black-ops Agents of Magic."

The marshal chuckled. "I didn't want to say anything, but BAM *is* much better than ARES."

The second case Diana opened held two standard Kevlar vests and a pair of illusion necklaces. *I don't want to waste our deflectors on anyone under a level-three.* She dropped one of each over her head and handed the others over. Cara mimicked the action and looked quizzically at her.

"One of our ongoing challenges will be to keep the federal side of things hidden while we work under the guise of the security agency. These change our looks. They're self-powered and take a voice command to activate." She wasn't sure how the necklaces were created, nor what level of magic was required to craft the artifacts, but had long since decided it wasn't worth worrying about so long as they worked. Bryant had said that they would work on both magicals and non-magicals, so she'd simply take him at his word.

And if they do need magic, there's no guarantee Cara lacks sufficient power, is there?

She flashed back to Bryant's first tease after she'd revealed her power. "You didn't tell me you had magic," he'd said. She laughed inwardly. Then she realized that the other woman was watching her and snapped the cases closed. "You put your hand on the pendant, say 'falach,' and you'll look like someone else for a while."

"Anyone in particular? I always thought Sandra Bullock was pretty hot."

She laughed. "Nope. Some sort of random average amalgamation of features. Who knows? Our magic techs are seriously impressive. So are the non-magic techs, for that matter."

She stowed the cases, and they slid into the car. Cara watched the scenery pass outside the window in silence as they drove, then finally broke it in favor of the inevitable questions. "So, why Pittsburgh? And why me?"

Diana turned left toward the river. "Pittsburgh, because the city is a hub for magic, both good and bad. I'm not sure exactly why it's so popular, but the revelation of the Cube can only make things worse."

Cara nodded. "The reveal to the media came a little earlier than expected—or so it seemed to me."

She scowled, sharing the woman's sentiment. "It did. We're still looking into how that happened. Let's simply say the rollout hasn't been without its issues." She swung the car across the bridge and turned right to drive along the river. "As for your other question, that's easy. You're skilled, you've proven you're tough, and you seem sane, despite your interest in joining us."

Her companion laughed. "Mostly sane, at least."

"Sometimes, that's the best anyone can do." Diana checked the GPS on her watch and swung the sedan into a gravel lot. Ahead was a large metal-walled building that had probably once been a factory dedicated to some part of the steel production process. Now, a hand-painted tattoo-inspired sign proclaimed it to be an auto body shop. The giant entryway spewed an unholy clamor of rock music, heavy clanging, and power tools through its open maw.

Diana took the lead as she stepped out of the car. Cara flanked her on her left. By unspoken agreement, they chose not to carry the rifles as it was too much firepower for such a public location. She activated her necklace and the other woman did the same and grimaced at the sensation as her features squashed and morphed into something plain and unattractive. Her skin was now pale and splotchy, her hair a frizzy orange, and her eyes had assumed a dull green shade that emphasized the freckles and patches of psoriasis along her neck. As a final touch, her nose had swollen to look more like a snout. Diana didn't want to know what *she* looked like. She sighed as she looked at her jacket. It was a luxury she would have to learn to live without when she was on missions. Wearing the same favorites was a rookie mistake, and this was the big leagues.

They made their way casually through the space and avoided eye contact as they sought their target. Diana's leather coat was loose enough that she could cleanly access the Glock in its shoulder rig. Cara kept her right hand on her hip to hasten the draw from the holster at the small of her back.

The car had an encoder and repeater, so the AR glasses were able to assist in the search. She spotted the bounty from a distance and nodded her head subtly in his direction. Her companion interpreted it and shifted to take a parallel path along the left wall while Diana continued down the center aisle. A few catcalls and a proposition or two tagged their progress, but nobody moved to harass either of them. Either there was a strict non-fraternizing policy or they knew something was up. Their target was working a dent out of a dark purple Toyota 86 when she reached him.

She halted across the hood from where he knelt and yelled, "Harold, we'd like to have a word with you." He didn't respond, so she stepped around and waved a hand in front of his face. He stumbled back, clearly alarmed, and yanked the earplugs from his ears as he straightened. He towered above her, a fact she did not enjoy.

I wonder if there's any magic to make me taller.

His bushy red beard was dirty, and a dark smudge of grease smeared across his cheek.

He looked at her and snarled, "What?"

Diana shook her head. She'd seen enough of the tough guy attitude in her life. Then again, they had interrupted his work on a very expensive piece of machinery. "Hi, Harold. Great first impression, by the way. We'd like to chat with you."

He swiveled his head and his gaze found Cara where she leaned against the far wall. From her position, she had a clear line of sight. He muttered an expletive and turned back to Diana. "I didn't do anything, Officer."

She put her hands on her hips. "Then why do you assume I'm with the law?"

The bounty coughed and pointed at her vest. It's obvious. You look like police."

Sadly, she had to give him points there. "Well, you're half right. Can we get out of the noise and talk?"

He frowned and failed to move. "Having magic's not a

crime yet, is it?" He gestured to the car as if to say, "Hey, I'm using it for good."

Diana shrugged. "No, but breaking into ATMs with it is. Magic doesn't give you permission to take other people's stuff."

His face went blank for a second before he marshaled his intellectual reserves and countered, "You can't prove it was me." Either those reserves were frighteningly limited, or he simply tried his luck with a feeble ploy—to what, buy himself time?

She raised a brow and withdrew her phone from her back pocket. He squinted at the screen as she held up the security camera footage of him smashing an ATM with a force blast.

Harold seemed genuinely surprised for a moment before he sighed. "Damn. That first fucking spell was supposed to fuzz the camera."

For a hairsbreath moment, Diana thought he would surrender, but he proved her optimism unfounded. An outstretched hand and barked command launched the Toyota toward Cara's position against the wall. Only a frantic jump over the hood saved her from being crushed. His other hand directed a pair of nearby power tools toward the second agent's face.

Diana called on her telekinesis and slapped the projectiles aside with a sweep of her left arm. She drew her pistol, but Harold had already fled, darting behind obstructions and coworkers to break her line of sight.

Shit.

"Stay on that side," she yelled to her partner and broke into a run. "I'll take the middle and right."

She pounded along the center aisle in pursuit, then flung herself behind a windowless car when a blizzard of lug nuts appeared. They rocketed above with the speed of bullets and struck the metal behind her. Various workers responded with outraged shouts mingled with at least one scream of pain. She weaved to avoid several of the bounty's force blasts. Glyphs glowed under the edges of Harold's now-unrolled shirtsleeves. If he hadn't already admitted to his magical abilities—and been caught on camera, of course—this would have been the damning evidence.

As if the flying steel wasn't proof enough.

Diana skidded across the cement on her knees as another salvo of lug nuts speared toward her head. A sharp ridge on the floor sliced a long gash in the side of her left boot, and she growled her annoyance. "Okay, punk. Now, it's personal."

With the increased anger came the familiar sensation as magic built inside her, and she grinned. She'd taken great pains to hide her gift before she'd joined BAM. Now, the terror she had once felt about it and the dreams that had plagued her nights had both faded. But not being afraid of it didn't mean she had proper control yet. Knowing it was there was comforting, though. A crash from the left was likely attributable to an attack on Cara, and she hoped the other woman was okay. Unfortunately, hope was all she could manage as she had no attention to spare beyond the deadly projectiles Harold launched relentlessly in her direction. Her mind cataloged them as she dodged.

Big-ass wrench. Socket set, in case. Socket set, not in case.

Her eyes widened and she flinched at the sight of a veritable wall of metal objects inbound. She crouched and raised her right arm in defense. Her wrist immediately glowed with glyphs, and a shimmering force barricade materialized to protect her from the hail of steel.

Captain America's got nothing on me.

She lurched into motion again and extended her pistol for a shot as Harold broke into the wide space at the far edge of the building, but the distance was too great.

Where the hell does he think he's going? If he dives in the river, I won't jump in after him. It's too damn cold for that nonsense.

For a moment, she wondered if aquatic shapeshifters existed or if she could find a mermaid to help patrol the waterways. Fortunately, he didn't try that route. Instead, he cursed and released a volley of spells at a chain-link fence with razor wire at its top. The barrier shook fiercely but didn't break under his onslaught.

Diana stopped, aimed at the tasteless image on the back center of his shirt, and shouted, "Okay, Harold. Give it up and get on the ground."

He turned frantically as Cara closed in on a separate vector with her pistol trained unflinchingly to deny him any chance to evade them for a running start. If he attacked, the other would be able to restrain him. At least, that was the theory. Unfortunately, standard tactics didn't mean squat to a magic user.

Harold threw his arms up and an invisible force spun the weapon out of Diana's grasp. Cara's followed the same example but to her credit, the marshal didn't hesitate. Instead, she charged the bounty instead. Diana lunged forward in response, lest he focus all his effort on her partner. He gestured at her and suddenly, it felt like she ran through mud. The technique was new to her and proved successful against her usual defenses. It demonstrated a level of control beyond what she could accomplish.

Damn. He's actually good at this.

Cara closed unhindered and delivered two sharp punches to his torso. The attack didn't impact him nearly as much as it should have.

He probably has some kind of close defense force going on, too. Why the hell is he only a level-two?

She made a mental note to talk to someone at police headquarters about their bounty categorizations as she continued to push against his spell.

The marshal threw a hook at his head that he blocked with a raised hand. It never actually touched her, yet the punch was guided away. A roundhouse body kick followed, and he stopped it with a gesture. She faked a backfist at his face before she spun to finally connect with a side kick to his ribs.

He staggered, then straightened with a condescending smile and rumbled, "All right, enough playing."

Harold thrust out both hands, and Cara was thrown back. The attack must have distracted him or required his entire focus because Diana found she could move at full speed once more. She covered the intervening distance in seconds and leapt in with a sharp blow aimed at the side of his head. He saw it at the last instant and shifted enough to catch the blow on the back of his skull, rather than his temple, so it glanced off the hard bone. In a frenzy, he whirled on her and made a punching motion with his hand. Time slowed for her as her reflexive magic kicked in instinctively. She tilted her head to the left and something whizzed past her ear, although she could almost see the invisible fist that she had narrowly avoided.

Diana flung herself aside to avoid his next blow as the world around her resumed its normal pace, then weaved and feinted in an attempt to keep his attention and make him miss. She spotted a tree stump ahead and dashed for the minimal cover it would provide. A heavy strike radiated pain through her back before she reached it, however. She sprawled painfully and struggled to recover. At least the blow had one benefit. The stump was now within reach. She crawled behind the remains of the tree as dark spots danced across her vision. After a deep, calming breath, she clawed the Ruger out of her boot.

She raised the revolver in a two-handed grip and rested it on the wood. Harold stalked toward her. His face was twisted with anger as his arms stretched before him. She tried to steady the gun and wished she could take a breath to still the trembling in her hands. He'd somehow restricted her ability to breathe, and she needed to take her shot quickly to break the hold he had over her.

Cara saved her from having to take the shot. She leapt stealthily from behind and delivered a brutal kick to Harold's right knee that dropped him to the dirt. The marshal stamped her foot on the man's calf, and his bone snapped. He screamed, and Diana gasped a ragged breath as her ability to breathe returned. Her partner bound him quickly with the zip ties provided and was smart enough to use a gag to prevent him from speaking. He'd not needed spoken incantations for any of his spells thus far so that might have been unnecessary. Still, there was no guarantee that he didn't have some nasty last-resort explosive something or other that could level the entire area in one massive blast.

She thought of that too. Good.

Her partner ran over to help her up. "Nice job distracting him so I could get close."

Diana laughed but it definitely sounded strained. "Yeah, sure. That's what it was. He's a bastard. You should've shot him, period."

The marshal shrugged. "I'm not sure where he threw my gun. Plus, isn't it always better to incapacitate them rather than kill them?"

"So I hear." She rolled her eyes and groaned, then shook her head at the moaning man. "He's secured, so let's call the wagon to take him away. Two Worlds Security Consulting just bagged its first bounty."

CHAPTER FIVE

Diana walked the few blocks from the agency to the restaurant and entered the front door. She ignored the glares and verbal protests from the line of people shivering in the cold as she addressed the hostess. "My group's here. I'm the late one." She navigated the loudly happy crowd with all the skills of a trained fighter. The space was built around a Caribbean theme, with a fancy glass and wood bar to the right and tables to the left. Two small areas in the back afforded at least an illusion of privacy. The rest of the floor space committed to a kind of upscale togetherness that reminded her of nights out in DC.

Well, everywhere but the Beagle, at least.

She chuckled at the memory as a stab of homesickness struck her and wondered how Lisa was doing. A rustle and vibration emanated from inside her purse, and she was sure Rath was enjoying the sights at least, if not the sounds and smells since he was buttoned up in his canister. She had rigged a Velcro strap that would hold the item at an angle near the top of her bag so his tiny mirrored periscope would let him see what was going on.

Sometimes, it's handy having a five-inch-tall partner. It ensures the element of surprise, anyway.

With a smile of greeting, she slid into the booth opposite Bryant and set the big leather purse gently between them. He was in business casual today—a simple pair of khakis and a light blue button-down shirt. "Cara should be here in a few minutes. She had a call to make."

He nodded. "Cool. It gives us a minute to talk about her behind her back. How was the first run?"

Diana shook her head. "That guy was a jerk."

Bryant laughed. "Seriously. You would think they'd simply go quietly, given our collective awesomeness."

"Exactly. Idiots." She grinned. "We learned a couple of things. Cara is as good as we thought she'd be. She kept it together during the whole scenario and delivered the blow that took him out of the fight."

"It's nice when reality matches the file, isn't it?"

"Yeah, she's gonna work out fine. I saw no obvious magic talent, but it could be she reserved it. Either way, Cara Binot is a keeper."

He seemed suddenly uncomfortable, and it wasn't a good look on him. She frowned. "What?"

He shrugged. "This is probably something I should have asked a while ago. You know your magic has to come from somewhere, right? It doesn't develop at random."

A ripple of remembered fear disturbed her peace, but it was nowhere near as bad as it would have been if he'd asked when she first joined BAM in DC. She took a deep breath and nodded. "Yes. I'm aware. Yours, too. Everyone's."

Bryant nodded. "You don't have to talk about it if you don't want to, but I'd be interested to know both personally and professionally."

Diana sighed, laid her elbows heavily on the table, and shook her head in one of her hands. "Elf. I'm part elf."

He made a point of staring at her ears. She rolled her eyes and laughed helplessly as she shrugged. "My mom told me after an…incident when I was a kid. She had power but chose not to embrace it, and she taught me how to keep mine in check."

He frowned. "She decided you shouldn't use it?"

She shook her head before he even finished. "Nothing like that. But she wanted me to have a choice. It's one of the reasons I shadowed the squad that was destroyed by the magic attack—to see if that was a useful place for me to bring it all together."

Bryant grinned, and a hint of the smirking chucklehead she remembered from their first days together broke through. "Now, don't you feel better with that out in the open, pointy?"

"Bite me, Bryant. Now, it's your turn."

He shook his head. "I'm gonna maintain the mystery and keep you interested."

She groaned. "Honestly, you are an idiot." She sighed and tried to remember what they were talking about.

Oh yeah, that's right.

"The bounty capture did point out one glaring issue, though. We'll need better intel on…well, everything. Trying to take Harold in the body shop was a really stupid choice on my part. We should have watched him for a while and approached him somewhere less crowded, but I didn't have anyone to put on it or any systems for recon."

Her companion grimaced. "That makes sense. Spooling up is always a challenge. Full demands with limited resources. I'll see if I can at least get you some tech to help."

"Speaking of which..." she began but was interrupted by Cara's arrival. Her idea of casual was identical to Diana's—a pair of black jeans and a colorful untucked blouse, although hers was in deep scarlet rather than electric blue.

The newest member of the team slipped into the booth beside her boss and reached a hand across the table while Diana dodged the long ponytail that circled into her vision. Cara's voice was playful. "Bryant, I've heard so much about you."

Diana couldn't help but smirk.

She sounds like a veteran BAM Agent already.

He looked uncomfortable for a moment. "What, and from whom?"

Cara smirked wickedly. "It's all good. Well, most of it. And a smart investigator never reveals her sources."

Bryant rolled his eyes. "Oh, you'll fit right in."

Diana laughed, and so did her purse. The other woman's eyes darted down and Diana grinned. "I thought it was time for you to meet the other part of the team." She pulled the sides of her bag apart. "Rath, pop the lid."

The top of the canister swung open, and the troll launched himself into a somersault and onto the table. He landed cleanly beside her arm and waved at Cara. "Hi. Rath."

The marshal laughed and sounded unexpectedly young for an instant, and a grin spread across her face. "Hi, Rath. Cara." She reached out a closed fist, and he bumped it with his own.

The server arrived at that moment to take their drink order, a twenty-something boy with tattooed sleeves and plugs in his ears. A hoop hung from each of the expanded holes. Rath released a small, "Oooh," and Diana's brain conjured a picture of the troll with piercings, spacers, and tattoos.

It wouldn't be a bad look, actually, but would set a minimum size for him.

The server turned to him as if magical creatures were part of his nightly routine. "For you, tiny dude?"

Rath gave a toothy grin. "Pineapple juice."

"Right on." The server departed, his attention already drawn to a nearby table with four well-dressed young professional women who looked like they'd been celebrating for a while. Diana felt Cara's eyes and turned to meet the new recruit's gaze.

The other woman shook her head slowly. "So, this is merely everyday stuff for your organization, is it?"

Diana exchanged a glance with Bryant, and they nodded as one. He answered, "Yep, basically. And it's *our* organization now since you're one of us."

"One of us, one of us," Diana added. Bryant caught the reference and smiled, but Cara didn't seem to. "This is nothing. Remind me to tell you about the tentacle jerk someday. Now that guy really sucked."

"They all suck," he said with a small smile.

She grinned. "That should be our official motto."

He spoke again. "So, Cara, I hear that you've been in any number of magical scrapes, so don't pretend otherwise."

The marshal laughed. "I've had a little more than my fair share, probably, but I wouldn't say it's a common occurrence."

Diana quipped, "So this will be better, then."

Cara nodded. A determined expression set her grin aside. "All jokes aside, I think so. I'm looking forward to it more than I did when I landed here."

Approving nods accompanied the arrival of their drinks and the placing of their dinner orders. Rath decided to branch out beyond fruit and cheese and ordered Caribbean nachos, which were apparently regular ones with jerk sauce on them. Diana shrugged.

It's your stomach, buddy.

She took a slow pull on her beer, a double IPA with the unlikely moniker of Sleighwrecker. It was divine.

"So, what's the long-term strategy here?" Cara asked.

Bryant laughed. "Protect Pittsburgh, defend the Northeast, and eventually, rule the world."

"That's a plan I can get behind."

Diana rolled her eyes. "In a slightly shorter timeframe, the goal is to get our locations up and running, add some support staff to the security agency, and find ourselves an experienced investigator who knows the town."

Cara nodded. "I can put feelers out through the Marshals, but I don't have any direct contacts here. It'll probably be expensive to identify the right person, much less convince him or her to join."

"Everything's expensive." Diana heaved a sigh.

They both turned to Bryant. He grinned back at them. "It's always pleasant to be gazed upon with such desire, even if it's only for the budget I supposedly control."

Diana laughed. "You'll always be my favorite moneyman."

Rath echoed, "Moneyman," and giggled happily as he sipped his juice through the tiny straw the server had thoughtfully provided. Diana had noted a little extra traffic near their table, doubtless hoping for a better look at the troll.

Even in this day and age, five-inch-tall magical creatures aren't an everyday occurrence at your favorite restaurant.

She pinched the bridge of her nose as the first symptoms of an impending paperwork headache stirred to life. "I have a thought on the investigator. I'll be in DC for a week for a whole slew of bureaucratic nonsense, but I have a meeting with my FBI mentor while I'm there. If anyone should have a line on a good candidate or can put us in touch with someone who does, it's him."

The other two nodded. Bryant took a sip of his drink —a local stout that looked more like ink than a beverage —and sighed happily. "Okay, here's the deal. While Diana's away, our construction teams will be in town and work on both facilities. We'll prioritize the security agency because she thinks we need the training space quickly, and I agree. We can't do all our practice in the field."

Cara frowned and gave an exaggerated pout. "But why?" Everyone laughed on cue except Rath, who no doubt believed in live-action training, Rambo-style.

Diana took over the conversation. "Anyway, within a

week, we should have the agency ready—physically, at least, with the core set up in the main building."

Bryant nodded. "That's the plan."

The other woman looked pointedly at Diana's wrists, and she shifted the gaze to the bracelet on her right hand and the smartwatch on her left. She said, "So, let's talk about gear. I've noticed mine is less impressive than yours."

Bryant barely managed to swallow his drink before he burst out laughing, and Cara raised an eyebrow at him. Diana shook her head. "You're such a child." She turned back to their newest recruit. "Don't worry. I'm sure to return from DC with presents. But this points to a bigger issue. After the investigator, our first priority has to be to add a tech to the team and get the labs up and running. Using rental cars as a quartermaster will not fly indefinitely, and logistics are very much not my bag, baby." The shared phrase brought Lisa to her mind, and she smiled. Seeing her best friend was one of the things she looked forward to most in her upcoming trip.

He inclined his head as if in agreement. "Well, you'll be with the big boss. Maybe you can convince him."

They paused for the arrival of the food, and each sampled their plate and judged it good. Rath was particularly excited by the new experience as he munched a fried plantain that had been intended as a garnish. Judging from his dreamy smile, it was the best thing he'd ever tasted. The sweet and spicy scents whirled around the table to add the aromatic layer that completed a fine dining experience and set the atmosphere for a positive outing.

Cara smiled innocently. "So, Bryant, you'll leave soon, right?"

He smiled as the troll and two women laughed. Then, the movement deliberately casual, he dabbed at his lips with a napkin. "That is correct. I have other cities to do initial reviews on and people to meet along the way. I don't imagine I'll be back for a few weeks, assuming nothing blows up here."

Diana growled. "Speaking of blowing up, how did the press get all that information about the Cube?"

Bryant grumbled, "Your guess is as good as mine. Still, it was bound to come out eventually, I suppose. As far as the public knows, it's merely a second Ultramax inconveniently located in their backyard. There's nothing to indicate that they know it belongs to us, or even that they've heard of ARES."

She shook her head. "It doesn't feel like a coincidence."

Cara set her glass down with a small *thump*. "There's no such thing as coincidence."

The others nodded in agreement. Rath's bushy hair waved like a paintbrush with the sheer vigor of his agreement. "There are no coincidences. Only the illusion of coincidence."

Diana frowned at his tone. "English accent?"

Rath smiled. "V for Vendetta. Excellent knives."

Cara leaned and lowered her tone. "So, neither of you has mentioned the Kemana. Is there a reason for that?"

Bryant's face slipped into an impression of theatrical shock. "My, my. You *have* done your homework."

She shrugged. "The Marshals have access to a lot, including the known sites."

Diana silently applauded the fact that the woman didn't assume that they knew about *all* the locations. "We'll have to connect, eventually. I'd like to be a little more established before we do, so we have something to bring to the table in any discussion. But they're definitely in our plans."

With the meal over, the dishes cleared away, and coffees delivered for everyone except Rath—who topped his fruit juice up and devoted his energy to more fried plantains—they discussed the future of ARES in Pittsburgh and beyond, and what the constantly growing number of magical bad actors meant for the world. They exited the restaurant bound by their common agreement that the unique position the agency held, comparatively unhampered by layers of governmental bureaucracy, would prove vital as the worlds moved ever closer.

CHAPTER SIX

It was beyond strange to return to her old bureau office, given all that had happened in the short time since Diana had left to join BAM. The clean walls, bright lights, and shining linoleum floors brought a smile to her face that widened as she passed through the open door into Tyson Samuels' office.

He came around from behind the desk, dressed as always for a job that paid much more than his did. Today's choice of fashion was a solid navy suit that fit his trim form to perfection. The gray at his temples seemed to have taken more territory from the brown hair that covered his head since she'd last seen him. He shook her hand and gave it an extra pat before he released it. Samuels was by-the-book, and any more expressive physical contact, like a hug, was reserved for outside the office. He *was* an excellent hugger, though.

She sat in the familiar chair across his desk and marveled at the complete lack of change in everything other than herself. "So, did you find someone decent to replace me?"

Samuels nodded. "Fresh out of the Academy. She jumped through all the low-level stuff to Special Agent on her first day." He delivered it with a perfectly straight face.

Diana looked at him in momentary confusion. "Really?"

He laughed. "Of course not. We're still using temps like I said we would, searching for someone who's the right fit. You left difficult shoes to fill."

"But fashionable ones, I hope." She stroked the well-repaired boot at the bottom of her crossed denim-clad leg.

"As stylish as can be. How are things with you? I hear rumblings from up north."

Diana sighed. "It looks like it'll be as much of a hotspot as everyone thought." He nodded. "Anyway, that's part of the reason I'm here."

He grinned. "And the rest?"

"I need a reason to visit with my Rabbi?"

He waved his hand. "Never. You're always welcome in this office."

She frowned. "The guards at the front didn't seem to agree."

"Being off the books has its advantages but also comes with a few disadvantages." He shrugged.

Her tone conveyed her frustrations only too well. "More disadvantages, so far. I know the FBI has constantly been budget-challenged and even more so since Homeland came online, but ARES isn't much better at the moment."

"Starting a number of new locations will do that to an organization. Growing pains. Give it a while, and you'll be outfitted like James Bond."

She grinned. "I'll hold you to that. If it doesn't happen, I demand at least an exploding pen from your people. Oh, and one of those Lotus submarine cars."

"Done and done."

Diana sobered. "Witty banter aside, I need to find someone who knows Pittsburgh and understands investigation—ideally, police procedures rather than a private investigator or something. It would also be good to have a person who speaks the language of the local PD."

Samuels leaned back in his chair and tapped his chin with a thin finger. "Any other requirements?"

She shrugged. "She or he should be in shape and have at least *some* combat training. We can improve on their skills, but it would be best if they had a set we could evaluate before we accept them. I guess amazing investigative abilities might balance that out, but we all have to be ready to do everything, and a dead investigator isn't much use."

He raised an eyebrow curiously. "Are you gonna make 'em run the gauntlet?"

She rolled her eyes. "How the hell did you hear about that? Oh, wait, never mind. Bryant." Exasperation colored his name.

Samuels nodded. "He said it was a storm followed by a rainbow but wouldn't explain further."

Diana groaned. "Anyway, about that investigator."

Her mentor laughed and leaned forward to tap the laptop keys on his desk. "It just so happens I *do* know someone. He did six years as an Army MP before being RIFed. Currently, he works in homicide for Cleveland PD but has only been there a year. Before that, he was in Pittsburgh for five, with three spent as a detective."

"That sounds great so far. Any magical experience?"

He shrugged. "The file doesn't say, and I haven't heard."

"But he's good?"

The man inclined his head. "He's trusted by the people I trust."

"That's solid enough for me." She stood and moved toward the door, then stopped and turned. "Lisa's having a small gathering at my place—well, *her* place—tonight. Do you want to come?"

Samuels shook his head. "We have tickets. Hamilton."

Diana whistled. "Those are hard to get."

He grinned. "I *do* know a few people here and there."

"Tell Ellen I miss her and that she needs to keep you in line better."

She walked away, accompanied by his laughing response. "Maximum oversight already achieved. No need for improvement."

Entering her home as a visitor was far stranger than revisiting the FBI had been. The door opened before she could knock, and Lisa stood across the threshold. They both grinned like idiots and grappled in a hug that threatened to bind them at a molecular level. Her friend pulled her inside and kicked the door closed.

Diana protested, "Hey, be careful. That's not a training door. It's an actual door."

Lisa swung her black hair dismissively. "Don't worry, my landlord's an absentee. She'll have no idea what we do to the place."

A bark was accompanied by a shout of glee as Rath dove into a triple somersault from the back of the couch to plummet into the cushion beside Max's head. The dog gave him an amused look tinged with exasperation.

Exactly. Now you know how I feel.

"I think he spends most of his time tiny simply because he enjoys the acrobatic opportunities it offers."

Lisa looked at him with something close to delight. She didn't have enough experience with him to be exasperated. *Yet.* "Count your lucky stars. Imagine if he did that at eight feet."

Diana shuddered. "He'll wind up breaking through the floor into the basement. What will your landlord say then?"

"She'll probably abandon me and move to another city."

She put a hand over her heart. "Ouch."

The other woman grinned and waved her into the kitchen.

Rath shouted, "Abandon!" as they passed.

Without looking back, Diana replied, "Shut up, you." That drew more laughter from the troll.

Lisa retrieved two Atlas Rowdy Ales from the fridge when she arrived, popped the top on one, and extended it to her friend. Diana took a long, satisfying drink.

"I haven't had the chance to sample Pittsburgh's craft culture yet. You need to come up," she said.

"You need to find some time," Lisa countered.

She nodded. "This is true. Still, you come up and I'll find the time."

They clinked their bottles in a familiar gesture of agreement. "Deal."

Diana jerked her head over her shoulder. "Did the

trouble twins behave today?" She'd dropped them off before heading out to her day of meetings after driving down that morning.

Bureaucracy sucks.

"They did great, although they were a little noisy during one of my calls." Lisa had agreed to work from home to keep an eye on the pair while Diana was in town. It wasn't so much that they needed watching but that she felt uneasy about being back in DC after the threats of retribution from her first adventure as an agent in BAM. Cresnan and his fellows were locked up in the Cube, but there were more of their organization somewhere out there. It was only a matter of time before they clashed again.

She sat at the counter where she could watch Rath practice his floor routine on the newly upholstered couch cushions. "No problems with Steve?"

Lisa slid onto the stool next to her. "He probably would've left me alone anyway after the alley, but that stuff you dug up on his company is a good insurance policy."

"I knew you wouldn't have told him about my job change."

"Not a chance. Sisters before misters."

Diana bumped her friend's fist in an act of solidarity. "Well, we closed their access off, so that's no longer a worry, and we have leverage if he ever causes trouble. I'd call that neatly wrapped up."

Lisa tipped her bottle and made an appreciative sound. "So, I took your spot at Jackson's studio."

"You didn't tell me that. Go you." She raised her brows in real surprise.

She nodded. "I really love it. It's great exercise, plus

you get to twist big guys into little puddles of submission on the ground." Diana choked on her drink, and her friend laughed. "It's more fun with the cute ones, of course."

After she'd recovered her composure, she wiped her mouth and pointed a commanding finger. "No dating inside the dojo. This means you."

Lisa rolled her eyes. "Witch."

Diana grinned. "Wench." The doorbell rang, and Rath and Max dashed to the door with excited shouts and barks, respectively. The Borzoi stood on his hind legs and put his front paws up so Rath could climb on his head and look through the peephole. Diana glanced at Lisa, who shrugged.

"Kayleigh," the troll chirped, and Max moved so Diana could let her in.

"Kayleigh, great to see you. Thanks for coming out." She immediately looked at the visitor's boots, which were shiny, black, and very similar to her own. "Are those the new versions?"

The blonde tech laughed. "I can't even get in the door and take my coat off before you ask. *That* is the sign of a true shoe fetishist." Diana backed out of the way and let her pass but she continued her examination. Kayleigh rolled her eyes. "To answer your question, no. These are the old pair. I'm still working on the new one. Other projects are sucking up my time."

She nodded in response, and Lisa materialized with a beer and handed it to the newcomer. "I'm Lisa. Sorry, Diana was too rude to introduce us."

Kayleigh laughed. "Kayleigh. I'm also sorry."

Diana rolled her eyes and turned to Rath and Max. "Do you see the abuse I take?"

The dog barked and the troll shook his head. "Sad. So sad." They all burst into laughter at his comically forlorn expression.

An hour later, the remainder of the guests had arrived. Lisa claimed a dozen was always best and didn't include Max and Rath in the tally. A few of Lisa's coworkers had joined them, some of Diana's FBI pals—she was especially happy to see Rodriguez, who'd been with her at the start of this magical adventure—and a couple of members of the DC ARES team. It was a rare social appearance for Nancy Blackwood, the DC team's second sniper. Even though most of the crowd used cover stories of one kind or another, everyone still seemed to enjoy themselves.

She noticed a conspicuous absence and made her way upstairs to the spare bedroom. The small room held a dresser, a television, and a queen-sized bed that was currently occupied. Kayleigh stretched out on the mattress and propped on her elbows with her face at the foot to watch a Marvel film with Rath and Max. The troll and the tech were both engaged in an animated discussion about Black Widow's gadgets.

"They were much better in the comics," she pointed out.

He nodded authoritatively, then looked at Diana. "Need comics. Must train."

Diana shook her head and bumped Kayleigh with her hip. "Move over, antisocial woman."

The tech groaned and shifted to the side. "I'm not anti-social by definition, but I don't do well in crowds."

"It's all good. Thank you again for coming out."

She stared at her with a perfectly sculpted blonde eyebrow. "I couldn't miss the chance to visit with Rath."

Diana nodded. "I have a suggestion on that front, actually."

Kayleigh forced herself to a sitting position. "No, you don't."

"Yes, I do." She nodded again to emphasize her seriousness.

"No. I am not becoming a field agent."

They both grinned. "Eventually, I'll convince you. But no, that's not what I had in mind."

Kayleigh wiped imaginary sweat from her brow. "What *were* you thinking, then?"

"I need a tech in Pittsburgh to get the labs going and make us lots of cool gear and stuff."

Her companion frowned. "I'm sure I can suggest someone."

Diana shook her head firmly. "I need a *great* tech. And you're the best I know."

"Ems is way better than me."

She slashed her hand between them. "No, Emerson is way *more experienced* than you. There's a big difference there."

Kayleigh grinned. "It's nice of you to say that, but I haven't heard that you're at the lab stage of your startup yet."

Diana shrugged. "It's my office. I have the budget. It's

simply a matter of making the dollars dance in the right way."

"I can't imagine leaving DC."

"Neither could I and suddenly, I have fantastic river views outside my office window. Consider it." She laid her last card down. "You'd be head tech and would get to pick your own staff as we grow."

Something sparked in the woman's eyes at that, but she still resisted. "I don't know, Diana."

"Think about it." At an explosion on the screen, Rath fell and rolled in a cackling fit. She stood and pointed at him. "And maybe explain to the little ruffian that explosions aren't always a good thing."

He grinned at her. "Boom. Big bada boom."

I really need to cancel my cable.

CHAPTER SEVEN

After a week of bureaucracy, Diana was beyond ready to get back into real activity. She entered the Sheraton's lobby through the big revolving doors and gazed at the high open area through the leaves of tall potted trees. To the right were conference spaces and to the left, the hotel proper with eight floors of balconies looked over the atrium. A circular bar filled the center of the room ahead and the afternoon sun filtered through the glass that made up the ceiling.

Cara sat alone on a tall stool at the bar, seemingly a business person having a late lunch.

She looks right in a suit.

The AR glasses that adorned her face were a new model, one of several different options they had acquired to assist in their multi-agency camouflage. If she seemed to talk occasionally into the microphone that dangled from her earbuds, an observer would put it down to ordinary texting or phone chat.

Which it is, only to someone closer than an observer might expect.

Her voice was clear in Diana's earpiece. "It's about time you got here. You've cut it a little close, haven't you?"

Diana angled for a chair at one of the low tables around the edge of the bar space. "You have a lot to learn about subtlety, Cara."

A soft snort sounded in reply. "Subtlety is overrated. Force, that's where it's at."

Her response was forestalled by the arrival of the skinny bartender with the spiky hair, who seemed disappointed when all she ordered was two coffees. He trudged away with an expression that suggested someone had hurt his favorite pet. "What's his deal?"

Cara's tone turned gossipy. "Well, his girlfriend left him, and he's not sure he wants to stay in Pittsburgh anymore."

Diana shifted position to watch the door. "You've gotten pretty personal with the bartender. How long have you been here, anyway?"

"Please. He told me that in the first five minutes. I think he's on a quest for moral support rather than tips at the moment."

"Then it's good you're the one at the bar. I don't do emotional counseling so well."

"It's not my strong suit either. I prefer shooting my problems."

She smothered a laugh. "That's probably not an appropriate way to deal with romantic entanglements."

Cara's voice held the satisfaction that came with having

successfully set someone up for a punch line. "It's worked so far."

Diana groaned as two things happened at once. The morose server dropped the coffees off, and the revolving door spun. She blinked, and her glasses performed their cyber wizardry to confirm that the tall man who strode into the lobby was detective Tony Ryan. He seemed average in most respects—neither fat nor thin, neither muscled nor weak, with nothing distinguishing about his facial features aside from the bushy hair that crowned his lip. It was a solid patch of ebony and seemed a natural progression from the man's dark skin. Cara's voice whispered in her ear. "I bet he grooms that mustache for at least an hour a day."

She didn't reply and instead, stood as the man approached. "Detective Ryan, I'm Diana."

He took the outstretched hand and gave it a shake—neither hard nor soft—and replied, "Tony." His heavy wool coat went over the back of the chair, and he gestured at the cup in front of him as he sat. She nodded, and he took a sip before he unwound the scarf from around his neck. "Thanks for the invitation—and the coffee."

"Thanks for coming."

He bared a set of perfectly white teeth in a grin. "When Tyson Samuels suggests I should do something, I tend to do that thing."

Diana laughed. "He *does* have a way with people, doesn't he? Let me guess, it went something like"—she dropped her voice and injected a dose of rasp into it—"'Got an opportunity for you. Get your ass to Pittsburgh.'" Her gruff impersonation made him smile wider.

"Yeah, that's about right."

They shared another laugh that ended quickly, and his eagerness to get down to business was obvious in his body posture. She was happy to leave small talk behind as well. "So, before we start, I need your word that what we speak about will remain only between the two of us, plus Samuels, if you require an outside opinion. He told me your word is gold."

Tony nodded. "I work hard to make it so. And you have my promise."

The bartender returned to refill their cups, and Tony thanked him. His immobile frown seemed impervious to social niceties. The detective's face showed he'd noticed, and Diana gave him the short version. "Bad breakup. He's down. If we're lucky, he'll stay away for a while." The last was for Cara, who she hoped would distract the boy while they talked.

Diana set her phone on the table and activated the comm jamming app. It would block most signals in the lobby other than the encrypted comms she and her partner wore. "I'm not sure what Tyson told you, but I'll go through the broad strokes quickly. ARES is an off-the-books op, with oversight that goes all the way to the White House."

She took a drink to soothe her throat.

Stupid winter.

"We have identified Pittsburgh as a growing hotspot for magical trouble, so we're establishing an office here. We need someone who has good investigative skills, knows the city, and can also kick ass. Samuels says you fit the bill."

Tony nodded and seemed to display clear confidence that he met all areas of the description.

"Right now, there's only me and one other on the team. *And a troll. And a dog.*

"Once you're on board, we expect to continue growing aggressively, both in the number of agents and support staff. We have a good location in the downtown, and it's mostly finished, finally."

He took her pause as an invitation to ask questions. "Is the new Ultramax part of your group?"

"It is. We'll claim it's identical to the other one in town and not as big an eyesore, but it does actually belong to us."

"I read that there are ongoing transfers in from around the country."

Diana rolled her eyes. "That wasn't actually intended for public consumption yet. When we think someone is relevant to the work we do, they're brought here so we can keep a closer eye on them. My team doesn't run it, but we'll act in support when needed. In practice, there will probably be a fair amount of interaction."

He nodded again. "What kind of ass-kicking do you expect to do?"

She grinned. "If it's weird, then it's us," she responded and smiled at his chuckle. "Seriously, though, if it involves magic, it falls under our mandate to either investigate or deal with."

"Budget?"

"Not bad and getting better. We'll run lean for a while, but you won't have to take a pay cut or anything."

He took another drink and leaned his long form back in the chair to stick his legs out the side. "Upward potential?"

She shrugged. "That would be more appropriately answered by the next higher layer of authority, but with the level of expansion ARES has planned, talented people will be needed. It's reasonable to think that if you have the skills, you'd have a good shot at one of those posts. But that's not a promise, merely an observation."

He sighed. "I do have a soft spot in my heart for Pittsburgh, and it is *way* too cold on the lake in Cleveland."

"So, I take it you're still interested."

He nodded.

"Then I have a couple of questions for you. First, what kinds of magic have you come up against so far?"

"When I was here in Pittsburgh, I saw it creep in at the edges of some of my cases. Nothing definitive, only suspicions about what might be going on at the root of certain situations. I've never actually had to confront a magic user."

Diana sipped her coffee and waited.

"In the military police, we had one guy who joined in ROTC and made his way up to active duty, then started using mental powers of some kind to steal stuff. The trouble is, magic doesn't make you smarter than any other chucklehead, and he screwed up when he tried to mess with the mind of his fence's girlfriend." Diana's eyes widened.

Not a good idea.

"It turns out he hadn't locked in as much control of the man as he thought and was shot while he tried to seduce her. We investigated, put the pieces together, and apprehended him while he was still in the hospital."

Diana recalled her own recent public capture attempt. "That seems like a dangerous play."

He shrugged. "We borrowed some intelligence types and had them dress up as doctors and nurses. He twigged to one, but the others had him sedated before he caught on that everyone in the room was a plant."

"Nice. Your idea?"

Tony nodded stoically. His lips never twitched. He stated a fact, but if he was prideful, he hid it well.

"Okay, next question. Why homicide?"

"I'm always looking for a new challenge, I guess." He shrugged. "Plus, I have a thing against people who are psycho enough to believe they have the right to take someone else's existence away from them."

"So, you're softhearted?"

He laughed. "My ex-wife would certainly argue against that sentiment. No, I simply think that sort of action should be confined to those who opt in, not the innocents on the periphery. I was a big fan of *The Wire*, you know? It's like Omar says. You only mess with those in the game."

Diana kept her eyes on his and maintained her neutral expression with some effort. "So, you don't mind when criminals off each other?"

Tony laughed. "Oh, hell no. They still have to go down. It simply doesn't make me quite as upset as when someone shoots a civilian."

She let her body relax.

Right answer.

"Okay, last question. Why are you interested in leaving? You seem to have everything where you want it to be."

His face settled into the most serious expression she'd seen from him. "Sometimes, it feels like things are getting worse instead of better. More crimes and more murders, whether magic-related and not. People seem unsettled at the new reality of the worlds coming together, even though they've had plenty of time to wrap their heads around it."

She nodded.

Tony continued. "If there's a chance to diminish the flow of trouble at its source rather than downstream, that seems like a worthwhile useful endeavor. Plus, Samuels told me I'd be a moron to refuse."

"That doesn't sound like Samuels."

He nodded a little sheepishly. "Okay, what he said was I'd be 'a fucking lunatic moron' to turn down the chance to join your team."

Diana burst into laughter. "Now that *does* sound like Samuels." A line of text appeared on her glasses and momentarily distracted her. "Okay, I thought of one more. Have you done any bounty work?"

"Nope. It's not part of my job, and I'm a little too busy to hang out my own shingle."

"But you could certainly handle the investigative side of tracking them down, right?"

He shrugged. "It's what I do. I take the pieces and put them together until the picture makes sense."

She inclined her head as she read both his expression and body posture. "And when the picture makes sense, punch the person it reveals in the skull?"

Tony grinned. "At the very least."

She shot a glance at Cara and smiled at the message that appeared in her lenses.

Looks good.

Diana turned back to him. "Okay, one more thing. Since you were an MP, I know you're familiar with our weapons and paraphernalia. We'll still run you through some tests to make sure your skills are sharp."

He nodded his agreement.

"We'll mix it up fairly often if recent history is to be believed. Is that a problem for you? I imagine the life of a homicide detective is a little slower paced."

"I hate to be bored." His grin widened.

She laughed and shook her head. "One thing I can guarantee, you will *not* be bored. You're in—provisionally—if you want it."

"I can take a leave of absence from work without a problem." He raised his cup in a toast. "Here's to living in exciting times."

CHAPTER EIGHT

Under cover of early morning darkness, Diana unlocked the front door of the security agency and swung it open to discover Bryant seated behind the desk. He fiddled casually with his phone, then looked up. "About time you got here, Sheen." His grin showed legitimate warmth, however, rather than his usual teasing.

Her own smile stretched her face enough that even she noticed it as she stepped into the room. "Missed you, too, BC."

He smiled at the old joke.

"I thought you were still out of town for a week or two," she observed casually.

"True. But I felt it was worth the trip to see your first training run in the new space. When I heard you'd requested BAM folks to play the opposing force…well, I had to be here." His jeans and t-shirt suggested he'd join in.

"And here I thought it was my sparkling personality. Do you want to take a look?"

He nodded and rose to join her as she walked to the

otherwise unremarkable door that led to the back. A wave of her watch in front of the sensor popped a hidden wall panel open, and she typed in the code to unlock the door. As she was about to lead the way through, the main entrance behind them swung open, and the rest of her unit entered.

Cara offered a bubbly, "Bryant, good to see you."

Tony walked forward and extended a hand. "Tony Ryan, newest team member."

"Bryant Bates, oldest team member." The group laughed as they wandered into the rear of the building.

When Diana had departed for DC, the base had been practically empty. Now, it was filled with a variety of rooms and goodies. The group stood in a preparation area that stretched to the back of the warehouse. A complicated computer terminal had been mounted on the wall near the entrance. It ran a custom ARES software program that created floor plans and structures based on strategic objectives. The people who installed it had set it up for their first run.

The system gave orders to a pair of bright yellow autonomous forklifts parked in the middle of the preparation area against the wall, neatly centered within the slashed warning lines that marked their home bases. There was a note that cautioned against having humans on the training room floor beyond the safe zone while the forklifts did their work, as they had no particular programming to avoid living beings. Diana had made sure to file that under the *very important things to remember* section of her mind. The far side of the facility held lockers full of equipment arranged around several benches.

The warehouse was filled with crates that had been stacked and attached with clever plates and grooves to maintain a sense of uniformity. These were a uniform dark-gray and were very sturdy without weighing a ton, which made it possible to arrange them in unique ways. Right now, they formed a solid barrier that cut off the remainder of the space, save for a single-file path that ran back six feet before it turned.

They all moved to the equipping area, and Diana unlatched the mounted cabinets to display sets of army laser training gear. Bryant checked his phone and reversed course toward the door. "The rest of the OPFOR's here." He opened it to reveal Gillians and Johnson from the DC team. Diana crossed and exchanged fist bumps and hugs with both of them. Bryant frowned. "Why didn't *I* get hugs?"

Diana raised an eyebrow. "Go away for long enough that I miss you, and you might. In your case, maybe a few months. Possibly a year."

He laughed and touched his chest to acknowledge the point.

She turned back to the newcomers. "I didn't realize they'd send the A-Team."

The other woman grinned. The expression transformed her strong face from aggressive to warm. "When the word came in, there were plenty of volunteers."

Johnson added, "It turns out most of us liked the idea of checking out the new unit. Blackwood wanted to come, but we couldn't be down both snipers at once."

Gillians nodded her agreement. "We've got HRT in

place as backup and the ability to request PDA support if needed. Those folks aren't big fans of ours, though."

Bryant laughed. "That's putting it mildly."

Diana frowned and asked, "Because of the lack of oversight?"

"Right on target," he affirmed.

Johnson clapped his hands. "Speaking of targets, how about we get to the shooting?"

She gestured for them to follow her back to the lockers. Her team had already donned the sensors, which strapped on above the knees and elbows, plus a chest piece and collar that would register strikes to the head. While the others suited up, fast-dressing Cara pulled a carbine from the wall and inspected it. "Pew, pew."

The room filled with good-natured laughter. Not only did this serve as a good test, but it also helped as a team-building exercise. Diana looked up from fastening her leg sensors. "I hope you guys can handle the high-tech nature of our gear. It's not quite the same as being pounded by a paintball."

Gillians laughed. Her voice was low and appealing. "Pain is a good teacher, though."

Johnson nodded and grinned. "I bet you won't forget to check for tripwires anytime soon after those claymores."

Diana scowled. Her first run at the ARES gauntlet still bothered her, mainly because of her mistake, but she would never forget how painful that deluge had been as the pellets exploded over her body. "Maybe there's a way to make the laser tag system reinforce the need to not do stupid things. Once we have a tech attached, we'll look into it."

Meanwhile, Cara had pulled rifle magazines—batteries, actually—and a pistol and matching mags from the cabinet. She slotted each into the appropriate spot on the light-weight vests, belts, and thigh holders.

In companionable silence, everyone geared up and were soon ready to rumble.

Bryant grinned. "See you inside, kiddos. Go Team Red!" His partners echoed the call, and the three of them disappeared into the aisle created by the stacks of crates on either side.

Tony looked doubtfully at them. "Are those things safe?"

Diana laughed. "Very. They're anchored to each other and the walls. They've been well tested, believe me." During the visit to DC, Rath and Diana had visited the ARES training facility at Emerson's insistence. The man had even gone so far as to escort them himself in a rare trip outside the bounds of his lab.

The troll did more than simply visit. He ran through the course at three feet, then tried it at full size. The exercise proved an eye-opening experience as she watched the troll leap from crate to crate and climb and tumble. He was less acrobatic in his largest form, but at middle size, he maintained all the grace of his tinier self with more force added to his blows. At the end of the session, Emerson shook his head. "This will never do. You'll need gear for your biggest form, too."

The troll had rewarded the scientist with a huge grin. "Is good. Must train."

Diana blinked to clear the memories and found her team staring at her with amused smiles. "Sorry. Woolgathering. Your fault for not bringing me coffee. What kind of subordinates are you?" They laughed and she grinned. "Okay, this scenario's a simple one. We go in, we try to survive, and if we take them out before they take us out, we win. If the sensor goes off, you can't use that limb anymore. If it's your head or chest, you're done."

Cara asked, "Only weapons? No hand-to-hand?"

She triggered her comm system and spoke in the most casual and innocent tone she could muster. "Bryant, Cara wants confirmation that hand-to-hand is okay. It is, right?"

His response came back immediately and enthusiastically. "Oh, *hell* no. We've all heard about what she did to that bounty."

Laughter sounded across the channel.

Diana grinned. "Gotcha. Switching to team." She flicked the selector and motioned her people to do the same. "Cara, you can be tactical lead on this one. We'll mix it up throughout the session and probably run it at least once with each of us in charge, then switch sides and play defense."

Cara nodded. "All right. I'm first, Tony is second, and Diana third. If we find an intersection, I go forward, Tony takes left, Diana right."

"Remember that Johnson is a sniper," Diana cautioned. "He likes to cause trouble from up high."

The other woman grimaced. "Enemy snipers suck. That's a really good argument for getting at least one set of gear that causes pain. It's not like we'd have to tell them ahead of time."

They laughed and advanced into the labyrinth. At an almost immediate right turn, Cara led them safely through it. A left followed, and she peeked her head around the corner. "There's a short staircase made of crates, so we'll have to either jump or climb."

Each crate was a two-foot square, so it wasn't a ridiculous leap, but the day would certainly qualify as a leg day if they had to traverse many of them. She gestured to illustrate the scene with her hands. "Beyond it is what looks like an intersection—a perfect choice for an ambush. I'll go through fast. You stay a beat or three back and see if they bite." They climbed quietly up the stairs before Cara surged up the final one and raced to the crossed corridors ahead.

The characteristic whine of a laser rifle sounded, but there was no answering buzz to signal a hit. Tony hurtled forward and to the left as instructed. Diana followed a step behind and focused on the right. She dropped when she saw the enemy, and the bolt intended for her nailed Tony as he turned to support her. Her triple-pull on her rifle's trigger fired to strike Gillians at chest and shoulder, and the woman sat with a grin. "Nice shooting, Diana."

Tony stepped beside her. His arm hung dramatically. "Couldn't you at least have killed me so I could get some rest?" They all laughed, and he set his rifle down and drew his pistol. "No reloads for me." He swung the "dead" arm for emphasis.

Cara's voice crackled over the comm. "Enough playing. Let's move." They fell back into line, and their leader adjusted their order. "Diana, middle. The rifle-less can bring up the rear."

He shot her a grin.

Diana was sure Bryant would have warned Johnson

against using magic, which made her concern about the sniper that much greater.

I can't allow myself to depend on early warning, but it's nice when it happens.

They advanced and the level appeared to widen at the end of the corridor.

"It looks like a room ahead," Cara whispered.

Diana whispered, "Yeah. That's not a good sign."

"I'm thinking run and gun since they probably have the sniper watching the entrance."

She nodded. "That's what I'd do."

Tony sighed. "I guess it's time for me to be the action movie sidekick and sacrifice myself for the team."

Cara grinned. "You know it. In addition to being one of Hollywood's favorite stories, it's also sound strategy."

He moved to stand beside her. "Suggestions?"

She patted him on the shoulder. "Run fast and keep running fast. It's important to identify enemies and shoot them, especially the sniper, but don't stop for anything. Find the room's exit and reach it. Then, once you're through, turn to eliminate anyone who follows."

Diana added, "As long as it isn't us."

"Right," Cara clarified with a laugh. "Please do *not* shoot your teammates."

Tony frowned. "Not even for fun?"

She shook her head. "Go in five." She counted down as he took position. The sound of laser weapons discharging followed as he pelted across the room. The marshal followed quickly, and Diana brought up the rear.

She immediately raised her rifle and looked for John-son. The barrel of his weapon protruded between two crates stacked high and to the right, but she couldn't get an angle on him. She hurtled in that direction while Cara went left. Dimly registered shots were immediately followed by the sound of a fatal strike. Return fire rattled from her side, a different pitch than their foes', and a shout of anger from Bryant put a smile on her face. A simultaneous beep declared a limb hit, and Cara cursed.

Diana continued to track right as she sought the sniper. She wasn't in time to stop his next attack. Another fatal shot chimed unmistakably, and Cara shouted an even louder curse. Diana thrust forward, acquired a target on Johnson in midair, and delivered a single shot to his head in the same moment he was visible. She'd already yanked her rifle around to eliminate Bryant when she landed, but he was nowhere to be seen.

Bastard.

She scrambled to her feet, kept her weapon trained on the doorway, and stopped beside Cara. Since she was dead, she couldn't share any useful information such as where BC had been wounded. Diana popped her magazine and swapped it with a full one. Her eyes locked on the entryway. The smooth exchange took only seconds, and she glanced at Cara. A broad grin stretched across the woman's face. "It's always nice when work feels like play, isn't it?"

Diana laughed. "Enjoy it while you can."

She nodded. "My rule for living. Now, go shoot that jerk."

From the corner of the room, Tony moaned. "I'm also dead. Heroically, even. Doesn't anyone care?"

They laughed, and Diana followed her opponent's only possible flight path. The passage rapidly became a tunnel created by boxes stacked high overhead, and her senses protested the claustrophobic space. Her instincts told her she was about two-thirds of the way through the warehouse when an opening appeared ahead. She held her rifle trained forward as she stuck her head in to peer in all directions.

It was a wide space littered with obstacles—some two crates high, and some three. She sprinted forward and flattened her back against one, noting as she did so that there was no exit other than the one she'd used.

Unexpected. And bad. He could be behind any one of these boxes, waiting for me to make a mistake.

She sifted through her options, which weren't many, and surveyed the room. It seemed that the stacks were arranged three or four rows deep. The only real choice was to move along an outer wall so she could at least be protected from one direction. She looked up and considered climbing to the top of other close columns of crates. While she quickly discarded that plan as tactically unsound, she stored it away as a last-ditch option if she was ever really in such a situation.

She stalked toward the right wall with her rifle trained forward and her ears open. When she reached the final stacked cover before it, she fished a spare pistol magazine awkwardly from her right thigh pouch with her left hand and took a breath. She flicked her weapon to auto fire and threw the magazine back the way she'd come, then dashed for the rear of the room. She raced through the first and second rows and found him in the third, already recovering from his instinctual reflex to turn toward the decoy.

She depressed the trigger, and his suit registered a fatal

shot. Bryant responded with a dramatic fall to the floor. She let her rifle dangle from its strap and crossed to where he lay turned on his side with his face down. Her laugh smug, she poked him with a foot to roll him over. "Okay, Bryant, that's one to nothing for me."

Her eyes widened when she saw his grin, and she heard the grenade tumble from where it had rested in his hand, secured by his body weight. *Again.* That was, regretfully, the only thought she had time for before the virtual laser spat death in all directions.

After an exhausting day of training runs—twelve in all— they took over the back room of a neighborhood bar Bryant had heard positive things about. Cracked paneling and band posters covered most of the walls. They shot pool and snacked on plates of appetizers while they waited. Diana took a sip of her local lager, pronounced it good, and watched Bryant line up his shot on the eight ball. "Miss it, Noonan. Miss."

He laughed and screwed the shot up, allowing Gillians back in the game. She gave Diana a thumbs-up. He came over and shook his head. "You suck, Sheen."

"No, *you* suck. What the hell was up with that grenade?"

He looked slightly sheepish. "Yeah, that was a little unfair. The DC folks brought them up—a present from Kayleigh."

They laughed simultaneously, and Diana said, "I'm glad you could make it."

His smile was familiar and oddly comforting. "I wouldn't have missed it."

They spent another hour together before Bryant and the DC crowd had to jet off to their various responsibilities. Diana and her team took seats at the bar for one more drink. Cara sat on her left.

"We have a strong core for the unit here," the marshal said.

"Agreed." Tony shuffled on his chair on her right. "And that training *was* fun."

Diana nodded. "It's good that we work well together because I think we'll be called to real action sooner rather than later."

The others nodded. Cara finished her drink, stood, and yawned. "I need thirty minutes in a hot tub, followed by a solid ten hours of sleep. But after that, bring it on."

CHAPTER NINE

Vincente set the power crystal statue carefully into his safe, closed the door, and spun the lock. He slipped the coin into a small pocket sewn on the inside of his black button-down shirt and secured the fastener to conceal it again. A little disgruntled, he shook his head.

Plans are not proceeding apace.

The sound from below alerted him that some things still ran on time, though. He crossed to the tall windows that comprised one side of his office. They were the best feature in the space and the rest was purely utilitarian—a metal desk, metal chair, and metal bookshelves on the wall over ugly paneling. The safe was the only quality item present, and he'd had to add it after he'd taken possession of the warehouse. The panes of glass overlooked the storage floor twenty feet below filled with pallets and crates of valuables. Some were legitimate but most were not. He turned and exited through the office's only door onto a metal staircase leading down to the lower level.

The business created operating funds by selling goods

of questionable provenance to anyone willing to buy. The warehouse itself had formerly been part of a steel mill complex and had access to the river and the nearby highway. It even had a rail line positioned beside it which made it infinitely easier to meet his customers' needs. Plus, only empty shells of buildings stretched for miles around, which assured the privacy he and his operations required. Gentrification hadn't quite reached this far upriver. *Yet.*

He deliberately held a scowl on his face but smiled inwardly when those who entered the warehouse separated into two distinct camps. The true believers stood on the left. Their leader Sarah was a highly skilled witch who devoutly believed in the vision Rhazdon had created for Oriceran and later, for Earth. Those with her varied in their levels of commitment, but the woman's charisma kept them all in line. They would be completely reliable provided that she was.

Those motivated by more mercenary interests gathered on the opposite side of the room. Their leader Marcus described them as, "Opportunists with a certain moral flexibility." The description always prompted a grin, even though he never allowed such an expression to reach his face. Aside from Marcus, they were little more than street-level thugs. The man bound them into a usable force, however, and they possessed the requisite skills to slip in and out of the circles that his customers inhabited.

Vincente nodded as he stepped off the metal stairs. Sarah was the muscle and accomplished at acquisition. Marcus was the middleman and forged connections that allowed them to sell the goods and reap the rewards they needed. It was a good arrangement. Of course, both groups participated in the occasional robbery, either for operating capital or for other items of interest. It was this that had brought them together today.

He arrived as the two faction leaders faced off in a heated argument, as they often did. Marcus was a wasp who snuck in to sting and then retreated to plan his next attack. Vincente often despaired over the thin skin that compelled Sarah to engage with him. At other times, he admired the restraint that kept her from crushing the man where he stood. Today seemed to be a good example of that restraint.

Marcus sneered. "That woman has not only been dead for twenty-some years, but she also lost. She seems like a strange bitch to worship."

Sarah scowled at his smirk. "We do not worship Rhazdon, as you well know, human. We simply believe in her vision."

He tapped his chin. "What was that again? To take the power from those who have it?" He shrugged. "That's noble. *Not.*"

She bristled. "Like you understand anything about nobility, street rat." The two groups drifted closer and hands inched toward hidden wands or weapons. That was enough of that. There would be no bloodshed this day.

Vincente stepped forward and clapped loudly. "Sarah, Marcus, thank you for coming—and thank you all as well." He turned and waved an arm at the gathering. "We will sit and discuss matters over here."

He led them to a circle of metal chairs arranged with a gap at each pole. As expected, one group took the seats to the left, and the others those to the right. An argument could be made that this lack of unity would lead to suboptimal results. The counterargument contended that pitting them against each other would bring out the best in all of them. Vincente didn't know which was best, and he didn't really care.

One has to play the cards they are dealt, and these are mine.

He found the exact center of the circle, pulled on his black vest to smooth it under his coat, and straightened his indigo tie. "We have been assigned two vital tasks from above." Only Sarah and Marcus were privy to the true nature of the Remembrance. The rest simply knew others were positioned higher in the food chain. "First, we must begin to set the stage for a larger undertaking. We will do this by inflaming the public against the new prison that has been built nearby."

A member of Marcus's group who was more impulsive and perhaps less intelligent than those around him piped up in a thick Pittsburgh accent. "Yeah, I heard about that. What, one wasn't enough?" A smattering of laughter followed his words. "Do you think it's gonna be a problem for us?"

Not for you, at any rate, my friend.

Vincente rotated to face the man. "No, not a problem. Instead, it's an opportunity. It is disguised and intended to be hidden. We confounded our enemies and sowed chaos by revealing it, which was the first part of our efforts. Now, with the right words in the right ears, we will alarm the populace and convince them it is a danger, that the magical prisoners housed there are a threat to their own lives and those of their children."

Another member of Marcus's crew added, "It's not like

we'll be lying." That drew dark laughs from both sides of the circle. Even Vincente's lips twitched.

"The second task is more important. Indeed, it is *vitally* important and thus more complicated." The groups fell silent, and he could sense them leaning forward in interest. "The nearby Museum of Natural History has received a shipment of antiquities discovered somewhere across the planet." He waved a hand to indicate that the precise location didn't matter. "They do not realize that stored among them are a number of powerful artifacts left by those who crossed over long ago."

He clasped his hands behind his back and turned to the magical side of the area. "They have hosted Oriceran exhibits before, and the place is appropriately well-defended. The Silver Griffins would have envied their equipment." A laugh swept through those he faced, as their knowledge of the magical history of Earth allowed them to appreciate the reference. "They have wisely employed magic to prevent us from simply creating portals into the building. We will have to do it the old-fashioned way."

Marcus sneered. "My people are *very* good at old-fashioned."

Sarah scoffed and tossed her mane of black hair. "Witches and wizards handled matters like this long before you were a child."

Vincente held his hands up before the sniping could devolve into a group discussion. "Focus, please."

The two leaders both nodded before Marcus spoke. "We can put the word out on the street about the new prison. While we do that, we'll get some heavier weaponry and maybe a line on people inside the museum to exploit."

Sarah added, "If we time the attack with an assembly in protest of the prison, it might distract the human authorities."

Vincente nodded. "Excellent. You two can work with your groups to plan it in a moment. First, though, I would like you both to join me in the office."

He led them up the stairs, which clanged with each footfall. Once inside, he directed them into the chairs on the far side of his desk but remained standing to gaze out the window. The minions below avoided one another carefully.

Sarah and Marcus were more silent than one would have expected, given the show downstairs.

But that's what it is—a show to make sure their crews stay loyal. In reality, they are only half as antagonistic and twice as smart as they let on. I would admire them if such cunning didn't pose a potential threat to my position.

He turned and raised his right hand toward them, then let it drop as he spoke. "I felt it was important to give you a glimpse of the larger picture. There have been setbacks to the branches of the Remembrance in other cities. This offers both challenge and opportunity. Challenge, because we are weaker due to their failures. Opportunity, because success will grant us and those above us the chance to rise in power and stature."

Sarah was the first to respond. "Just say what you need, and we'll make it happen."

Marcus nodded his agreement.

Vincente paced the boundary of his medium-sized office—ten steps in one direction, turn, then ten steps back. His words emerged slowly as products of deep thought. "Some time ago, we identified a new enemy, an organization that has risen in power to the point where we now must contend with it. It is called ARES. It was the undoing of certain plans in Washington, DC, and is the driving force behind the second prison that has been established here. We can only assume that there will be a greater presence of organized opposition to our efforts because of it."

He unconsciously flexed his right hand in a fist with each step. It was the only outward sign of his anger. "We have acted against them in subtle ways—intercepted shipments, thrown up distractions, and even undertaken a personal attack on an agent. But we will need to do more."

Marcus barked a laugh and scratched the short brown beard that matched his hair. "No one's been able to defeat the combined strength of my weapons and Sarah's magic."

He nodded but frowned as he addressed his subordinate. "It doesn't do to be overconfident. Overconfidence leads to assumptions, and assumptions lead to defeat. We must redouble our efforts on all matters, including discovering if anyone knows details about this organization."

The other man laughed. "I'm not real friendly with any politicians. I bet, though, that with a little money, we could make some quality friends." He rubbed his fingers together to illustrate his point.

That drew a smile from Vincente. "That's a good idea, but one already worked on by others. For our part, buy more eyes, ensure we know what's going on in our streets, and remain alert for these newcomers."

He paced in silence until Sarah finally built up the courage to ask, "Is there anything else?"

With a sigh, he stopped and turned to them again. "Yes. I didn't fully express how important it is that we succeed from here on out. It was not said in so many words, but it was nonetheless made clear that lives will be forfeit as a result of *any* failure, no matter how small." He closed his eyes as he recalled the less than pleasant conversation with his superior, one of the most aggressive figures in the Remembrance. It was the only sign he would show of the unpleasant feelings that rose as a result.

He opened them again to see both of his lieutenants pale. They were likely imagining the methods that would be used for their punishment.

Certainly not a clean or fast death.

"As such, *I* will join the raid. You both will run all plans by me for approval. Get to work setting the stage. We need to move as soon as we can be assured of success."

He turned to the windows again. "Go." He knew the dismissal wouldn't be questioned. He contemplated the vast stores one floor below him. The money he could make from those goods would equate to a small fortune. But those riches wouldn't buy him even a second's mercy if he failed his superiors.

CHAPTER TEN

Diana pulled the nondescript black SUV into the parking lot outside an equally unremarkable office building. Cara rode shotgun, and Tony sat in the back. Both passengers gazed around appreciatively as they drove through the city on the way. The marshal discovered new parts of it for the first time, while Tony renewed his acquaintance. They entered through the front doors into a sparse lobby that contained only a mammoth desk with a bored security guard behind it. "Can I help you?"

"We're here to see Anderson Stevens." There was no person by that name at the facility and the statement was simply a code to inform him that they weren't random visitors. He straightened with a nod and reached for something hidden by the counter in front of him. A panel on the top of the desk slid aside to reveal a glass surface.

"Palm prints, please."

They complied one at a time. Diana had set the visit up the day before, so there had been ample opportunity to draw their biometric records. Hers, of course, was already on file from her previous trip.

I wonder how Sasquatch is doing. Hopefully badly.

The guard gestured them toward a door on his right, and it unlocked to admit them into a small anteroom. Once inside, the door closed behind them and another opened ahead. A new, no-nonsense alto voice said, "One at a time, please."

She recognized the cylindrical transparent wall before her and stepped forward. The oval rotated to seal her inside, and she extended her arms without being asked to do so. In addition to another biometric palm scan and the buzz of detection devices, a sharp pain stabbed into her index finger as the system sampled her blood. The barrier ahead rotated open, and she walked through.

Dang. She sucked on the injured digit. *I wonder if they replace the needle between uses.*

She waited in another featureless room while her team cleared security. Tony came last and rubbed his fingertips together. "I hope they change that needle."

Diana laughed and shook her head. "I'm sure they do. Well, *reasonably* sure."

Cara rolled her eyes in silence. The door opposite opened, and they passed through it to be greeted by Warden Murphy's thin, hard, and smiling face. She wore a sharp blue suit, a white shirt, and low heels.

She extended a hand to Cara and Tony in turn. "Evelyn." Once greetings were exchanged, she turned to Diana. "Full tour, right?"

"Plus a chat."

Murphy nodded and gestured them forward. Another

featureless door opened, and they emerged into a large oval area. A guard post made from the same transparent material as the security quarantine was positioned in the middle of the space. Four officers in black uniforms were stationed within, one facing each quadrant. They sat on tall stools with monitors to the left and right but a clear view out over the space ahead. Elevators broke the smooth curve of the walls in four places, each with oversized doors that could accommodate many passengers.

Above them, a pair of gun turrets whirred and tracked their steps. Tony gestured at the weapons. "That's some serious security. Should we be concerned?"

The warden chuckled. "Well, they're only stun cannons on this level, so no need to be *too* worried. Plus, your ARES credentials will cause them to disregard you as a threat, so long as you're not doing something obviously destructive."

Tony laughed. "Is there anything our watches can't do?"

Cara sounded distracted as she gazed at the barrels above. "They could use a fitness tracker. Even cheap smart-watches have fitness trackers."

Diana shook her head. "I'll put that in as a feature request. I'm sure they'll get right on it, given its *obvious* importance."

The warden laughed, raised her wrist with a smile, and spoke into her own smartwatch. "Open two."

The doors to an elevator with the big number two painted on them slid free, and the party stepped inside the mostly featureless plastic box. Murphy gestured upward. "The Cube has four floors above ground—mainly offices, storage, and such. There's nothing vital, except for our entrance point on the main floor. And, of course, there's a backup exit if that should be compromised. Underground, we have five levels, each of them at least two stories high."

Diana gestured at the thick plastic shackles set at elbow height all around the elevator. "Prisoner restraints?"

The warden nodded. "The elevators have anti-magic emitters, as does most of the facility. However, we find it's handy to make sure prisoners can't cause more mundane kinds of trouble on the way down, especially the larger ones." She stared at Diana.

"Is the Kilomea your largest?"

"Yes. Not our most troublesome, though. The out-of-towners have begun to arrive, and some of those convicts are real challenges."

Cara looked from one woman to the other. "Wait. You're saying the Kilomea *isn't* a real challenge?"

Diana laughed. "Well, talking to him is certainly an epic task, but beyond that, not so much." She tried not to picture the Diana-shaped dent in her car.

Her teammate's eyes widened, but she didn't reply.

The elevator halted and the door slid aside. Murphy led them into an oval that matched the one above. "This is the highest underground floor. We call it level one. The above-ground levels are A through D." She gestured as she spoke. "It's separated into two halves. That way is the infirmary and it's very specialized holding cells. On this side, we have the interrogation rooms."

Tony looked interested, and the warden led the way to the closest chamber and used the panel beside it to pop the locks. Tony and Cara soon disappeared inside. Sounds of approval came through the open door, and the woman in the corridor shared a grin.

Cara emerged first. "That chair looks solid."

Tony followed her out. "It's certainly not like any of the interrogation rooms I've ever worked in."

Diana nodded. "It's lots of fun because the chair releases electric shocks."

The others looked unexpectedly uncomfortable, and Diana felt the need to explain. "What? Sometimes, a prisoner requires some extra persuasion. You try talking to a Kilomea and see how you feel about a little buzz then."

Murphy laughed and led them back to the elevators. She raised her watch and made the same request as before, and they entered. The warden pressed the button for level two. Tony asked, "Any staircases?"

Murphy shook her head. "Nope. They're too much of a security concern. The only way up or down is these four lifts."

He whistled. "It seems unsafe for the workers as well as the prisoners. "What about a power outage? What then?"

She pinned him with an unflinching look. "There's a backup power source to the backup. Look—sometimes, you have to choose between safety and doing the job right. Our people are carefully recruited and have knowingly made the decision to accept the risk."

"How do you ensure they stay loyal?" Cara asked.

"They're under voluntary surveillance. It's part of the gig."

Diana winced. "Now that makes *me* a little uncomfortable."

The warden shrugged. "There are too many examples of people on the inside working with criminals on the outside. Until we can develop unhackable robots with all the skills of humans, it will be a constant dance between privacy and security. We might have taken it too far. Time will tell. But I comfort myself with the knowledge that at least the oversight isn't kept a secret from them."

The opening doors forestalled additional comments. Murphy led them left out of the central elevator area, which was identical to the floor above. They walked a short distance, turned right, then right again. Diana took note of the dual turrets mounted at each corner with one barrel facing in either direction. Others were positioned at regular intervals in long stretches of the corridor.

The warden caught her interest. "Stun cannons are everywhere. These are either controlled from the booth in the center or can be put into motion-sensing mode after interaction hours. We have heavier artillery if needed, but those require human intervention at every stage. They're too powerful to be automated."

They arrived at an area with a blue floor instead of the ubiquitous institutional beige. Short hallways led toward the center of the facility, providing access to sets of four cells, a pair on each side of the spoke. Heavy doors sealed each one. Murphy knocked on one and it resonated loudly in the combined space. "Prisoner storage. We can hold twenty-four each on levels two, three, and four." She raised her watch to her mouth and said, "Guard post two, this is Murphy. Is two-three unoccupied?"

The answer was instant. "Affirmative."

"Open it, please."

The door swung wide as the locks retracted with a smooth *whir* and a sharp *bang*. It was a reasonably sized room—bigger than Diana's office at ARES DC had been.

The impression was immediately utilitarian in the same white as the elevators, the corridors, and almost everything they'd seen so far. A bed stretched along the left side with built-in shelves above it. A toilet and sink were installed on the back wall of the cell. The right held a desk. Soft lights shimmered above. Diana squinted for a closer look. "Blue light?"

Murphy nodded. "It's allegedly similar to sunlight and supposed to help keep people calm. I honestly don't know if it works, but we'll take any edge we can get."

Tony ran a hand along the desk where it met the wall. "Is this seamless?"

The warden grinned. "It is, and it's built out of super-heavy-duty plastic. Each surface of the room is the same. The bed is attached as well, and the facilities are of the same material. There's nothing to break off and use as a tool, and anyone who has powers involving metal manipulation is out of luck, even if they manage to overcome the emitters. Fortunately, we haven't found any magic users who can do much with plastic yet."

Cara peered at the place where the bed met the wall. "It seems like it will make replacing anything that breaks difficult."

"Yeah, I'm not sure they thought that one through all the way from start to finish. I guess we'll cross that bridge when we come to it."

She led them out, and the cell banged closed behind them. Diana quickly identified the cameras she knew had to be there. The small discs were almost identical to the ceiling surrounding them. Further along, the hallway opened into a large common area that made up the rear portion of the level. A basketball court stood in one third, some basic exercise gear in the middle, and tables had been set up on the far side.

The warden did her tour guide impersonation again. "This is where the prisoners are permitted to gather for a few hours each day, more or less, depending on their own particular issues and the degree of risk. Level two is our lightest security, and it increases at each descending level. Anti-magic emitters generally keep them out of trouble. We have books and board games, plus projectors for television and movies. The opposite side is identical to the cellblock we just left." She led them through another heavily secured door that accessed the lobby via a small hallway that was secured with its own stun turret.

When she spoke into her watch again, the elevator doors parted. After she pressed a button, Murphy said, "We'll skip three and four, since they're the same as two. They merely have more turrets, an increased guard presence, and fewer privileges. Four also houses the guard station for five."

Diana was impressed. "It seems you've addressed everything." She faced her team. "What do you think?"

Tony nodded in agreement, but Cara frowned. "Is this the slowest elevator ever, or is it my imagination?"

The warden grinned. "No, it's not your imagination. They are deliberately slow. It's security again." She pointed at the ceiling. "There are broad beam stun guns mounted above, and also nerve gas for anyone who can't be subdued the easy way."

Cara shook her head. "Some of this stuff seems as dangerous to the guards as it is to the prisoners."

The warden shrugged again. It seemed to be her stock response to questions about concerns for those employed there. "It's set up so that only human intervention can trigger lethal action. That's why we're so concerned about the reliability of those who work here. There are many who think a completely automated facility would be the best way to go, particularly cost-conscious politicians, but the very idea makes me shake in my boots." The door stopped, and she gestured ahead. "You'll see why."

The bottom level was very different than the others. There was no central guard post, only a pole with turrets attached. Several pointed in each direction, and they weren't all stunners. The weapons made mechanical sounds as they swiveled on their axes. The warden led them out of the lobby a touch more quickly than on previous levels. "This is where the most problematic prisoners are confined. We can't rely on anti-magic emitters here, because these either literally cannot survive if cut off from their magic or have become so attuned that they go catatonic when deprived. While catatonia is good for security, it's decidedly less good for the long-term health of our guests."

Cara's laugh was a mix of disbelief and sarcasm. "Is that something we're concerned about?"

Murphy stopped, turned, and stared at Cara with a neutral gaze. Her voice wasn't accusing but far from warm. "Our mandate is to incarcerate these prisoners as securely as possible while ensuring whatever quality of life we can provide, given those strictures. So, yes, we are concerned with their health."

The marshal raised her hands in a gesture of appeasement. "No offense meant. It's a little overwhelming, I'm afraid."

The warden nodded, and the chill in her voice lessened. "I felt the same way. We're used to it but will hopefully never get *too* used to it." She repeated the procedure to unlock and open one of a pair of cells on a short hallway identical to the ones they'd seen. The inside mirrored those above in size and furnishings, but there was only a single unit on each side of the corridor on level five. "We have significantly increased physical defenses here. The walls, floors, and ceilings are extremely thick. It takes up a lot more space. The level itself is extra-high to accommodate it, so it's not really obvious to the eye."

She led them to where the common area would have been on the other floors. Instead, they discovered a holding station for six-foot-tall plastic machines with four articulated arms and heavy black treads to roll on. The tops were the same white as the cells.

"We don't have any humans present on this level. There's a post on four where the guards control these robots. Everything here is done by remote for fear of magic abilities we aren't aware of being used to harm the guards or escape. It's overkill for the prisoners we've seen so far, but they designed the facility against all contingencies, and this is what they came up with."

Tony stared at the devices like he appraised them for his own use. "So, until you get that special prisoner who has the ability to control machines, we're in good shape."

"Right, but nothing lethal can happen on this level—or any other—without direct human intervention."

Diana shook her head. "Other exits?"

"Not here. Level three, and it's an exit only. Anyone trying to get in without first disarming the traps from inside using physical switches in the tunnel would collapse it and seal the access off."

Murphy took them back to the elevator, called for it to open, and pushed the button for level A. "So, any questions?"

There were none. There really was nothing to say. Diana was sure the others thought the same thing she did.

Please, never ever let me be sent to the Cube as a prisoner.

Ten minutes later, they all sat around the conference room table with bottles of water and cups of coffee at hand. Diana started the ball rolling. "So, what would you like to see from our team?"

Warden Murphy took a deep drink from her mug and released a contented sigh. "We have most things covered. There are contingencies in place for almost any kind of attack on this building. The underground levels can be sealed off at the touch of a button and separating them from one another is equally as easy. We're as close to impregnable as we can be." She knocked on the table with a fist.

"But?"

The woman grinned. "Right. *But*. We would hope that if something did happen, your team would deploy in defense of the facility. We'd have to adapt in the moment to figure out how best to work it."

Diana turned to her people. "Any thoughts?"

"Not about the Cube," Cara replied. "But this might be a good time to talk about interfacing with the local PD."

Tony nodded. "I've been in touch with my old boss. I can be the conduit for influencing how bounties are prioritized, so both we and the warden can have a voice in that."

Murphy shrugged. "I can't see how that's a bad thing."

Diana added, "At least we should make sure that level threes aren't listed as level twos." Cara barked a laugh, and the others looked confused. "All right, I need a private word with Warden Murphy."

The others said their goodbyes and left the two leaders alone. Diana swiveled to face her squarely. "So, I want to know if you have any problem with ARES, especially the lack of direct oversight. I can see where that might be an issue for you."

The woman chuckled. "I may be a bureaucrat, but that doesn't mean I think bureaucracy is the solution to everything."

Diana persisted. "I'm aware that you spent some time with the Paranormal Defense Agency, though. They're basically by-the-book."

Murphy shrugged and took a sip of her coffee to delay her answer. "That's one of many reasons I didn't stay with them. Sometimes, in order to get things done, you have to color outside the lines."

She nodded, satisfied, and stood. "Call anytime." She extended a hand.

The warden rose and shook it. "Hopefully, I won't need to. But if anything goes wrong, count on it."

CHAPTER ELEVEN

Rath watched the clock eagerly. Diana had a rule that he wasn't to wake her until seven in the morning on Sundays. He'd checked the calendar to be sure, but it was Sunday, so he had to wait. Most of the previous two hours had been spent watching the kung fu channel, practicing moves on the couch, and adding his own acrobatic elements to them. Max surveilled him with droopy eyelids the whole time, but the troll imagined that he, too, waited for the magic moment to arrive.

Sundays were for training *together*.

As soon as the clock's hands clicked into position, he ran to the opposite side of the couch, ready to wake Diana. She passed him on the way to the coffeepot with a wave. Her voice was scratchy. "Twenty minutes, Rath. Let me wake up."

He performed a happy backflip. "Okay, twenty." The Borzoi stretched lazily and rolled onto his side. "Good, Max. Rest twenty minutes. Then train." Rath spent the time making his preparations. He slipped on the bandolier

Emerson had created for him. Most of it was ornamental, but the little armor piece held several tiny throwing spikes for him to use. His paired needles slid into the cross-draw holster on his back. He had grown proficient at drawing and sheathing them after considerable practice. Now, he accomplished the action without a thought.

When the clock read seven-fifteen, he climbed to the floor and poked at Max until the dog rose obediently. Rath pulled himself into place on his collar and looked around expectantly. Diana appeared, wrapped in layers of exercise gear, a hat, and a heavy gray sweatshirt designed to ward off the February chill. A black backpack completed the ensemble.

He shook his head.

Will be slower. But good for strength.

They went outside and engaged in their separate warmups. Diana stretched on the porch railing, Max sniffed around the perimeter of their small yard, and the troll grinned. He had warmed up inside already. Finally, it was time. He could see it in the sparkle in Diana's eye. She said, "Ready, boys?"

Rath struck a noble pose with his head pulled back and chin angled up. "Born ready."

She laughed. "Okay, then. Three, two, one. Go."

Diana surged to an early lead in the race and bounded down the hill toward the University. Rath had to poke Max many times to move in the right direction. Apparently, waking up was hard for him, too. But once the animal found his stride, it was glorious. He loved the feel of his mount beneath him and reveled in the blur as the world whipped past. It was one reason he stayed in his smallest size so much. It made everything that much more *fun*.

They reached the bottom of the hill with Diana and paused to cross the big street. Few cars were on the road, but they still waited for the white glowing person to replace the red *X*. After they traversed the five lanes, the dog surged into first place. Rath laughed as Diana fell behind. As they rounded to the library, she called, "Okay, Max is too fast. He has four legs. I only have two." They jogged to a stop. Both runners panted moist clouds into the chill air. She looked at the troll. "Hand them over, short stuff."

Rath slipped out of his bandoliers and surrendered the armor and weapons to her, then made sure she set his weapons carefully into a pouch attached to the backpack.

He flipped into the air and landed in his larger form but stopped at middle size. Diana had explained that the height was called three feet. It offered what he considered the optimal balance of acrobatic potential and power.

She nodded, grinned, and broke into a run without warning. The second part of the race had begun.

He bared his teeth. "Good job, Max. Keep up." Rath dashed after her. She couldn't match his speed, even with his smaller legs. He left his friend and savior laughing as he passed her. When she finally caught up again a full minute after he had arrived, he hung upside down from a set of horizontal metal bars in the place called the park.

Diana fell onto a green wooden bench with a laugh, rotated her ankles, and massaged her calves. "Too much office work these days, Rath. Running hurts."

The troll bobbed his head, which made the world look very strange from upside down. "Must train."

"You know, it's funny you should mention that." She slid the backpack off her shoulders and set it on the bench beside her. The zippers rasped as they opened, and she extracted his utility belt. He grinned and nodded. A somersault took him off the bars, and he jogged over. She handed him the pouch-covered black strap, and he fastened it across his hips. With practiced movements, he secured the Velcro straps of the holsters around each leg. She offered the batons, and he slipped them home.

They were angled for cross draw but could be pulled with the same-side hand as well. He checked to ensure they were set to safe mode.

It would be wrong to accidentally shock while training. The edges of his mouth curled in a grin. *Wouldn't it?*

Diana knew Rath was up to something, but given the wicked smile on his face, she reasoned that she probably didn't want to know what. She retrieved her own batons from her backpack and stood. They had practiced enough together to be comfortable using the real weapons instead of padded ones, and both were able to pull blows at the last second when they chose to do so. They focused on technique for most of their training. When they did choose speed, they usually switched to the foam versions, because the battles occasionally got a little exciting.

I suppose that's an appropriate word for having a manic troll somersaulting around and smacking you with things.

They crossed to an empty patch of frosty grass, and Diana spun her weapons to loosen her wrists. Rath practiced drawing his several times and impressed her with the smooth way the baton went from holster to full extension in one quick flick of his wrist. She wouldn't want to face off against the troll for real, even though he'd be about the only opponent she'd ever taken on who was more height-challenged than she was. "Start us off, Rath."

He needed no additional urging and waded in with batons a-whirl. She'd taught him the eight main attack vectors, and they generally stuck to them during warmup, varying the order to keep one another on their toes. She reacted to each incoming blow without needing to think. Frequent practice allowed her to avoid, redirect, or block each swing. Her counterattacks were more difficult because of his size, which benefitted the troll so long as he protected his head. She snaked a baton through his defense with a clever curve and tapped him on the skull.

Rath growled and increased his attack speed.

Damn. I always underestimate how fast he really is.

She worked hard to defend herself, but eventually, one slipped through and rapped her on the knee.

He paused, did a celebratory backflip, and grinned at her. "One to one."

She sat on a dry patch of ground and held a hand up. "Two-minute rest."

Her gaze drifted to check on Max, who was busily sniffing the playground. *He has lots of kids to smell, even in the winter, I guess.* The place was usually deserted on Sunday mornings, which is why they chose it for training. Not that Diana would have worried about the combination of dog, troll, and children. But parents occasionally seemed nervous about the idea when the pair was around. She turned to Rath. "I have a question for you."

He crouched until they were eye to eye. "Okay."

"It seems to me like you don't want to get as big as you can. Is that true? Is there a reason for it?"

He shrugged. "Bigger is less agile. Acrobatics are more fun than pure strength."

It's funny how well he speaks when he chooses to.

She tilted her head and considered his words. His fighting style *did* rely much more on speed and dexterity than it did brute force. And she could imagine, assuming one was skilled enough to have a choice, that cavorting around like a damn fool might hold some appeal. She managed a smile. "Okay, I can see that." Her stomach twisted painfully as she forced the next sentence out. "But to be clear, I'm not holding you back, am I?"

The troll grinned. "Nope. All is good." A canny expression slid onto his face. "But maybe more Maxes would help."

The tension flooded out of her, and she growled playfully. "We will *not* get another dog, Rath." The troll laughed at her, and Max gave a timely bark. "It might make sense for you to train in a bigger form, though, don't you think? In case something happens that requires extra strength?"

His thought process was visible, but he seemed reluctant to respond. She fumbled in the backpack and pulled out four foam cylinders—two sized for her and a pair for someone taller than her—and held the larger versions out to him.

After a moment, he grinned. "Is good. Must train."

A short while later, they were set. Rath towered above her at over seven feet tall, not counting his neon-purple hair. His belt and shock batons rested safely in her backpack, and they each whirled the foam sticks as they prepared to battle. Max sat beside the bench and watched the pair curiously.

I imagine this isn't something you see every day. She laughed inwardly. *I hope no easily shocked people wander by.*

She lunged at her opponent with a yell and aimed for his legs. Logic said they would be his weak point as he adjusted to his height. He skipped to the side, brought one baton down in a curling sweep, and flicked the other at her head. She ducked below it and stopped, then turned to face him. His gaze was intent. He was clearly focused on whatever he felt in the new form.

Diana moved in straight and slow, and they parried at close range. It resembled their usual training but with more effort and energy and the foam allowed for full-force attacks. His height prevented him from attacking her legs, though.

Aha! The tables have turned.

Her head, however, was another matter. She was forced to focus on defense against his flurry of headshots to the exclusion of making any offensive moves of her own.

She backed away to evade the blows and thrust back into the attack. She flicked her fingers without thinking and used her telekinesis to bump his leg out of the way. He staggered, and she scored a hit as she ran past. She laughed as she turned. "Okay, not fair. I know."

Rath grinned as he moved in fast. She blocked the first blows, but when he brought a kick around that connected to her thigh with enough force that she stumbled sideways, her smile immediately matched his. "So, that's how you want to play it?"

He nodded.

"Your funeral, pal. It's on." She lunged and used a mixture of physical attacks and telekinetic blasts, then practiced redirecting his blows with pulses of magic. Every so often, she threw in a kick to keep him worried about that possibility, but in a real fight against an opponent with batons, she'd focus on weapons before she went hand-to-hand. Finally, during a particularly vicious pass, he disarmed her with two simultaneous sweeps of his rods.

Diana staggered back as he advanced and chopped down with his batons in what would be a battle-ending strike to her head. She knelt and threw her arms up, imagining a movie scene where the hero blocked with a quarterstaff, and a shimmering force appeared between her fists to impede his weapons. He blinked, and despite her own very real surprise, she spun into a sweep that knocked the troll's legs out from under him. It felt like she'd collided with tree trunks, and she regretted the bruises she'd have before the action was even finished. But it was successful, at least. He landed on his behind, looked at her, and echoed peal upon peal of laughter as he shrank to his three-foot size again.

"Diana. Fighting mode. Is good." She fell back onto the cold grass and laughed with him.

Is good. A groan followed almost instantly as the troll yelled, "Round two!" and flipped ninja-style to his feet.

Right. Fighting mode. Must train.

CHAPTER TWELVE

The lower level of the main ARES facility was finally finished. Diana nodded in appreciation of the excellent work the construction crews had accomplished. The core took up half the floor. There was no need for the option to secure it as they did in the DC office, so there were no tracks for the mounts or movable walls. But otherwise, it was identical. The center display and mounted monitors looked crisp and efficient as they displayed data on the looming threat.

The others were already gathered. Cara and Tony stood within the technological oval and both wore the new AR glasses they'd received. Each human agent now owned two pairs, one for ARES missions and another for their roles as security consultants. Rath had his own set sized for his three-foot form to use inside the base with ridged ends to hold them in place, but they had agreed it was probably a bad idea for him to wear them in the field. They were expensive, and size-changing trolls were not part of the eyewear's operating specs. He followed her to the rest of her team.

The separate displays showed satellite views of the block surrounding the museum, and the main display table provided the blueprints of the building. Tony motioned in the air to interact with the image and zoom in or expand various parts of it.

We should call him Tony Stark. Heh.

He looked up as she neared. "Howdy, boss. This looks like a mess."

Cara nodded. "A *serious* mess."

"That's pretty much our mandate." She laughed and dark chuckles answered her as she gestured at the arrayed information. "Has anything changed in the twelve hours since we last reviewed this?"

The other woman shook her head. "Same old. It's far from ideal."

"That's also our mandate." She waved for them to follow, and they crossed to the armory near the entrance door. Working quickly, she moved from one black metal cabinet to the next and used her palm print and the numerical code to unlock them. The locks would respond to any member of the team, but she felt a certain pride of ownership and wanted to do it herself.

There were five, each about six feet tall and four wide, a couple of feet deep, and securely attached to the wall. A pair were dedicated to weapons, two more to armor and defensive items, and the last to specialty gear. Dark plastic benches were arranged in front for equipping lower-body defenses and boots. There was more than enough room in the area and also in the cabinets since the space was designed for eight agents rather than the three-and-a-half currently assigned. Another similarly sized portion of the chamber on the opposite side was conspicuously empty, reserved for whatever other needs might appear as their purpose evolved.

Diana set the pieces of her own equipment on the bench. She sat and began to strap on the black shin and thigh guards. The ARES armor preserved mobility and flexibility at the cost of pure coverage. So far, it had proved a useful trade, as she found herself dodging twice as often as she was blocked.

Exoskeletons would be nice, even though that's not really our area. Hell, maybe battle mechs.

She pictured Godzilla marching in from the river, her team in giant robots waiting to fight him, and laughed inwardly. "Okay, so everything suggests that the initial alert from ARES DC is correct, and there will be a move on the museum in the next two to five hours."

Tony refastened a piece of his own gear with the harsh tear of Velcro. "How did they come by this information all the way down there?"

"Cyber wizard."

The pair looked confused, and Diana laughed. "Our data geeks prefer to be called cyber wizards, although the term is also used for those rare beings who can merge tech and magic into computer systems. In this case, it was cameras, basically. The Pittsburgh Police surveillance grid identified an increased street presence around the building. We've been piggybacking the feeds since we set this place up. It seemed random at first, but our computers picked up enough repetition to distinguish a pattern and alerted the techs. When they pulled other sources for closer examination, they caught some suspicious cell phone conversations—unencrypted, apparently, so very amateur—which led them to more people to watch. Ultimately, they had sufficient information to generate a rough timetable."

Cara tilted her head. "So, why don't we have a better one?"

Diana shrugged. "They switched to radio silence. It seems there are some smart bad guys in the mix, too."

Her agents both nodded. She knew they'd both had sufficient of their own experiences with criminals to be well aware that they lived on the same intelligence spectrum as everyone else.

But a reminder never hurts.

The other woman checked her watch. "The protest this evening is supposed to start about three hours from now. That seems like a convenient coincidence."

"No coincidences," the troll interjected crisply.

Diana nodded. "I'm with Rath. No coincidences. It's too handy."

She stood, slipped the vest over her head, and secured the Velcro tabs at each side. They were the same models she'd last used in DC, slimmer than the SWAT versions and equipped with built-in anti-magic deflectors and electrical absorption. The front held two magazine holders for the rifles and a pair for the pistols, all made of non-conductive plastic to avoid interfering with the vest's function. She had requested the addition of a Bowie knife sheath like Bryant's. The weapon's weight was comforting at her lower back. "I talked to the Warden on the way in. The

Cube is on high alert, but she doesn't think they'll call for us."

Tony made another adjustment to his vest and shrugged to settle it properly. "She has the direct line for police support but said she didn't need that either." He shook his head in reluctant admiration. "SWAT snipers are already in position at the museum, but they can only cover front and back since the side streets are too narrow for long-gun deflection. The rest of the unit is posted about a block away in an unmarked truck, waiting for something to happen."

Cara drew her Glock from the shoulder rig she'd removed and placed it on the bench beside her. She slipped it into the hip holster on the utility belt that rode her hips. "We coordinated with local forces a lot in the Marshals, but we rarely used them, except as perimeter control during takedowns. Having them set to go in with us is strange."

Diana nodded. "When we're at full strength, we'll probably choose to use our own teams and not local forces too, except as backup on the odd occasion. Until then, we need the extra firepower. SWAT will take point until serious magic shows up. Then, we'll move into the lead. They'll follow once we've cleared the way. At least, that's the plan."

"And if there's magic from the opening bell?" Tony asked

She shrugged. "That's why we get the big bucks."

Rath had been quietly putting on his own gear. He perked up at her words. "Rath needs big bucks. More Maxes."

They all laughed, and she shook her head. "No more, Rath. You can keep nagging, but I won't change my mind."

She turned to the other humans in the room. "If he had his way, there would be an army of attack dogs with us."

Tony grinned. "Actually, that sounds like a good idea."

Cara nodded. "I agree. BCOM. Black-ops Canines of Magic. Maybe it's time to think out the box."

Diana rolled her eyes. "Two things. First, you're both traitors and deeply unhelpful. Second, no." She rummaged in the tech locker and withdrew the special item she'd carried back from DC, then sat beside the troll. "Emerson sent you a present—something in addition to your standard gear."

He peered up at her with an eager grin. She extended the canister-covered bandolier and set it diagonally across his chest. It fit perfectly, naturally. Diana was convinced Kayleigh had surreptitiously scanned Rath from head to toe while they did the comm fittings. She then pulled out a pair of headphones for him that looked like ones a DJ might wear. The flexible strap that connected them was designed to expand if he changed to a larger size, so he wouldn't lose contact. A microphone curved around the front. She positioned the unit on his head. "All good?"

The troll gave her a double thumbs-up, and the sight was so unique that she broke into laughter again. "Top grenade is pepper, middle is sonic, bottom is flash-bang." Rath nodded. Emerson had wanted to make the last one incendiary, but Diana had vetoed that idea. Maybe after he practiced for a while, she'd told the scientist.

Maybe never is more like it.

"So, here's the plan. The four of us should stay together as long as possible. Ideally, we won't have to split up. If we do, Rath and I will be a team, and you two will be the second one." She reached into the top area of the tech cabinet, which was outfitted with a second lock. She released it with a fingerprint and a code and withdrew three carbine magazines marked with a bright blue stripe. "We each have a single magazine of anti-magic bullets, secured at great effort and expense." *And more than a little peril.* "Don't waste them but don't be afraid to use them either. You all are worth the cost."

They snickered, and she grinned as she passed them out. She slotted hers into a chest holder on her vest. Tony and Cara had already donned their weapons. Diana retrieved the other item in the small safe, counted out six Ruger rounds for each, and handed them over. She drew her revolver, cleared the standard bullets, and replaced them with the anti-magic versions. The discards went into the weapons cabinet.

She slipped the backup gun into the off-center holster at the back of her belt. "Grenades as you want. Load 'em up. But be sure to warn the rest of us when you throw them." As the troll started to move, Diana said, "No more for you, Rath." He grinned at her but didn't appear at all apologetic. Instead, he looked fierce in his vest and utility belt with the batons ready in their holsters on each side. He had refused any additional armor, claiming it would reduce his agility. She couldn't argue. The balance point between raw protection and gear weight low enough for mobility was different for everyone.

Diana crossed to an unmarked crate against the far wall and opened it with the standard routine. SWAT-issue stun rifles bigger and blockier than their own carbines waited patiently for someone to use them. Each had a spare battery in a holder on the side of the stock. She handed one each to her team. "So, we'll play by SWAT's rules at the start. It's our guess they'll send the magicals forward and use humans as guards against us. If we can disable them without killing them, great." She hefted the gun. "At the first sign that these don't get the job done—" She paused and pointed at them. "And I do mean the *first* sign, ditch the stunners and go loud."

The others checked the new weapons in silence. The gravity of what they were about to undertake had quietly settled into the room. Cara seemed to take it more in stride than Tony, who wore an expression stuck somewhere between disbelief and concern. Rath didn't seem bothered in the least. He merely flexed his hands like he wanted to feel his batons in them.

Diana clapped and startled her team. "There's been nothing to suggest they'll do anything other than break in and head for the basement vault. That will continue to be our base assumption. If they do something unexpected, we'll adjust as we go. One thing to remember is that even though they're likely to have the numbers, their training shouldn't be anywhere near SWAT's level, much less ours. We should be able to eliminate the pawns without excessive trouble."

They nodded confidently as Diana continued. "When we reach the magicals, that's where we need to be focused and do our thing. I have the most recent similar experience, so I'll take lead. Once we're in the heat of it, target choice is yours unless I say differently. We have the gear, we have the smarts, and most importantly, we have each other to depend on. That's an advantage the other side won't be able to match." She finished with a grin. "When the mission is over, I'll buy the drinks."

Tony laughed. "That bar tab could be a little expensive, boss."

"Work hard, play hard. But don't forget, there are no days off for the Black-ops Agents of Magic. Even though it seems like a big deal, this is simply another day for us. Let's get to it."

CHAPTER THIRTEEN

B AM Pittsburgh deployed from a pair of boring gray sedans a little over two blocks from the museum. It was still early evening but already dark thanks to the persistent cloud cover, and the area was devoid of foot traffic.

The comms carried Cara's quiet comment perfectly. "Everyone's probably at the protest."

Diana nodded. "Yep." A telltale glow in her vision indicated an incoming request, and she warned the team. "Adding in local SWAT." With a couple of taps on the side of her glasses to navigate through menus, an encrypted channel was established with the Pittsburgh Police Department's SWAT division. Not for the first time, Diana wished there was an AET unit in town. Despite being a reasonably big city, Pittsburgh still carried a risk-avoidant attitude about certain things, and it seemed the advanced anti-magic version of SWAT was one of them. It had never been said in so many words, but she was sure that was a reason for locating an ARES bureau there.

"This is Sheen, ARES Actual. What's our status?"

A deep baritone responded instantly. "Lieutenant Donalds, SWAT Commander. We're posted as planned, ready to enter on the northwest corner."

"We'll be there in ninety seconds. Any sign of activity?"

A quiet male voice answered. "This is sniper one. No action in the back."

A younger-sounding and notably more excited person reported in. "Sniper two. It seemed there was motion near the eastern front entrance, but it turned out to be nothing."

Diana exchanged glances with Cara, and they pushed into a jog. She checked left to make sure Rath still paced beside her. His three-foot form kept up easily. Tony, whose day-to-day routine hadn't involved quite as much physical training, gamely brought up the rear a couple of strides behind. She tripped her mic. "It could be illusion magic. There's probably no way to tell until we get inside but it seems likely they're timing this with the protest."

The SWAT leader's voice responded. "Which began for real about fifteen minutes ago."

She cursed. "Earlier than expected, right?"

"Affirmative. Apparently, they couldn't wait to start shouting at the office building."

Tony joined the conversation with a laugh and heavy breathing. "I talked to the warden again just before we rolled out. Murphy's convinced she has all she needs if this is a decoy and the Cube is a target. Not coincidentally, the prison received an additional shipment of drones today. *Armed* drones."

Diana's voice contradicted her words. *"That's* reassuring." She shook her head to clear everything from her mind other than the impending mission as they rounded the corner to the front of the building. She deactivated her mic, raised a fist to circle her team, and gave them the signal to kill their mics as well. Rath bumped into her leg, and she smiled and shifted her expression to neutral.

"Okay, game faces. We start nonlethal, but only so long as it's abundantly safe to do so. We won't trade one of us to prevent some scumbag from receiving the consequences of his actions." Cara and Tony nodded. Their expressions hardened as they individually prepared for what was to come. Diana turned and led them at a jog toward the entrance as she reactivated her comm. "All right. As we agreed, Donalds, your people lead. We'll bring up the rear until magic beyond your ability to manage shows up. Best case, you handle the whole thing and we get to watch."

The deep-voiced lieutenant chuckled. "Perfect."

Ahead, a fully geared unit materialized from hiding places among the architecture and landscaping outside the front of the museum. By the time SWAT was lined up on both sides of the entrance, Diana and her team were in place behind them. Donalds unlocked the door with keys he'd acquired from the museum's curator. The appropriately cautious woman had argued during their call that she should bring in additional guards to lie in wait for any thieves, but the two leaders had persuaded her that doing so would simply ask for a bloodbath, given the nature of the opponents. They had reassured the executive that they had the matter well in hand.

I really hope we have the matter well in hand.

The time for thinking ended abruptly as the door swung wide and the SWAT team flowed into the building.

Shouts of contact rang out. Diana crossed the threshold and took stock of the situation. Ahead was the opening to a large exhibit that looked to be filled with ancient facades and statuaries. An event hall stood off to the right, separated by a set of eight glass doors.

The SWAT team had already leapt into action down a long, wide corridor on the left. Its walls and floors were made of polished marble. Pedestals supported smaller statues and precious objects at precise intervals. Lighting modeled after gas lamps hung above and the gun barrels that protruded from the more distant pillars glinted in the dim illumination. The weapons clattered as the enemy fired first. She flung herself behind a pedestal on the right wall as her mind cataloged the opposition.

I see a mix of rifles and pistols—maybe a handful, depending on how far back along the hall they go. We clearly outnumber them, which is basically what we anticipated.

They had decided that the thieves would need to prepare for an incursion from any of the museum's many entrances, so initial resistance would be light and scattered. She had guessed, and the SWAT lieutenant had agreed, that the enemy would have surveillance outside the building and a mobile response group ready to supplement small delaying units positioned at each breach point. They had considered splitting their own people but discarded the notion early on. Overwhelming force seemed like the right play for the situation.

It usually is.

Grunts sounded as bullets struck Kevlar, and one of the SWAT troops collapsed, the victim of simultaneous attacks from multiple opponents. The sizzle of stun rifles filled the air, and several enemies dropped their weapons when the limbs holding them numbed. The distraction that resulted from the disarming was substantial enough that the officers could advance and subdue the remaining defenders.

As the last opponent was disabled, a multi-forked bolt of lightning hurtled down the hallway and struck the lead SWAT component. Three of the four troops screamed in pain and alarm as they fell. The second group rushed to drag the wounded clear as a wash of flame followed on the heels of the first magical attack. The sprinklers activated and drenched the party.

"Isn't that lovely?" Diana muttered under her breath, momentarily glad she'd bound her hair in a ponytail before the mission. In a louder voice, she commanded, "ARES, forward." They shoved ahead in a staggered line and dove behind the nearest cover as another sweep of fire filled the center of the wide hallway. It seemed less intense than the last, possibly because of the water from the sprinklers. The lightning storm that followed, on the other hand, looked even more dangerous. Whether that was simply a natural reaction to mixing electricity and water or an actual danger, Diana neither knew nor cared. She simply ran faster once it sizzled past.

Rath and Cara were a step behind and one to each side when a wizard and witch appeared ahead. Diana raised her stun gun and pelted forward to hurl bolts of energy that streaked at the wizard. The wave of a wand dissipated the blast and she let the rifle fall to her chest with a curse. Its positioning prevented her from drawing her carbine with the anti-magic bullets, so she snagged her Glock from its hip holster instead. She raised it and fired a triple burst at each enemy in a continuous track from left to right. As expected, their shields raised. Cara's pistol barked beside her, and Diana shifted her aim to the wizard once more. The sizzle of a stun gun nearby confirmed that Tony was doing his part, but to negligible effect.

They maintained a steady barrage as they closed and forced the magic users to focus on defense. The wizard found a momentary hole and thrust a lance of lighting at Diana, but she weaved right and Rath somersaulted over it. They both avoided injury and it smacked into the wall behind them with a sizzle and pop and reduced a nearby statue to dust and shards. The witch on the other side of the hallway had retreated from Cara's bullets and no longer had a clear angle to attack her. She continued to backpedal and opted to send a wash of fire at Rath, instead.

The troll stopped on a dime and vaulted into an acrobatic roll that enabled him to avoid the fiery cone that reached for him. This gave Diana the opportunity she needed. In the moment of distraction, she dropped and fired at floor level. The anti-bullet shields were often less comprehensive than a full-body shield, and the witch's didn't fully cover her. The bullets pierced her foot, and she collapsed with a cry. The agent holstered her pistol, switched smoothly to her stun rifle, and pulled the trigger. Despite the pain of the wound, the witch had the presence of mind to interpose her shield and deflect the blast, which drew another growl of annoyance from Diana.

Heaven save us from competent enemies.

Rath took advantage of the witch's focus on his partner to circle and deliver a jump kick at her head. His descending feet smacked her skull against the marble floor with a resounding crack, and her wand tumbled from nerveless fingers. They turned to the wizard together, but Cara was engaged with him and Diana couldn't risk a shot. The woman had closed to hand-to-hand combat and hurled punches and kicks at her opponent. Tony stepped beside her with his rifle trained on the pair but was also unable to intervene.

The wizard generated small barriers to intercept his adversary's attacks with flicks of his wand and retreated a step at a time. The concerned look on his face changed to fear when she used the wall to her left as a launchpad to hurl herself at him. His hasty shield slowed her in midair but wasn't strong enough to prevent the inevitable collision. The elbow she'd thrown as she vaulted finished its arc and connected with his temple. The sharp snap as she rode him to the floor and landed on her knees atop him indicated broken ribs, without a doubt. His prone body slumped and she celebrated with a victory curse.

Diana mopped the sprinkler drizzle from her face. The SWAT team had joined them in the combat zone, which lay immediately outside the gift shop. She checked the map in her AR display and stroked her watch to zoom in on the image. "Okay, the most likely enemy path is through the souvenir store, then through the dinosaur exhibit, and finally, down."

Donalds nodded. "Is it worth going around?"

She zoomed the blueprint out to make sure she hadn't missed anything in her pre-op reviews and confirmed that she hadn't. "This way will be the hardest for them to defend. A single enemy could keep us bottlenecked along the other approaches, so it might be safer in the long run, but we'd take forever to get there."

Tony sounded annoyed, perhaps because he had been stuck on the sidelines of the earlier fight. "They're deliberately stalling. Those two magic users could've run after the first attack, but they wanted to make sure we spent time here."

Diana and the SWAT lieutenant spoke together. "Bastards." She glanced at him and finished for them both. "Through the gift shop we go."

An officer who'd taken a lightning blast was still down, and Donalds told another to stay with him and apply a healing potion, until the officer could be extracted. The third member looked shaky. An ugly red welt ran diagonally across her face from the left ear, but she held her stun gun at the ready. Diana wondered if this wasn't the appropriate moment to more lethal weaponry, but it wasn't her call to make. They obviously had their orders to minimize lethal force unless unavoidable, given that some of the protesters might simply be innocent people swept into something they didn't fully understand. If they somehow flooded the building, stun guns were the preferred option.

The lieutenant detailed a trio to secure the area outside the gift shop. One faced the hall to the left, one the hall to the right, and the last guarded the staircase opposite its entrance. The stairs were not a viable option for the team because they led to an easily defended bottleneck a floor below.

They reestablished their marching order, and SWAT moved into the store. The lead officer reported, "Clear," and the blue-clad troops advanced to the antechamber positioned before the next exhibit. The BAM team entered the room as the officers left. Cara beat her to the punch and yelled, "Illusions present!"

Diana and Cara both intoned, "What is hidden, let it be found," and a shimmer appeared behind the cash register. Her first thought was, *Ha. So she does have magic.* Her second thought was, *Holy Hell,* as Rath dashed past, executed his now signature somersault over the counter, and delivered his perfect two-footed kick into the face of the suddenly visible wizard who had brought his wand to bear on the women.

The troll and his target vanished behind the desk with a resounding crash, and Diana heard the snick of batons extending, followed by the snap of the stun element built into the tips. The first time was surely essential to render the mage unconscious. The second might have been useful, assuming the enemy was particularly tough. The third sizzle, though, seemed like overkill.

"Rath!" The troll darted around the side of the counter with a smile on his face. She shook her head, and his grin brightened.

You're a loose cannon, short stuff.

Warnings of contact sounded ahead, and she dashed through the mineral exhibit into the Hall of Dinosaurs. The troll dropped behind to cover Tony. The enemy had deployed in force among the skeletons. She counted at least six in the time it took to find cover and avoid the flurry of lead that peppered the display she now crouched behind.

"Okay, enough playtime," she growled. She unclipped the stun gun's strap and set the weapon aside.

Diana raised her rifle and rotated the selector from safe to semi-automatic. She positioned the barrel on top of the concrete barrier that formed the exhibit's base and sighted through the leaves of the tall artificial plants it contained. Three pulls of the trigger forced the closest enemies into cover. The SWAT team advanced but quickly found themselves at a stalemate with the foes ahead as they engaged in a vicious exchange of fire.

The attack from above shouldn't have been a surprise, but it was since she'd dismissed it as a threat because there was no one there when they'd entered the room. Whatever magic users had since crept into position announced their presence with a blast of fire directed at Tony. The detective cursed as he stumbled away in panic. The pops of his anti-magic deflectors being consumed mixed with that of renewed enemy gunfire.

"Tony, fall back," Diana ordered.

He scowled as he complied.

She announced, "Switching to anti-magic rounds," and let the partially-expended magazine fall as she slapped in the expensive replacement. Calmly and precisely, she sighted the wizard on the balcony. His expression displayed the kind of smugness that only came with perceived invulnerability. She smiled and depressed the trigger three times. The bullets plowed through his hasty shield unhindered and blood blossomed from the trio of center-mass hits, while the recoil from the impact catapulted him back. She moved her rifle to the next target on the platform, but the lack of spells or obvious magical attack implied that this one was simply an ordinary scumbag who fired his rifle at the fighters below. A little disappointed by that, she set her finger outside the guard.

Dammit. I can't waste them. I have to figure out who's pulled our supply down, the sooner the better.

Diana drew a deep breath, scanned the room, and grinned.

She moved into position for a clean line of sight to the far wall. Hanging there, mounted against a thick window, were the bleached bones of a huge prehistoric fish. The largest were two-and-a-half times Rath's current height. She reached out with her telekinesis and yanked one free from the rest, then hurled it at the enemy above. He scrambled back with a shout and ducked beneath a heavy glass and metal partition as the bone smashed to splinters.

You didn't expect that, did you?

The opposition's gunfire ceased momentarily as they reacted to the shards of fishbone that rained down on them. The BAM team was not affected, fortunately, and used that lull to strike. Diana raced up the center aisle, snatched more fish bones telekinetically, and raised them high before she cast them down at enemies who hid behind the displays. Cara sprinted wide to the left and fired sideways at those she passed. She vaulted over a planter and slid into cover before the enemy could react. Rath followed in her wake and found a foe to batter and shock with his batons.

The assaults from above and the side disoriented the defenders enough that SWAT was able to take advantage of the moment. Working methodically and efficiently, they cleared the remaining adversaries in a series of quick advances. A pair of wizards on the balcony announced themselves by a sudden shower of sharp-pointed icicles that forced the team back into cover. The opposition seemed content to hold them in place, and the steady hail of ice javelins made it dangerous to move.

Rath, clearly excited, grated over the comm as he said, "Big bones guy. Ramp. Shield?"

Diana immediately understood his plan. The skeleton of a Tyrannosaurus Rex filled the right side of the space, and its head towered above the second-floor balcony. It was a jump the troll could make easily but far too dangerous to reach without protection. She searched for the power she had used only the other day in her training with her partner, but magical energy proved elusive. In this situation, she hadn't built any anger at the enemies—the trusted go-to that triggered her power—and only had a dispassionate need to get past them to the real threat.

She reached deeper and a flush rose in her cheeks as power threaded into her limbs. It was only an echo of what she'd experienced before, but it would be enough.

Hopefully.

She yelled at Cara. "Give us cover!"

The marshal's voice was calm in her earpiece. "Affirmative. Switching to anti-magic rounds."

Diana waited briefly, then stood. "Go, Rath." She reserved a minimal amount of focus to flick away the descending icicles near her with left-handed telekinetic nudges. Most of her concentration followed her extended right hand as it tracked the troll's charge while she pictured a curving barrier above him. It almost became visible as the sharpened spikes struck, shattered, and rolled off.

His arms and legs pumped furiously as he barreled up the beast's spine with both batons clenched in his fists.

Cara's counter-fire joined the mix. Apparently, the enemy was smart enough to learn. Her target chose to duck rather than shield himself. The spiked deluge diminished at least by half, and SWAT was able to evacuate their wounded. The wizard who hadn't taken cover was at a bad angle for the marshal. He twitched his wand and the frozen rain careened sideways. If he couldn't break the shield, he would go around it.

The troll thrust into the attack in a spinning twist and landed cleanly on the head of the T-Rex, then launched himself at the mage feet-first. The man swatted him with a slab of ice and redirected his opponent's momentum to the side.

As it had so many times in the past when Rath had been in danger, the rage burned through Diana. She smiled as she hurled a blast of force at the wizard. Since imagination seemed to help shape her power, she visualized the attack as a high-speed baseball. The blow struck his shoulder and glanced off.

There's a reason I'm not a professional athlete.

Despite the initial failure, the attack still bought the troll the time he needed, and a series of cries filled the air as he smacked the mage with his batons. He vaulted upward and stabbed both tips into the middle of the wizard's chest. The man twitched like a fish out of water. Rath turned a vicious grin on the balcony's other inhabitant and advanced.

The second gaped with horror at the troll who now stalked in his direction. He brought up his wand but hesitated as he debated his choices between threats. In that moment of hesitation, blood spattered from the man's arm, shoulder, and head.

Diana didn't wait as the final combatant fell and vanished from sight. She ran to the next exit and followed Cara deeper into the museum. "Rath, find your way to us," she instructed over the comms.

The troll sounded as cheerful as ever. "Yep. Will."

Tony closed the distance as he hurried after his teammates. Fortunately, he was about six feet away when the trap triggered and dropped a wall of stone that separated the dinosaur room from the one Diana and Cara had entered. They skidded to a stop and cringed at the impending collapse of the museum, but it didn't materialize.

The agent's voice had transitioned from his earlier annoyance to the angriest tone she'd heard from him. "I'm cut off."

Diana snapped, "We can't wait. Go another way, if you can. These assholes are still trying to delay us. We can't let that happen. It's time to show them what we're really all about."

CHAPTER FOURTEEN

Cara's longer legs put her in the lead as they descended the stairs at breakneck speed. The comms whistled as something in the lower portion of the building interfered with its signals. They crossed one level unopposed and entered the next. Ever the nimble acrobat, Rath soon caught up and kept pace a step behind the duo. The troll was dirty and his hair looked more like an old duster, but he still wore his ever-present smile.

With the comms down, Diana chose to go for safety over subtlety. They already knew the fighters were coming, after all. "Ignore the comm. Keep moving," she said

Cara threw a thumbs-up as she reached the bottom of the steps. Two corridors branched, one left and the other right. Each woman took a moment to check their map before Cara bolted down the right branch. It ended in a ninety-degree turn. She slowed as she neared it and set her back against the inside surface. Diana and Rath soon caught up. The troll tapped his batons together impatiently.

I know the feeling, little guy.

The marshal stuck her head around the corner and withdrew it quickly to avoid the rattle of weapons fire that followed. She put her fingers on an incendiary grenade but Diana stopped her and pointed to the sprinkler system above. Cara nodded and selected a flash-bang instead. She hurled it blindly down the hallway and bolted forward when it detonated.

Two thugs along the same lines as those they'd faced upstairs writhed on the floor as a result of the combined light, sound, and concussion.

"Rath, tie them quickly and catch up." Diana didn't wait for an acknowledgment. She pelted after Cara, who had already almost reached the next intersection.

The marshal repeated her quick surveillance of the next area. No gunfire followed. "It looks like we found the snack bar. I saw tables and a counter. There are no visible enemies, but there are tons of places to hide."

The leader nodded. "Let's do two. I'll throw the flash and you follow with the sonic. When we get in, I'm right, and you're left."

Cara nodded and primed her grenade. Diana threw, and her teammate rolled hers a second later. They both surged into action before the munitions detonated, counting on their glasses, earpieces, and training to protect them from the grenades' effects. True to their suspicions, several hidden enemies staggered in disorientation. Two presumed mundanes were armed with rifles, and a wizard held his wand in a limp hand. The sonic must have gone off at his feet, given the man's dazed expression.

The marshal raced to the gunmen and ripped their

weapons away, then kicked the backs of their knees to force them down. It didn't take her long to zip tie them. Diana seized the wizard's wand from his hand and stowed it in the back of her belt, then knocked the combatant senseless with a leg sweep and trussed him. Before they finished, Rath had rejoined them.

The trio was about to exit the room when two enemies emerged from the doors at the rear, having watched the fight play out. Diana had a moment to berate herself before they waved their wands and summoned two portals that ejected a flood of two-foot-high furry creatures.

Monkeys. How cute. She squinted. *Okay, monkeys with giant fangs and claws. Not so cute.*

Rath growled and raced into the attack without hesitation. She ducked behind a nearby trash container as one of the wizards aimed a shadow bolt at her and barely missed.

With a muttered curse, she raised her gun and fired a triple burst at the nearest monkey. The anti-magic bullets shredded it instantly. She had a moment where she considered drawing her pistol to see if the animals could be destroyed with normal rounds, but the witch fired lightning bolts at Cara and the situation became too dangerous to worry about being economical.

The troll disabled his opponent with two powerful swats to the head, then charged at the closest wizard. Time slowed for Diana, and she scanned the field to determine the cause. It didn't take long. The storm-wannabe witch wore an evil grin on her face as she directed her wand at the unsuspecting troll.

Oh, hell no.

Diana pulled the trigger and six rounds thumped into

the woman. The corpse fell back against a wall and left a red trail as she slid into a crumpled heap.

Time didn't return to normal and Diana panicked at the very real fear that Rath was still in danger. A flood of rage burned through her, and she released the rifle to free her hands. The first yanked the man's wand out of his grasp. The other punched forward to strike him with a blast of force that rocketed him against the wall. The satisfying crack of bones greeted her ears, and she smiled wickedly.

Time sped up, and she retrieved her weapon and picked off four more monkeys before it clicked empty. She dropped the magazine and slid in a replacement filled with normal rounds, then swung the carbine to assist Cara. She'd already defeated three of her simian opponents and was in close combat with two others. They hopped and scampered about her and their wicked claws swiped and slashed with vicious intent. The woman dodged and wove, but her hands and face had already gained several bloody scratches. She deflected a creature that swung at her eyes and whirled to deliver a spinning kick to the other airborne menace. Its new momentum was stopped abruptly by a support pillar in the center of the room. It fell and tried weakly to climb back to its feet. Rath ran in its direction.

The fight ended with simultaneous blows from Cara's foot and Rath's batons as they dispatched the remaining creatures. The marshal swapped her empty magazine for a standard one. "Well, those were some expensive little bastards."

Diana nodded. "When we're done, we need to go back and claim everything these jerks have on them as our own.

Maybe there's a local pawn shop with access to high-end magical technology."

Cara laughed and her expression was rueful. "Didn't you promise me big budgets and awesome tech?"

"I think I specified *eventually*. How about we simply agree to blame Bryant?" She moved toward the exit that led to the rest of the floor's functional areas.

Cara nodded as she stepped into position beside her. "Deal."

Rath spoke up as he joined them. "Deal. Stupid bouncy Mirennas."

Diana wanted to catch her breath or to at least wipe the grime off her face, but there was no time. The enemy's strategy was clear—delay the teams with cannon fodder while they did their nefarious thing, whatever that was. The BAM agents advanced through another series of twisting corridors until the narrow passages opened into another room. They repeated the grenade procedure from before, but an instant after they'd thrown them, the ordnance rolled back into the hallway.

The agent cursed as she and Cara dashed forward to escape the blast range. Even with their precautions, exploding grenades were *not* something they wanted to be near. The room was dedicated to exhibit preparation and an open space housed four large rectangular metal tables with thick bases that rose to stomach height. The top of the room was a huge transparent affair that allowed visitors above to watch the workers below. A thin railing discouraged guests from stepping on the ceiling itself, although Diana imagined it would easily support them if they did.

The glass was comprised of two-foot squares supported in a heavy black grid.

The enemy was well prepared for their arrival. No rifle-wielders were present—*maybe the bastards finally ran out of them*—but three wizards and a witch stood at the back of the room to block the only other exit. They'd spread out to avoid the possibility that any individual attack would impact all of them at once. There was a frozen instant in which the opposing forces took stock of one another before the BAM agents raised their rifles and fired a series of single rounds at their enemies. The targets flicked their wands out casually to deflect the bullets. The two women sighed, let their carbines fall to their vests, and closed in for hand-to-hand combat.

Cara went left, Diana right, and Rath simply sprinted directly ahead at a witch.

Diana shouted, "Are you sure you don't want to give up now?" The two on her side of the room laughed mockingly and thrust their wands at her. She slid to avoid the beam of concentrated light that slivered above her and shards scattered from the point of impact. A stinging sensation on the side of the neck brought a grimace but she thought nothing more of it as she pressed into the attack. She'd faced worse before.

The other wizard reacted to her slide evasion and launched a trail of small shadow orbs in her direction. Diana twisted away from the first few but couldn't evade them all. The last two struck home and her deflectors absorbed them. One shattered and another went fully dark. The other pair were also faintly colored.

Okay, so we have a couple of powerful scumbags.

She bounced up and extended her right hand to aim a bolt of force at one of the shadow mages. He gestured with his wand in a *Z* pattern, and a swirling ebony barrier sprang up in the bolt's path. A whooshing erupted as the magics met, and her attack was sucked into the void.

Diana reached for her Ruger but was forced to abandon that plan as another beam of light sought her out. She ducked behind a nearby table, which proved no protection as the beam burned through it an inch above her hair.

She rose and stretched her arms. *Let's see how you bastards like this.*

While Rath focused his fury on the witch in the middle, Cara had one-on-one odds with the wizard who remained.

Lightning sizzled at her, and one of her deflectors popped. Kayleigh had explained that the deflectors created an aura, which was why they intercepted the magic before it reached her electrical protective vest. She ignored the attack and continued her sprint. Her opponent scowled and rotated his arm to make circles with his wand. A coherent rope of crackling power lengthened with each spin to puddle on the floor.

He flicked the lightning whip, and it snapped an inch away from her eyes as she backpedaled frantically.

Damn.

He retracted it and spun it out again with a flick of his wrist. The whip descended toward her in a curve and she instinctively threw an arm up in defense. The attack was too swift to avoid, and two more magic deflectors blew.

Double damn. He's actually good with it.

She ducked behind a table and the vibrant rope curled over the top to lash her shoulder. Her last deflector and several resistors were destroyed, even though it had seemed like only a glancing blow.

With no choice, Cara clawed for the Ruger in the holster at the small of her back, drew the weapon, and fired as she brought it up. She pulled the trigger three times as quickly as she could. Two shots missed as the wizard spun reflexively to avoid the bullets, but the third reached him before a hasty shield replaced the whip and caught him in the thigh.

He fell to one knee but maintained enough composure to fire another blast of forked lightning at her. She ducked. This time, the table proved adequate and from her temporary haven, she looked right and caught a glimpse of Rath's engagement with the witch. The enemy held her wand like a knife in her fist, the point down, and a shimmering blade of force protruded from the end. Rath delivered enthusiastic blows with the batons, but they no longer sparked. The woman was skilled at defense and deflected his blows before she delivered a kick to his chest that hurled the troll to slide back several feet.

The marshal's jaw clenched in anger, and before she had time to think about it, she used her left hand to hurdle the table and fired the revolver's last three bullets at the wizard who had already launched his attack on her. His blast sizzled all around her as the remaining resistors were consumed in a crackling medley of soft pops. The vest didn't absorb all the spell's power, though, and she landed hard to twitch and shout as the sparking energy bit into her flesh. The sight of the trio of holes in the wizard's chest tempered the pain, and she was almost able to enjoy the way he slumped to his knees and fell forward onto his face. She closed her eyes to focus on staying conscious while the lightning wreaked havoc on her nerves.

———

Diana stretched her left hand toward the table in front of her and thrust her right at the one that lay beyond it, several feet closer to the enemy. The various objects on them—bones, tools, and a heavy microscope that unfortunately looked very expensive—rocketed at her opponents. They focused on defense. The shadow wizard flung himself to the floor to avoid the barrage, while the other man's blasts annihilated them before they reached him.

Oh, that's cocky. You're first.

The residual rage that still lingered flared a little at his arrogance. Diana dashed in a curve around the tables until she had positioned the light-user between herself and the other wizard.

He tracked her motion and released destruction along her route, and she had a moment of fear that her attack might have been a bad idea before the residual anger that still trembled inside her found a new melody. Suddenly, the key to transforming her passive defensive power to aggressive use was clear. There were still so many questions, but she was out of time. It might only be a theory, but it was the only hope she had. She drew a ragged breath and channeled the energy within onto a different path, and time slowed.

With the first step, Diana felt exactly how draining an intentional and aggressive use of her defensive magic could be. Her limbs became heavy as she drove herself forward. By the second step, she feared how much more energy the effort sucked from her. Nonetheless, the delay allowed her to dodge the incoming blasts and drive her fist squarely into the wizard's face. She released the power with a gasp of relief, and time resumed its normal flow.

As soon as his falling form cleared her line of sight, she thrust her right arm forward to hurl a force blast at the other wizard. It did little more than ruffle his long dark hair. He rewarded her effort with a contemptuous sneer and extended his wand toward her.

Uh-oh.

Rath's patience with the stupid witch had run out. His training had not included much in the way of knife fighting, which he now realized was a definite lack.

Rambo uses knife. Must train.

He shook his head at his own blindness as he rolled out of the way of a vicious thrust. He tried a double outside-in slash action with his batons, one from each direction, in the hope that she would have to choose a side to defend. She accepted the blow from one and blocked the other with the shimmering blade that extended from her wand. Her smile pure evil, she delivered another resounding kick to his chest and he tumbled into a nearby table. Pain blossomed in his back.

Anger came with it to add to the flow of emotion he felt

from Diana that had pushed against his mental barriers for the last half-minute. Now was clearly not the time to focus on retaining his smaller size. This particular opponent required his full capabilities. The troll surrendered to the flow and rose slowly to his feet.

Everything diminished as he grew to his full size. The Velcro tabs on his vest separated, and the two halves fell away.

Emerson. Good design.

His belt parted in the same fashion and fell from his hips. The witch propelled a force bolt at him that struck solidly. His chest hurt but the attack did little damage. Gunshots and breaking glass erupted above, and she threw a hasty shield up to intercept the new and unexpected attack. He waved at Tony and grinned. The investigator had found another way through and now had the woman pinned in place with well-timed bullets. Rath bared his fangs and stalked forward with cold deliberation.

The color seeped from the witch's face as she cast two more blasts at him. He chose to dodge rather than meet the attack head-on. The truth was that he hadn't practiced enough with this larger size to engage in real acrobatics and so he twisted aside rather than engage in his usual fighting style.

By the time he reached her, she had adapted her magical construct into a longsword. The troll was not afraid. The weapon was a no greater threat than the knife had been to his smaller form. She swung wildly and he stepped through her guard to seize her arm and stare into her eyes. He enjoyed the moment as fear twined into her expression for only an instant. Then, his fist collided with her face and the thin woman sagged in a boneless heap.

He turned toward Diana's fight as Cara flashed past him in a run.

The last wizard now circled away from Diana but continued to launch balls of shadow in a relentless attack. Her deflectors were all dark or shattered, and she cried out in pain as one of the orbs curved in the air to follow her evasive maneuver and strike her shoulder. She spun like she'd been punched by a troll twice his size and folded over the table, then fell back. There was no time for subtlety. Rath rocketed forward to intercept the mage as the man went in for the kill, but Cara beat him to it.

With a shout that snapped Rath's head around, she hauled her hand back and flicked it forward at her side with her fingers outstretched. Five glowing darts erupted. The troll had enough time as they traveled to realize they were composed of compressed fire that flickered a bright red and orange. They struck the mage in the spine, and the way he arched and screamed suggested that there was both force and burning involved. The wand slid from his fingers as he fell to roll desperately in an effort to smother the flames. The wounds themselves were already seared shut, but the darts continued to burn.

Diana staggered to her feet and kicked him in the head as the last flames flickered and died. She turned to Cara, her face streaked by the beads of sweat that trickled over the dirt. Fresh tear-streaks washed some of the grit away from her cheeks. She choked out a hoarse, "Thank you."

"Are you okay?" Tony called over the comms. She gave him a thumbs-up. Now that they had line of sight, the private network's backup seemed able to activate. "I won't jump unless you have magic that will make it non-bone-breaking."

She laughed, then gasped and hissed in pain. "Maybe Rath could catch you. What do you think, big guy?"

The troll grinned and shook his head. "Probably could, but bad idea. Might drop. Tony's breakable. Here, you look like you need this." He tossed her a healing potion.

"That stuff's not easy to make. We only use it in emergencies."

"Have you gotten a good look at yourself?"

Diana sighed, made a painful circuit of the room to collect the fallen wands, and limped to stand by the door. She caught the rifle Cara threw to her. "Okay. See if you can get down to us some other way. We'll move on."

CHAPTER FIFTEEN

They reached the secure room in the same moment
that the heavy round door swung open.

It's like a bank vault in a fifties movie. Bizarre.

The five enemies present turned to face them. Diana
categorized them instantly based on body language. Two
moved to protect the other two, and that pair drifted
toward the central figure in the arrangement. The leader,
seconds in command, and *their* seconds. She shouted,
"Down on the floor—now!"

They didn't comply, of course.

They never do. A girl can dream, right?

Replicating their pattern from the previous room, Cara
went left, and Diana cut right, while Rath attacked down
the middle. The leader stepped into the vault and vanished
from sight. His two lieutenants blocked access to whatever
was inside and raised their wands at the seven-foot troll
who bore down on them with cold intent. Diana pulled the
trigger of her rifle until it clicked empty. She hoped for a
lucky shot on the wizard on her side and sighed when the

bullets bounced harmlessly away. While she'd expected a shield, it would have been nice for her not to be right for once.

Shadow magic reached for her in the form of waving tentacles that emerged from the wizard's wand. She threw herself to the side in a frantic evasive maneuver and dipped her head to avoid the one aimed at it. The barbed spikes along it sent the reality of their murderous intent home.

Shit. These bastards are tougher than the others were.

She clicked the release strap for her rifle and dropped the weapon behind her. It was useless now.

The mage dispatched a continuous flow of tendrils to grasp her. Fear and anger surged within at the memory of being trapped by a similar attack. The emotions emerged from her hand as a shuddering bolt of force that she dragged in a line across the wizard's body. He staggered at the unexpected series of blows, and his spell faltered. She rocketed forward again and flicked her left fingers to knock his wand free, but he held on stubbornly and whipped it in her direction.

The dark tentacles uncoiled again. This time, they were narrow and cylindrical and entwined themselves into a thick bar. She avoided it with a backspin to the right and leapt at the wizard. Diana registered two things in mid-flight. The first was the broad grin that stretched across her adversary's face. The second was the short wand in his off-hand that she hadn't seen. It fired a thin cone of shadow directly at her heart.

Cara was exhausted and the blast she'd delivered in the previous fight had drained her. Offensive magic always did. There hadn't been much occasion to call upon that power in the Marshals, and training beyond the basics had seemed a poor investment of her time.

I guess I was wrong about that.

Her rifle clattered as she forced the human duo ahead of her to duck for cover under their hastily prepared bulwarks—a pair of rolling carts from the vault. Still, the ancient stone blocks that had been stacked inside them proved adequate to shield them from her bullets. She raced forward and slid to a stop on her knees on the opposite side of the obstruction. By her reckoning, she was closest to the one she'd identified as the low man on the totem pole. She paused to take a breath and froze when the barrel of his weapon appeared in the open area underneath the cart, two feet away from her face.

Rath was buffeted by chill blasts from the witch on the right. They struck with surprising force and almost burned. Trails of icicles were left in his fur from the places contact had been made. After he'd absorbed the first strike, he decided avoidance might be the better choice.

The man on the left raised a rifle and fired at him. The bullets hurt where they scraped along the outside part of his arm. The impact twisted him slightly as the metal projectiles furrowed through his flesh. He bared his fangs at the pair and angled toward the one who had shot him.

The next ice bolt caught him in the head. The

momentum snapped it sideways and he staggered as he lurched aside. The man ahead now raised a pistol and fired. The gunman's face seemed different—almost exultant. Rath knew better than to remain where he was, so he instinctively somersaulted to avoid the shots. Unfortunately, he'd forgotten that his large form wasn't nearly so acrobatic, and two more bullets found their mark.

He had never been shot with anti-magic bullets before, he realized, as the rounds burned into the muscles of his thighs. The troll went down hard and the momentum carried him in a tumultuous roll back the way he'd come. This was the first serious pain he could remember since being locked in the cage with its magical and mundane torments. His eyes latched hatefully on his opponent, who now lowered the pistol toward Rath's slowing form.

The cone of shadow struck Diana with enough force to overwhelm her. It wasn't only physical, although it was sufficient to alter her trajectory and spiral her into a painful landing on her side. The magic struck at her very essence, and its tendrils sought to consume the life inside her. Her energy ebbed, and she could almost see it flow out as the shadows surrounded her. The wizard struck again and more darkness poured over her prone form in a continuous assault. She thrashed impotently. For a moment, she feared it was all over.

What a stupid way to die.

The anger at her own failure provided the necessary spark, however, and her vexation ignited as the vital catalyst to heat the molten pool that lay within. Heat spread slowly through her to push the shadow back, although it didn't quite eliminate it. Conscious thought ceded to raw animal instinct as she rose in a fury and thrust both hands out. The shadows that had sought to engulf her recoiled. They jerked slowly into a lazy orbit around her. Then, they coalesced around her clenched hands before she drew both arms back like an artillery unit launching its payload.

Two shadowy spheres rocketed from her fists. The wizard appeared to have no reflexive defense against his own power. Whether it was fear or shock that paralyzed him, the end result was the same. He careened in a flailing tangle of arms and legs and crumpled against the wall beside the vault door. She grinned. He would have some serious bruises, if not broken bones, after the brief unromantic encounter he'd experienced with the marble surface.

Diana looked at her hands like they belonged to someone else.

What the hell was that?

She didn't have time to wonder further. Anger boiled again when she saw the bullets pierce Rath's legs and he reeled in agony. A closer threat demanded her attention as the witch near the vault swiveled her wand at the downed troll. The agent extended her arms again, but the shadows didn't come.

Okay, then. Have this, instead. No one hurts my friends, bitch.

She cocked her right arm and threw it forward, and a familiar bolt of force erupted, directed at her foe. The woman somehow sensed its approach and managed to lean back enough that it collided with the door beside her with a loud *clang*. Diana strode toward the witch. Her fury manifested in the form of a glow around her left fist and the ball of force that hovered above her open right palm.

Cara leapt over the barrier as the man fired. She landed on top of him and kicked his rifle away. She had to give him credit for quick reflexes, though. He rolled and regained his feet in a tense crouch with weapons drawn. His left hand held a combat baton that he flicked to full length as she readied herself. The right gripped a long knife that resembled a medieval dagger.

She slid forward and led with a front jab at the man's face and almost lost her fingers as he brought the blade around in a quick slashing motion. The marshal dropped into a spin to sweep his feet from beneath him, but he jumped aside to avoid it and lashed a kick in response. She blocked and shoved it away, then struck with a short left hook to his ribs before he could recover. It was the only blow she'd managed to land so far, unfortunately. She shook her hand, which had *not* enjoyed the impact with his Kevlar vest.

Not the smartest choice, Cara.

Mindful of his skill, she stepped back and assessed the threat before her. His stance was perfectly balanced, ready to attack or defend. He seemed content to wait for her to move, which was consistent with Diana's belief that the enemy merely wanted to delay them. They'd certainly succeeded thus far, and whoever was in charge now had unhindered access to the vault while they struggled with these hindrances.

Cara had a multitude of options to deal with knives, combat batons, and almost any kind of melee weapon, but they all required her to have something to use as a blocker. She gritted her teeth and accepted the reality that she would either have to take a blow or a cut directly. It was a sobering thought, but she forced the fear down and braced herself for the attack.

Her opponent grinned and twitched the dagger in a cocky invitation.

She yelled defiance and flung herself at him. Her attention was focused on two things—control the knife and protect her brain from the baton. Anything else, she would endure in order to get inside his guard. He surprised her when he skipped forward, and she threw her right arm up to block the blade stroke and managed to halt it far enough away that it couldn't circle to catch her in the back of the head. His skip hampered the strike and it lacked sufficient force as it encountered her low left block.

The strength behind might not have been strong, but it was enough. The pain that radiated up her arm from the point of impact made it clear that the limb had taken significant damage and could no longer be trusted. She faked a punch to his chest, and he flinched to avoid it. His avoidance lowered his head enough that the elbow strike she threw immediately after caught him on the temple. He staggered, and she repeated the blow rapidly in the same spot and he collapsed in a clatter of extra gear. Cara snatched the dagger up and spun to aid her teammates.

Rath turned his tumble into a tackle and snapped out a long arm to knock the man's legs out from beneath him. He raised a fist and pounded it down on his opponent's head. The fighter rolled away toward the center of the room. The troll tried to rise, but the pain in his legs prohibited it.

The enemy regained his feet and Rath growled at him, then began to pull himself across the floor with his burly arms in an awkward crawl. His target retrieved the pistol that had been knocked free by the tackle. The troll pushed up to his knees, ready to make the desperate attempt to hurl himself sideways, but dropped instantly as Cara shouted, "Rath, down!"

He sensed something whistle past him. His adversary went wide-eyed and instinctively blocked the thrown blade with the only thing he had. The pistol and the knife clattered to the floor, and a long cut on the back of his hand quickly welled with blood. He shouted a curse and sprinted into the vault. En route, he caught the witch alongside by the sleeve and dragged with him. Rath resumed his crawl as both Diana and Cara raced forward. The heavy safe door swung closed much faster than it should have and left them on the outside with no means of entry.

Diana threw her hands up in frustration when she recalled what had happened and what that likely meant. "The

AGENTS OF MAYHEM

bloody monkeys were summoned. The bastards can use portals in here."

Cara swore, and Rath groaned. Diana knelt behind beside him and examined the wounds on his legs. "One of the bullets is still in there, and I'm not sure that's a good idea. Hang on. This will hurt." She yanked the medpack from her belt and rolled it open with a flick of her wrist.

The painkillers and stimulants were unusable since she didn't know how the troll would react.

We have to get a med tech, too, a really good one.

She fumbled for the surgical tweezers and the antiseptic spray and sterilized first the surgical implement, then Rath's leg. Finally, she bent to take a closer look at the injury. She tapped the stud on the side of her glasses a couple of times to increase the magnification, and her view improved. "Cara, I need light."

In the moments before she arrived with the needed illumination, Diana saw the edges of the wound already looking a little better. She shook her head and looked at Rath's face. "You are a formidable fighter, young one."

He grinned. "I try."

Diana laughed and supplied the rest of the long-standing joke. "Do or do not. There is no try."

He barked once in pain as she seized the bullet with the tweezers and yanked it out of his thigh. Once she was confident the wounds were clear, she wound them with gauze and sealed them with duct tape.

She noticed Cara's labored breathing and looked at her bent form. "Are you okay?"

The woman nodded. "My left arm's hurt—maybe fractured. I have a couple of other bumps and bruises. You?"

159

"My whole body is a giant bruise, but nothing more than that—assuming the damn shadow magic doesn't have any lasting effects, that is."

"Those bastards sucked."

Diana couldn't help but chuckle as she recalled Bryant's response when she'd been the one to say those words. "They *all* suck. So we have to do better than we did today."

The heavy tramp of booted feet heralded Tony's arrival with the SWAT team. The looks on their faces crushed her last hope. One way or the other, the bastards had gotten away. She gritted her teeth.

That's only round one, assholes. Ask the Kilomea how round two goes.

CHAPTER SIXTEEN

The scene outside the museum was remarkably calm and ordered, given what had recently transpired. The wounded among the SWAT team had been stabilized and transported. A pair of ambulances with their back doors ajar served as havens for Cara and Diana while EMTs administered to them. They put the marshal's arm in an air cast and told her she needed to go to the hospital for an X-ray.

Diana received bandages and surgical glue with a couple of quick butterfly adhesives to hold the wound in the side of her neck closed until it healed. There wasn't anything that could be done about the contusions. Finally, they were both released from the paramedics' ministrations, and the two met their teammate in the center of the crowd of police and emergency vehicles.

Tony was the only undamaged one. He seemed to be self-conscious about it, and his voice was quiet as he asked, "Is Rath okay?"

Diana nodded. "His wounds were in better shape by the

time he stowed away in his capsule, and I re-wrapped them after he shrank." She patted the belt pouch where his defensive container hung during missions. "He said to tell you that you need to be faster, Tony."

The other agents broke into tired laughter, and she shook her head. "He's something. Let's get out of here."

She led them to her vehicle, and they clambered inside. A SWAT officer would return their spare to the lot at street level outside the ARES building. She drove the short distance to one of her favorite restaurants she'd discovered in the area, a breakfast place that stayed open into the early morning hours.

They passed the old register with its cash-only signs and seated themselves in a booth far from the door of the mostly vacant space. The seating was covered in cracked vinyl, with antique jukeboxes mounted on the wall above each laminate table. Tony flicked idly through the pages of song selections as they settled. The server was there before they were fully organized. Compassion colored her features at their clearly exhausted conditions. "Coffee, I'm guessing?"

All three nodded, and Cara added, "Plus one Coke for me."

The woman smiled and took their omelet orders. Ham and cheese for Tony, western for Cara, and black-eyed peas, greens, and ham for Diana. She also requested a side order of cheesy potatoes. Rath couldn't actually make an appearance in such a public place, but she'd make sure he had a treat waiting when he was ready to eat.

After her initial visit to the restaurant with Bryant, this

had become her favorite breakfast spot, and she was working her way through the menu options.

Cara turned her head to where Tony sat on her left. "So, where the hell were you?"

It might have sounded aggressive if she'd said it on the first day they'd met. Shared experience had since revealed that they all possessed deeply sarcastic senses of humor. He laughed. "Sunbathing on the roof. It was relaxing."

They chuckled briefly before his smile morphed into a frown. "When the wall came down and cut me off, I looked at the map and found another route. It took forever to get across the museum to the staircase as a fairly large group of guards had locked down the main one outside the gift shop. I still had to take out a couple of those assholes along the way."

"Magicals?" Cara asked.

Tony shook his head. "Idiots with rifles. I got the drop on them because they were talking when they should have been watching."

Diana pushed the hair out of her face. "There were some significant differences among that group of criminals. Some were scarily competent, and others seemed like it was their first time actually firing a gun."

He sighed. "Street thugs and gangbangers, for sure. Cheap cannon fodder, but effective."

"Well, they bought them all the delay they needed, even though we knew they were doing it. It shows that someone smart was in charge."

Cara nodded. "I'd say the last three were the core of the group."

Tony interrupted. "Hey, who's telling the story here?"

They laughed, and he folded his arms in a dramatically offended fashion. "Anyway, the second guy almost got me, but he forgot about recoil. The first shot hit the vest, and the rest missed." He shook his head. "After that, I moved as quickly as I could until I wound up above you. I didn't realize you'd gone down two levels. I thought you were only down one."

"Comms died when we reached the bottom, so we couldn't tell you," Diana explained. "We need to ask the techs for a solution to that."

Cara nodded. "Relays, maybe."

He slapped his palms gently on the table. "Honestly, you two, can I finish?"

She resisted the impulse to plague him again with another interruption and offered a nod instead.

"After I shot through the glass, I ran down the staircase on the other side. I called SWAT for help on my way down. But, as you know, I got there too late to make a difference."

The marshal raised an eyebrow at him. "A committed teammate would have jumped."

"A committed teammate would have had two broken legs and not been of use, anyway," he countered.

The waitress found them grinning as she slid their food and drinks onto the table. Cara reached for her Coke and almost knocked her coffee over with the air cast around her left arm. She winced, likely at both the pain and the near accident. Diana asked, "How bad is it?"

"The painkiller from the kit seems to be wearing off, so it sucks a little more than I'd like." She shrugged, then flinched. "I'll head to the hospital after we eat. Food is more important."

Tony interjected, "I'll drive you, just in case."

She nodded her thanks. "You know, boss, we really need a medic and something in the way of medical facilities if we have to keep this up."

Diana nodded. "They said we'd be in the fire, but I'll admit I didn't expect it to come so soon. Or so hard. It makes me think that not only were they right to open an office here in Pittsburgh, but they underestimated how much it was needed."

She shook her head and tapped her fork against the plate. After a furtive glance for reassurance that they were unobserved, she popped the lid of Rath's canister. His nose twitched immediately like a built-in meal sensor and his grin broadened. She positioned his cheesy spuds beside the bag, and he shifted so he could snack within his mobile home without drawing attention to himself.

"Unfortunately," she continued around a smile at the troll's murmurs of enjoyment, "there are too many trade-offs. We need to kick the budget up, and you know what that means."

Cara sighed. "Bounties, bounties, and more bounties."

"At least we can make sure they're properly categorized and be compensated appropriately," Tony pointed out.

Diana nodded. "That's all you. Shout if you need anything on that end but otherwise, run with it."

"I have it under control, boss."

She pushed away her frustration with another bite of her delicious omelet. After a sip of equally tantalizing coffee, she set her fork down and retrieved her phone. "I'm tired enough that I'll take notes. Item one, med facilities. Item two, bounties. What else?"

Together, Tony and Cara said, "Anti-magic bullets."

Diana laughed. "Do you actually know how expensive those things are?"

The marshal shrugged. "More expensive than our medical bills or having to replace us?"

"I agree totally. I'm only messing with you. It's high priority. There are a few kinks to our supply." *Like a menace out there, hunting for us.* "Hopefully, Emerson can do something about that."

Tony looked confused, and she waved a hand. "Head tech in DC. I forgot I'd only told Cara about him. He's working on a different way to make anti-magic rounds that should cost less. There's no real information on the timetable, though. In any case, I'll harass Bryant about it."

He nodded and returned to his breakfast. Diana grinned when he piled the omelet on top of a piece of toast and shoved a huge bite into his mouth.

Every op I've ever been on, the first meal after tastes twice as good.

"Okay, what else?" she asked.

Cara finished chewing. "Portable anti-magic emitters?"

"I don't think those exist."

"Okay, then. A tech who can *create* portable anti-magic emitters."

Diana laughed. "Actually, I'm already on that. Well, the first part, anyway."

Tony dropped his utensils onto his empty plate with a clatter. "We need a reliable backup unit. Not necessarily people who will be on the front lines with us, but ones we can trust to watch our back—like SWAT did, but with more skills and better weapons."

The other woman nodded. "Like a mini-AET squad."

Diana added it but shook her head. "I'm not sure how we can make that happen. I'll have to pass that one along."

"More agents," Cara suggested.

Tony countered with, "More investigators."

The marshal turned to him as if his response were a challenge. "Access to the city's surveillance grid."

His tone upped the competition. "Shotguns that'll work against magicals and non-magicals."

She raised her voice. "More grenades, and more kinds of grenades." She held a hand up to silence his counter and turned to her boss. "Okay, seriously, we need more agents, and we need to spin up faster. All signs point to trouble."

Diana nodded and underscored that where she'd already written it in her notes. "Finding quality people is hard, and we have to factor training time in. I don't know if it can happen more quickly. We've already sent feelers out, but we'll keep trying."

Tony grinned. "I have one more. How about some brass knuckles for those who insist on going hand-to-hand?"

Cara gave him a half-lidded look that told Diana the finishing blow was about to strike.

"Faster teammates, so they don't get stuck behind falling rocks. As Rath would say, 'Must train, Tony.'"

CHAPTER SEVENTEEN

The following week passed in a haze of normalcy. No further revelations appeared in the media to concern them, and no whispers rose among their contacts of impending events.

Cara nursed her fractured arm—which remained in a splint to keep it supported—and ran things at the office. Tony and Diana used their necklaces and alternate weapons as disguises to increase the profile of Two Worlds Security Consulting by apprehending bounties. Thankfully, the necklaces definitely worked for non-magicals too, something Bryant had told her. She hadn't fully believed until they tested it on their newest team member since her first test on Cara was moot given her magical abilities.

They chose AR-15s and Sig-Sauer pistols instead of the more identifiable BAM gear and hid their unique vests under their clothes. It left them less well-equipped than their regular choices but was still adequate for the level-two and -three crooks they rounded up to deliver to the

Pittsburgh police. By the end of the week, they had caught four, and Tony had improved his connections in the city in the process of tracking them down. Only one had been captured in a public place, and Diana had simply snuck up from behind to stun him with a taser rather than making a scene.

Rath had fully recovered but had yet to go back to his more rigorous training regimen. Some days were spent at home with Max, while others were spent with Diana at the office. He seemed more tired than usual and didn't show any real inclination to train. She assumed it had something to do with his healing process and that he'd let her know if it was anything serious.

Ha. Maybe he's found a new movie series. He loves his binge-watching.

Still, he professed to be excited for the night out they had planned. She weaved the Fastback through narrow back streets. Instinct guided her unerringly toward their destination, a restaurant in one of the city's up-and-coming neighborhoods that boasted the best burgers in town. "We'll be the judges of that," Cara had replied when Diana suggested it, and they all agreed such a bold statement required verification.

She backed the car into a convenient parking space against the curb and threw the keys into her purse. Rath unclipped from his booster seat in the back, having decided on his three-foot size for the evening's activities. He wore a T-shirt they'd found in the local comic shop with the logo of a band from the 1980s on it. When the troll had chosen it, Diana had immediately approved. "You can't go wrong with the Sisters of Mercy."

She had worried about Rath's visibility but decided that if ever a place to feel comfortable wandering through crowds with him existed, the gallery crawl was it. The monthly event attracted the artistic and art-appreciative to the borough streets. The prohibited traffic and permitted open-air entertainment created an atmosphere of jovial acceptance. The early March night was unseasonably warm, which seemed to have everyone in a good mood, judging by the throngs they passed on the way to the restaurant.

When they pushed through the door, they found the others already seated in a booth. Rath slid in beside Tony, and Diana sat on the end across from Cara. Drinks materialized before them, delivered without a word by a harried server with a septum piercing and dark beard. Diana tasted hers and looked at Rath with a grin. "Is good. Must drink."

The whole table laughed, and the troll inclined his head in regal acknowledgment. Their waiter spun past again, they ordered, and he dashed away. A warm evening apparently meant great business. The rectangle of seats around the fancy bar in the center was completely filled, and the booths on the periphery were likewise occupied. A line had formed beyond the entrance. Diana asked, "How long did you have to wait?"

Tony shrugged. "I got here about fifteen minutes early, and we only had another five after Cara arrived."

The other woman nodded. "It's a nice night for standing outside, though."

He laughed. "Enjoy it while you can. Pittsburgh's weather is the weirdest. And that's saying a lot, given that I've spent the last year in Cleveland."

Cara grinned and sipped the colorful cocktail she'd ordered. "You know the city best, Tony. Tell us something about it."

He lowered his Guinness from his lips and banished the foam from his mustache with a swipe of his tongue. "Okay, here's a good one. So, when I first arrived here and hadn't learned the town yet, I got a call to an area called Blawnox. Or, as they pronounce it here, Blah-nax."

Diana sputtered into her drink at his impersonation of the Pittsburgh accent. It made him seem unconcerned with pretense. An oversimplification, no doubt, but she liked the idea.

"Anyway, we arrived, and two guys yelled at each other on the street. A big guy, the bodybuilder type, sat on the hood of his beat-up car, which he'd stopped right in the middle of the road between parked cars on either side. The other scrawny older dude sat on a folding chair in an otherwise empty parking space."

Diana shook her head. She'd been warned about this particular Pittsburgh idiosyncrasy early on. Tony continued, "It turns out, in this town, a chair in a parking spot means it belongs to the house nearest it. It's not only a reservation. No, these people view it as a sacred tradition. To the man in the chair, the guy in the car essentially demanded to park in his living room."

They laughed, Cara more incredulously than the rest. "So, how did it turn out?" she asked.

"When I showed up, both men shrugged and claimed to be having a conversation. A conversation audible from down the block, apparently, since we were called in—and which included many colorful words—but a conversation, nonetheless. We told car guy to shove off and park somewhere else, and he did it without further protest like he simply needed to be heard or something. The person in the chair then offered us beers and invited us to stay."

They all laughed again, and Diana shook her head. "It's a unique place, to be sure."

Tony nodded. "And that's only the start. There are a hundred stories like that."

Their food arrived, and they spent the next minutes in silent appreciation. When they'd all eaten at least half of their meals, Cara finally broke the comfortable silence. "Okay, I'm buying it. This is the best barbecue burger I've ever had. And that's saying something since Fort Benning had its share."

He grinned. "I agree. Best in town."

Diana rocked her hand. "It's not the best bacon and bleu ever, but it's up there." Tony threw a napkin at her, and she caught it. She laughed as she whipped it back at his face, then turned to Rath. "Opinion?"

He looked up from where he munched happily on mozzarella sticks, dipping them in three different sauces in rotation—marinara, cheese, and gravy. Diana's stomach twisted a little at the combination. "Is good. Must eat."

They finished the meal with more conversation and laughter, then emerged and turned left down the avenue.

I think this is the most relaxed all of us have ever been together. We'll need to make this a tradition.

Small businesses lined the block on either side. The food and drink sellers had positioned portable counters at the edge of glass garage doors that served as the fronts for the restaurants when closed but were now open thanks to the good weather and happy crowds. Several bars had the same arrangement. Galleries were interspersed among them, some with multiple styles of art and others dedicated to one specific type.

They wandered through the entrance of the photography gallery and held up the admission bracelets they'd purchased at the restaurant. The exhibit featured candid shots of everyday people, and they took turns to make up stories about the characters in them. By the time they'd worked their way around the displays, the tales had grown truly outlandish. Cara claimed the last was a space vampire, and Tony groaned. "There's no such thing."

Diana grinned. "Don't be so sure. What about Area Fifty-one?"

He rolled his eyes. "Unless you're telling me that ARES runs Area Fifty-one and you've been there and seen stuff in person, I call shenanigans on you."

They passed through a gallery devoted to paintings and another filled with modern sculpture. Diana feared the latter, as Rath seemed *very* interested in some pieces and spent much of the time hopping up to see the ones that towered above his height from a better perspective. She needn't have worried. His agility was remarkable.

Hell, he could probably jump from the top of one piece to the next without knocking them off their pedestals.

As they walked down the center of the street, surrounded by diverse folks engaged in their own conversations, laughter, and the pleasant spring atmosphere, she realized that the town was growing on her. It felt surprisingly like home, the same way Colorado Springs and DC had.

Now, if I could only convince Lisa to get her ass up here, everything would be perfect.

A tiny part of her brain added, "and Kayleigh," but she shushed it. Tonight was for fun, not work.

Rath fell in love the moment they entered the comic book art gallery. The walls held oversized pages, and the space was arranged in a labyrinth to create the most available wall surfaces for them. Each corridor displayed a single story, with covers and back material at the start and finish. The first contained a superhero book, and he was clearly interested but not necessarily excited. The second and third shared tales of samurai and Shaolin monks.

The samurai called to the troll, judging by the way he bounced up and down to get a better view of the panels. The monks, though, entranced him. Rath stared without moving for long stretches. The only sign of consciousness was the occasional swivel of his head and a sidestep to a new panel. He studied the panels with the intensity of one determined to memorize every detail.

By the time they reached the end, his posture subtly imitated some of the positions the monks had used in the comic's combat scenes. Diana guessed the troll was so wrapped up in the experience that he didn't even notice. The final corridor showed a tale of espionage drawn in the noir style. While the content clearly failed to engage him as much, he admitted to liking the drawing when she asked.

Diana's heart swelled to see him so happy. "I guess we'll have to spend more money at the comic book store, huh, Rath?"

He nodded. "Take out my paycheck."

She immediately laughed, one echoed by the other humans in the little group. "Will do, Rath."

It had been an almost perfect evening, she mused as she emerged onto the street a step behind the others. Her phone buzzed, and she raised it to see a text from Bryant that contained only three words and a link.

Check the news.

Dread seeped into her as she clicked the link. After a short delay, a video from one of the local stations appeared. It showed a tall man with thin hawkish features and perfectly groomed hair. The banner at the bottom proclaimed him to be a lawyer named Stuart Young. His angry words assailed her ears a moment later.

"The officials of the city of Pittsburgh have not been honest with us. We didn't want the first prison, so they hid the construction of the second. Worse, the *new* prison is not a regular Ultramax. It's for magicals as well. They have already begun to send the worst of the worst here, which makes the city less safe. Less safe for our workers, less safe for our students, less safe for our senior citizens, and most concerning, less safe for our children. I call upon the community to join me in protest."

She sighed.

Dammit. There goes the neighborhood.

CHAPTER EIGHTEEN

Diana stared out at the river from a private office on the fifth floor when Bryant arrived. She turned and waved him toward the conference room. The coffeemaker had already done its thing, and he prepared two mugs while she sat at the table with a sigh. He slid one across as he lowered himself into the chair opposite her. "So, how about that news?"

She chuckled darkly. "You are a *serious* buzzkill, do you know that? I had a really great night before you got involved. You owe me."

"It ruined my evening, too. I've set up alerts for all our potential offices, and that one popped up as a story everywhere there's an Ultramax. I wouldn't be surprised to see national coverage today."

Diana shook her head. "It seems like it would take a leak from the inside to have that much information."

Bryant took a sip, then returned his mug to the table. "I asked the warden about that." All traces of mirth had left his face. "She says one of the guards is missing.

Surveillance showed him going into his house and never coming out. When he missed a shift and they went to check, the place was empty."

"So, magic?"

"It seems like it. Or some fancy technology that defeated both the drones and the interior security system."

Diana drummed her fingers in irritation. "Is there anything we can do about it?"

He shrugged. "I've told Warden Murphy she has my full support, whatever she needs. She says it's under control. Her history suggests betting against her isn't usually a great choice."

She rose and crossed to stare out at the water again. The sense of escalating danger wouldn't allow her to stay still.

I should schedule training. The rest of the team might feel the same way.

"Have we discovered what they were after at the museum?"

Bryant joined her with his coffee mug in hand and stared off into the distance. "Nope. The curator found several artifacts missing from a shipment they had just received—a new tomb unearthed in Egypt, he said. They hadn't identified any of the items as magic, but they also don't have a permanent magical on staff." Diana turned with a questioning look, and he shrugged. "Budget problems, same as everyone. They have a wizard on retainer, but he's abroad at the moment. He was scheduled to come in next week after they'd done the initial cataloging to prepare for it."

Her words emerged in a growl. "Our enemies seem very well informed."

"No argument, there. Secrecy is a difficult thing with all the technologies and magics that have risen to threaten it. At some point, you have to quit worrying about whether every buzzing noise is one of those techno-magic surveillance insects and merely live your life."

She turned to face him and leaned against the window. "Did we manage to ID the three who escaped?"

He shook his head. "They destroyed the security room on their way down, so there are no recordings. But even if there were, there's no guarantee they're in the system. They seem too sophisticated to have been caught before. We identified a number of the others, but nothing's led anywhere useful yet."

Diana thought back to the interview at the Cube. "But we think it's the Remembrance, right?"

"It's the smartest move to assume so. Since we know the group is active here and interested in acquiring magical artifacts—like the followers of Rhazdon before them—it seems likely."

She returned to the table, sat on its edge, and took a slow sip of her coffee. "So, I've been a little too busy to study as hard as I should. Do you want to give me a refresher on Rhazdon?"

Bryant leaned his back against the metal frame of the floor-to-ceiling windows and coughed to clear his throat. "Rhazdon is a figure out of Oriceran history who popped up a couple of different times to cause trouble. The first time, all the records said he was male, and those in charge basically had to fight a war to shut him and his followers down. The second spilled over onto Earth, and we discovered Rhazdon was female."

Her skepticism slipped her grasp and burst into reality on her face. "That's a significant mistake."

"The royal family apparently likes to keep their secrets close. Anyway, she came around at the end to fight with the forces of good, but the damage had already been done. Her legacy lived on and apparently, is still alive today."

"And what's that all about?"

Bryant shrugged. "It's not an atypical story. She and her followers believed that those in charge looked down upon them and that the group's members didn't have enough power—or, at least, didn't have the amount of power they *deserved*."

"So, your average everyday oppressed revolutionaries?"

"Far from average, but yeah. Their beliefs weren't entirely without merit, given the centralization of political authority that comes with hereditary monarchies, but still, they took it solidly to heart."

Diana sighed. "It's very easy to see oneself as being repressed. That message will resonate with a lot of people, both on Earth and Oriceran, I would imagine."

He grimaced and nodded agreement. "But what we *don't* know is what the ultimate goal is this time around. It seemed clear the other two times—a major power grab, with an understanding that magical ability was the primary determinant of a person's value. Now, with this particular branch's use of mundane humans, and inept ones at that, it seems a little different. Unless they're willing to simply use the non-magicals and plan to cut them out at the end of the plan. That's always a possibility."

She set her empty mug on the table. "Were you aware of this group when you chose Pittsburgh?"

Bryant frowned. "We weren't, which is essentially a problem in itself. Our intelligence should be better than that. No Agency had a line on them, not even the PDA."

Diana paused while she considered whether she had more to say on the topic, then changed the subject. "Well, I guess it'll be what it'll be. Did you get my team's post-Christmas list?"

He laughed. "Yeah, I did. It made for some entertaining reading. I've already argued that headquarters needs to allocate more money and manpower in your direction, so there should be at least a little help forthcoming. But your best route will probably still be to manage it yourself."

She scowled. "That's no way to run a railroad, BC."

"We told you it wouldn't be an easy gig. Didn't you believe us?"

"Yeah, but I thought the problem would be humans and dragons, not dollars and dimes."

"Welcome to the big leagues, Sheen. We'll make a bureaucrat out of you yet."

She barked a laugh. "No way that's gonna happen. My place is in the field."

Bryant nodded. "So's mine. And look at me now."

Diana took a moment to do exactly that. His wardrobe had improved since he'd taken the regional SAC job, and if she didn't miss her guess, tailored suits had replaced the off-the-rack outfits he'd worn in DC. It was a fine outfit with charcoal pinstripes and a deep purple tie atop an eggshell shirt. Her mind wandered, and she pictured the two of them talking like normal people instead of federal agents engaged in life or death situations. She couldn't help the tug pulling at her mouth as a smile formed on her lips.

Her phone's vibration jarred her from her thoughts and made Bryant cross the space between them and stand beside her. She looked down, and her eyes widened. Wordlessly, she showed it to him, and he read it out loud.

"The lady requests that you come to the fountain at your earliest convenience."

She took it back and verified her initial impression that it had been sent from an unknown number, then raised her eyebrow in an unspoken question.

Bryant shrugged. "I suppose we should have expected this, given the news. The only person in town whom I know of who's referred to as 'the lady' is the leader of the Kemana."

Diana looked at her jeans and T-shirt, which were a poor match for his sartorial splendor, and said, "Give me five to change."

They pushed through the main doors of the lobby six minutes later and turned left toward the park. The green space nestled in the triangle where the rivers narrowed the city's land to a point. A tall fountain stood on the spot, which had just been restarted after its long winter break. She had her doubts about the decision to run it so early in the Spring, but she didn't control the city, so she let it drop. Besides, there were more important matters to attend to.

They walked briskly along the path. She kept an eye on her side of the park while Bryant's experienced gaze roved the other. She kept her voice low so it wouldn't carry.

"Is there anything I need to know?"

"Think of it as a magical version of the city. All the

things you see up here, expect to find similar versions down there, minus our ubiquitous technology."

"It's underground?"

Bryant nodded. "It is. We're not sure how far. We tried to check a few times in different places, but nothing we used would detect them. The Kemanas were built on magically active sites so those who wished to do magic on Earth would have a place to draw power from."

She'd known that much, at least. "Why Pittsburgh?"

He shrugged as they made their way under the raised highway access ramp that separated the front and back sections of the park. "There must've been a reservoir of energy here that they found useful. Maybe it's tied to the rivers—some magical version of hydroelectricity. I have no idea, and the leaders of the various Kemanas haven't seen fit to share that information with us."

They abandoned the meandering walkways and cut across the grass toward the fountain. Aside from a few wanderers walking near the river, the area was deserted. The clouds diffused the late afternoon sun to impart a vague sense of sameness to the atmosphere. The water jetted straight up, seemed almost to hang in midair, then crashed down as if the flow were driven by currents, rather than streams.

When they stepped onto the pavement that surrounded the basin, her bracelet grew cold against her skin. She looked at Bryant, and he nodded. They slowed and drifted their hands toward their holsters. Hers was at her lower back and his rode under his left arm. She flicked her boot to verify the comforting weight of the Ruger holstered inside.

Casually, she swiveled her head to provide her glasses with a good view of the area, but they didn't identify anything on the initial pass. After several moments of slow walking, though, they identified strange deflections in the falling water and sketched the pattern on her visual field. It revealed a rough cone shape, similar to an umbrella. She turned toward it, and a being stepped free from its illusion. The liquid continued to flow around him but not touch him. His hands were held at a forty-five-degree angle to each side as an indication of his peaceful intentions.

As if you need a weapon in your hand to be dangerous.

Neither agent altered the position of their own hands as they vectored to intersect with him. He was midway between their heights, with straight brown hair pulled back from his face and gracefully pointed ears. When they reached speaking distance, he spoke in a cultured voice with an Elven accent.

"I did not wish to alarm you, but nor did I wish to be seen by a casual passerby." He waved at the couple that disappeared from view along the closer of the two river walks. "I am the lady's emissary, and I am sent to inform you that she will grant you an audience at noon tomorrow."

Bryant inclined his chin toward Diana, and she turned to face the elf. "Please tell the lady we are happy to attend."

The elf nodded. "Seek the hourglass for entry. Your friend will know the place." With his message delivered, he vanished as seamlessly as he'd appeared, and the illusion of water droplets danced yet again. Diana turned to Bryant, who shook his head and made the sign for silence, followed by the one for surveillance. They walked back without speaking. Despite the persistent feeling that events conspired to limit her options in every direction, a contrary part of her mind refused to be discouraged. That tiny voice of wonder and adventure sang ever so softly.

We're off to see the wizard....

CHAPTER NINETEEN

Diana had decided, and Bryant agreed, that she should be the contact person for the Kemana. Only she, Tony, and Cara descended the stairs from the main street level to the parking lot that ran along the river. The nearby wharf was now open and housed an assortment of poorly parked cars filling every available space—one more reason to appreciate their personal underground garage.

Tony looked uncertainly at his boss. "Where's Rath?"

She pulled her coat a little tighter around her neck against the chill breeze coming off the river. "I thought bringing him might not be the best first impression, and I'm hesitant about the reception we'll find. I feel better having him safe at home."

Cara grinned. "Of course, safe at home is a questionable description with him, isn't it?"

"Hopefully, he and Max aren't getting into too much trouble." She chuckled as she led the way to a darkened section of the wharf. "He told me there's someone at the University who wants to talk to him. I'm sure nothing can go wrong there." She rolled her eyes, and her teammates laughed.

They stopped at a metal gate that led into a small alcove. Its purpose was unexplained, and she wondered what others thought of it. Spray-painted icons surrounded it. Her bracelet felt chilled but not freezing, which suggested the presence of an illusion but not a particularly powerful one.

She whispered, "What is hidden, let it be found," and a clearer set of etched runes appeared, looking for all the world like those around Tolkien's Doors of Durin.

Diana touched the image that resembled an hourglass made of triangles, and the gate glowed briefly before it opened far more smoothly than its appearance would suggest was possible. She checked to ensure they hadn't been noticed, then motioned the others inside and pulled it shut behind them. The area behind the gates was difficult to make out and seemed to be somehow diminished. Given the fact it was beyond an illusion designed to protect this entrance, it made a certain amount of sense.

Ahead, the brick wall that had been the back of the alcove had vanished to reveal a large staircase leading downward. Cara and Tony both stood aside to let her lead, and her lips twisted in a smirk. "Cowards."

"Privilege of rank," he replied.

"And age," the marshal finished.

"You are both insufferably rude." She raised her chin and descended. After what felt like three or four flights of stairs, they reached a heavy wooden door. A panel slightly higher than Diana's eye level—*why am I surprised?*—opened, and a Kilomea lowered his head to peer at her.

The guard didn't speak and opted instead to wait patiently.

"We come at the invitation of the lady," Diana said with as much formality as she could muster.

The massive being spoke in an unexpectedly soft and cultured voice. "Names." She gave herself a mental smack for assuming it would be otherwise.

If anyone knows not to stereotype, it's you, shorty.

"I am Diana Sheen. With me are my two subordinates and escorts Cara Binot and Tony Ryan."

The Kilomea nodded and the panel slid shut. The door opened with a low creak to reveal more of the tunnel and additional stairs. He sounded almost warm as he intoned what struck her as a formal greeting.

"Be welcome in the Kemana of Stonesreach. Do no harm, and no harm will be done to you, by the word of Lady Alayne You will find the lady in the palace."

Cara stepped closer to speak softly into her ear. "And we trust this?"

Diana gave the signs for silence and surveillance and advanced without a reply. It would have been rude to wear comms, and the danger of their hosts noticing was too high.

Still, I wish we had them.

They walked for about ten minutes before the Kilomea led them through another gate. Diana's legs burned after five. She tried not to think about the fact that they would need to walk up these same stairs to leave. Finally, they stepped free of the tunnel and slowed to a stop. She almost pitched headlong out of sheer wonder.

Bryant had described it as another downtown, but her

mind hadn't grasped the sheer size involved. It was undoubtedly the largest cavern she had ever seen in person or on television, let alone heard of. It stretched for at least a mile ahead. She performed the eye sweep that would call up her glasses' display to find out for sure, and they failed to respond.

Of course, no signal. I bet our phones don't work either. Still, it was worth a try, and now we know for sure.

Two varieties of stalactites hung from the ceiling. One looked like traditional stone generated by the vagaries of moisture and minerals. The others were comprised of glowing faceted gems that emitted a purple light that spread across the entire ceiling. She heard an indrawn breath behind her and echoed it as the magical potential of the place washed through her. She hadn't noticed the emptiness inside her until the crystals' power filled the hollow space. It felt incredible.

So that's what Bryant meant about magic fuel. Wow.

The lower portion of the cave formed a bowl, and she grimaced at the number of stairs that lay between them and the bottom. The layout resembled a child's drawing of sunbeams. Streets of varying widths flowed away from the semi-circle that held the palace grounds and reached all the way to the sides and back. Terraces climbed the slopes everywhere, except behind the palace, and each was dotted with what appeared to be small houses. She noticed a shimmer of motion below and realized it was foot traffic. Again, she reevaluated the scale of the place and shook her head. "We should've brought an energy bar or five."

Tony moaned. "There has to be an elevator to take up, right?"

Cara slapped him on the shoulder. "Not to worry. It's probably an Uber-like service, only made of people who can fly."

Diana laughed. "Dragon express. Fifty percent discount if you get burned on the way."

Their escort raised a skeptical brow but otherwise, remained silent. She took a deep breath and resumed the descent. Groans sounded behind as her team followed.

The stairs were precarious enough that they had to go slowly, but they finally reached the bottom twenty minutes later.

It gives credence to Cara's idea, really.

The staircase ended at the widest street, which carved the bowl into two equal halves. It appeared to run unbroken to the palace. People flowed in both directions, and Diana took a moment to recover her breath and her wits before moving on. The revelation of the Kemana equaled the surprise of the discovery of her magic so many years before.

She turned to her team. "Okay, this is far, far beyond my experience. I presume it's beyond yours as well?" They both nodded. "Right. Here's what we'll do. We walk straight to the palace, so we don't lose our way. A reasonable speed should get us there about fifteen minutes before noon, assuming no time or distance-altering magic are employed between here and there." She grinned. "I know, that's a huge assumption, but we have to start somewhere."

Cara squinted at the ivory building across the cavern.

"It seems there'd be no need for it, except as a defensive measure, and then you'd think it would be active, not passive."

Tony nodded in agreement, and Diana chuckled. "We have two priorities. First is to get a sense of this place, as we'll probably visit fairly often, assuming things go well. The second is to not tick anybody off. I know that might be hard for you, so I'm officially asking you to dial it back a little." The offended looks the comment inspired warmed her heart, and she spun to lead them on before they could muster a counter-insult.

They merged carefully into the foot traffic on the right lane of the main street. People walked far enough apart to avoid bumping into anyone and so they would have time to react to unexpected actions committed by those in front of them. Despite this, the total number of travelers still doubled or tripled what she'd estimated on the city streets above. She identified beings she was familiar with—dwarves and elves walking alongside wizards and witches. She also noticed goblins, Kilomea, and several other creatures she didn't recognize.

Trees and other plant life, some green and some vibrantly hued, filled the gaps between the shops that extended along the side of the street. They appeared to fill spaces that would otherwise connect one road to the next. Diana assumed the foliage would be thin enough that they could cut through, if necessary, but it would probably be frowned upon. Every so often, a narrow footpath would thread through the flora, and she guessed that would be the authorized shortcut.

She studied those walking toward her from behind the

anonymity of her glasses, which she had polarized to appear dark from the outside. They wore sharp suits and attractive professional dresses. It was odd to see pointed ears and long hair combined with business attire, but she imagined they would go to the surface from time to time, and it might be easier to use partial illusions, rather than full ones. As far as she knew, *all* these people were on their way up, although there didn't seem to be anyone actually climbing the stairs.

Diana stepped out of the flow of traffic and onto the sidewalk to admire a store window. Swords taller than she was made up the left part of the display. They descended in size and type to the throwing daggers on the far right. The metal gleamed in the white light emitted by a gem that hung above them, and all appeared to be exceptionally well-crafted. Each bore etchings and symbols in a language she couldn't recognize.

The next store was filled with food, and a display outside held what seemed to be fruit in colors and shapes she had never seen. The diamond-shaped one that reflected the purple light from above especially caught her eye. She turned to make sure her team still followed. Cara stared into the blade shop with what came close to adoration, and Tony kept his hands planted in his pockets while he carefully avoided getting too close to anything or anyone. She met each of their gazes in turn and tilted her head in a question. They nodded, and she faced forward and continued to their destination.

They're fine. Quit worrying, the mental voice that popped up at such moments argued.

Yes, but first impressions matter, she countered.

We're making a fine first impression. Also, shut up.

She was certain she imagined the snickering as her internal conversation fell silent.

At the next window, she paused and peered inside. At that point, her brain slipped into a vapor lock. The space held an assortment of boots made from materials she didn't recognize and fashioned in gorgeous styles she had never seen. One pair was tall enough to reach her thighs, while another looked like it would be as soft as silk. That pair's material somehow managed to look tough and luxurious simultaneously. She'd lost track of how long she had stared when Cara bumped into her gently. "Keep a move on, boss."

Diana sighed. "We need to find out what kind of money they use down here. And I need to go back to that shop."

The three rejoined the flow and walked abreast. Cara shook her head. "Sure. *That* won't be a telltale or anything."

She frowned. The other woman had a point, but she wasn't willing to give up on the idea either. "Okay, maybe only in the evenings when the light isn't good. And at home, of course. Oh, and the office would work."

Her voice trailed off as she identified a gathering of some kind up ahead that caused the steady movement in the street to become unpredictable.

That could make us late.

It looked innocent enough, but who could say? She led the others down the footpath to the right. They merged onto another street so dramatically unlike the previous one that she could hardly believe they existed so close to one another. The artificial light didn't seem to penetrate as well. Only two people could walk abreast, and the shops seemed somehow sinister, less welcoming, and more intimidating.

She turned left and increased her pace. Halfway toward the next big intersection, a throaty laugh carried to her, and she couldn't resist turning to find the source. A tall woman leaned in a nearby doorframe.

Correction, a tall elf. The pointed ears are a dead giveaway.

Diana's eyes widened as her brain connected the dots. Not only was it an elf, her dark skin and pure white hair marked her as a Drow—one of the more dangerous Oriceran races according to everything she'd read and heard.

The woman said something in a language Diana didn't understand, and when she failed to respond, the Drow rolled her eyes. "Oh, very well. I will speak your simple tongue. Welcome to Stonesreach, humans." Her voice made it seem as if they were anything but welcome.

She put on her most polite face and banished the frost from her tone. "Thank you. I am Diana."

The elf nodded with a small smile that transformed her features from neutral to predatory. "It is foolish to give up information so quickly, *Diana*. Although it is true, I already know *so* much about you." Tony and Cara stepped near, one behind each of her shoulders. She sensed their willingness to act if it became necessary.

"Oh? What do you know?"

The woman gave a lazy grin and paused before she replied. Diana used the moment to assess her. She wore a black tunic with intricate embroidery that ran down the left and right sides. This particular female was curvy, unlike other elves Diana had seen.

Definitely a head-turner.

The Drow wore what looked like leather pants and high boots that appeared to have been made the old-fashioned way. They glinted oddly in the light. Diana pushed aside her envy over the footwear as the elf spoke. "The male behind you is nervous. He has no magic, so he has every reason to be so."

Diana felt Tony's body tense.

"The woman, on the other hand, clearly does have magic." She tilted her head to the side and her eyes lost focus briefly. "Magic that speaks of fire and heat. *Elven* magic." Diana looked at Cara, fearing she would be upset at the knowledge being so casually shared.

I know I would have been.

Cara simply shrugged.

The Drow rose from her perch to face Diana with her full height and took a step forward. "And you, their leader, are different. Your power is a ferocious thing that comes in many flavors. You are one who bears watching." She stepped back and extended her arms on either side as a thin smile blossomed over her face. "All of you are welcome in my shop. Anything you may need, I have. Or I can get, for the right price."

She marshaled the wit to reply to the sudden change in attitude. "We have no time to browse at the moment, but perhaps we'll come back."

The elf shrugged her shoulders. "As you please, *Diana.*"

She led the others toward the castle and looked back only once. The Drow leaned against the wall of her shop and the same confident smile played on her lips. Diana shuddered and faced forward again hastily. They took the next path that crossed to the main street and found themselves in an area filled with restaurants. Beings of all kinds sat at tables with food or drink before them, many of whom were involved in animated conversations. It created as jovial an atmosphere as they had seen since their arrival and relaxed her jangled nerves. Even better, their destination was in sight.

The remainder of their journey was smooth and uneventful. They arrived at the foot of the steps leading to the palace at the appointed time, and all three companions groaned in unison at the sight.

Diana shook her head. "Every day is leg day in this town."

CHAPTER TWENTY

She led the way up the shallow but seemingly endless steps at the front of the huge building. They swept out in a graceful curve at the bottom and narrowed slightly as they climbed. At the top, six people could easily walk side-by-side without jostling one another. The palace was white, accented only by a few variations in the form of off-white features in the stone. It reminded her of marble.

But marble doesn't have that faceted glow.

It most certainly wasn't local, in any case.

An ornate pair of double doors at least a story high stood before them, flanked by two figures in gleaming armor. Diana slowed, hoping to demonstrate that they weren't a threat. A closer inspection revealed the guards to be elves with long hair in different shades of blond cascading down their shoulders from beneath the circlets they wore. Each gripped a tall spear in the hand farthest from the door. Their other hands hovered near the sword sheaths at their belts. Their bodies were encased in chain mail woven from a metal she couldn't identify.

Quiet, Diana. This is not the time for a Lord of the Rings reference.

Her inner voice added a defiant, *Mithril,* in the appropriate accent, and she sighed inwardly.

The doors swung wide with no reaction from the guards. The emissary she'd met the day before stood beyond the opening and beckoned them through as the guards relaxed their pose. "Thank you for coming, Agent Diana Sheen. I am to take you to the lady directly." He turned and strode away, apparently assuming they would follow.

The inside of the castle featured the same material as the outside, although every block was polished to reflect the soft geode-based lighting above. Paintings and tapestries hung on the walls, separated by intervals of bare stone. It reminded Diana of the gallery crawl only a few nights before. The event seemed much farther away than that, given all that had happened in the interim. The art ran the gamut from portraits to landscapes to depictions of presumably historical battles. She recognized some of the new creatures they'd encountered in the city. Others were completely alien. Elves featured the most prominently.

They turned the corner and entered a spacious throne room. The cavern's purple glow filtered in from windows on the side and the transparent surface above. Support pillars rose at intervals to connect the floor and ceiling. A raised dais that supported a pair of ornate thrones was the room's only other architectural feature of note. The smaller seat was empty, but the larger one held a Light Elf dressed in elegant finery and bedecked in jewels at her wrists, throat, ears, and brow.

Tony breathed a soft, "Wow," from behind, and Diana silently agreed.

The emissary stopped them several feet from the base of the platform, then turned to address their host. "Lady Alayne, the human representatives you invited have arrived."

The woman nodded. The unreality of the moment relaxed as she smiled and her expression conveyed warmth, caring, and a kind of purity that Diana couldn't quite put her finger on. She expected to feel her bracelet chill to indicate the presence of illusion, but it didn't. The woman's personality was simply that powerful.

"I would like to formally greet you as the leader of the Kemana Stonesreach. From this time forward, unless you are informed differently by myself or my emissary, please consider yourselves welcome in this place. Do no harm, and no harm will be done to you." They nodded solemnly in response. "Might I request the pleasure of your names and titles?"

Diana nodded and spoke first. "Diana Sheen, Special Agent in Charge of ARES Pittsburgh."

"Detective Tony, Ryan, Agent."

"U.S. Marshal Cara Binot, Agent."

The lady rewarded them with a smile. "Thank you for accepting my invitation. As much as Ciannon enjoys amplifying the formal power the head of the Kemana holds, I am well aware that you could have declined." The emissary scowled, and she laughed.

Diana smiled. Maybe this relationship wouldn't have to be so rigid after all. "We appreciate your thoughtfulness, Lady Alayne. We would have requested a visit, but we've been a little busy since reaching town and didn't want to presume a welcome."

Alayne nodded her understanding. "That is appropriate." Then, with a suddenness that surprised them, the edges of her mouth turned down. "The new prison in the city above—the Cube, I believe you call it—is causing trouble for magicals and non-magicals alike."

She nodded. "It appears so. However, it is necessary."

The elf's head tilted to the side, her expression shifting between curiosity and skepticism. "Why?"

The question set her back on her heels. The truth was that she had taken the presence of the Cube as a given and never really considered *why* it was essential. She shrugged. "This area of the country is a particular hotbed of magic. Our data shows that this is the closest large city to the center of it, which makes putting the prisons here a logistically sound decision. Also, having it near an ARES bureau is a logical idea."

"Why not in the country's capital?"

Diana grinned. "No one wants to put that substantial a number of detainees in such close proximity to so many legislators, Lady Alayne. The politicians might corrupt the prisoners."

Alayne's laughter seemed almost to vibrate through the crystalline fixtures of the throne room. "Very well said, Diana Sheen."

She hesitated, then decided to simply go ahead. "May I ask a question, Lady Alayne?"

The elf's lips twitched, and she replied, "I believe you just have." A small wave indicated the lady's permission to proceed.

"What do you know of the Remembrance?"

The lady exchanged a frown with her emissary and sighed. "Too much, I am afraid. In Stonesreach, we hear talk of their ideas. It is not Rhazdon, of course, but others trading in her beliefs. We are not sure whether they are true believers or are simply using her principles as a tool to gain followers and power. In the end, the distinction is largely irrelevant."

Diana nodded. "That corresponds to our knowledge. We have identified a hierarchy with unknown members at the top overseeing others on Earth." She tried to keep the note of hope out of her voice. "Do you know what their goals are?"

Lady Alayne shook her head, and the gems that dangled from her ears swayed in time to refract the purple light. The sight made Diana wonder.

Can you wear power stones and always carry a refill of magic with you?

Her musings were interrupted as the lady spoke. "We understand they are seeking artifacts and presume it is with the goal to distribute them amongst their followers to increase their magical capabilities. It is likely that these actions are meant as a form of preparation to initiate some act of importance to them."

She nodded. "That sounds very much like what we believe, Lady Alayne."

"If they continue as they have been, they will attempt to sow chaos wherever possible. We expect the monster attacks in Europe are connected, although we lack clear proof. Of course, the protests against the prison here are their doing." She said this as if it was beyond question.

"Of course," Diana conceded. "Do you know anything about the mysterious figures at the top of this organization?"

"Removed as we are from those on Oriceran, we are not privy to this information. We are only sure it is not a single leader, as it was in Rhazdon's time, but a group with a shared purpose. Like Rhazdon before them, they embrace any follower, so long as they share their belief in the primacy of magic and possess the will to act toward that end."

"It sounds like we need to get back to work, then. We were already reasonably certain that the event at the museum was part of this, but your words have removed whatever small doubt remained."

The lady nodded. Her emissary stepped forward without instruction, and Diana remembered that she had a final question to ask. "May we have permission to finish the connection between the Kemana's tunnel and the one from our facility you are doubtless aware has been reaching toward it?"

Alayne grinned in confirmation of that knowledge. "Granted. However, please connect beyond the outer door. It would not do for anyone coming through your tunnel to have unfettered access. In truth, the guard's primary responsibility is not to keep visitors out but to send a warning ahead of those who enter."

Diana nodded. "Thank you, Lady Alayne."

"You are welcome, Diana Sheen, Tony Ryan, Cara Binot." She nodded to each of them in turn. "Please visit us as often as you feel the need. We have no wish to see all the gains our people have made together destroyed by those with limited vision."

The emissary hustled forward during their polite farewells and escorted them from the building, then vanished behind the closing doors.

Tony sighed as he peered out at the city. "So, about that elevator?"

Cara added a humorless laugh. "I didn't see one, or any dragons for rental."

Diana looked at the immense staircase on the opposite side of the cavern and exhaled. "Leg day has just become leg *week*, people. Start walking."

CHAPTER TWENTY-ONE

A chill wind rippled through the broken structures. They were gray with scorches of black, cracked and weathered by the years since their partial destruction. The stone remembered the battle of long ago, a conflict that ended in a loss for the followers of Rhazdon.

A crackling echoed from the collapsed forms and rebounded from the columns and pedestals that still remained, however decrepit they had become. An oval of energy formed in the air, then filled with darkness. The nominal leader of the Remembrance, first among equals, stepped through. The rift sealed behind him, and the wizard gazed suspiciously around the chamber. His wand was held low in a pale hand. Only the stones were present to greet him, and they were far from welcoming.

Dreven nodded in satisfaction and advanced toward the round basin set in the middle of the ruined courtyard. His dark purple robes ended an inch above the ground, and heavy, warm boots showed beneath. He used his wand to clear the littered path before him. Debris and dirt that had accumulated since his last visit swept easily aside under the force of his magic. When he reached the fountain, a swirl and flick of his wand gathered the algae, leaves, and other detritus that had settled in the water. The residue of the magical conflict from long before ensured that though it struggled, life would not gain a stronger foothold there than it already possessed. While they had not yet succumbed, the mottled trunks of the trees indicated clearly that they fought a losing battle.

Not unlike the humans.

A final twitch of his wand sent the collected debris elsewhere, leaving only clean liquid that shivered beneath the caress of the breeze.

He strode to his position at the northernmost point of the circle created by the fountain. The wind sifted his hair like wind chimes. The long braids he had tied it into were less pliable than his unbound hair would've been but still not heavy enough to resist nature's force entirely. At the appointed moment, four portals appeared a notable distance from one another. Various beings stepped through each and crossed the distance to take their designated places around the fountain

A dwarf had arrived with a metallic *clink* that suggested armor under the robes and cowl that partially hid his face. He took his place quickly on the left.

Next in line stood a female Kilomea, whose bulk was larger than the greatest male of the species he'd ever seen. Her massive teeth and broad, bony forehead communicated a love for violence. The mammoth sword handle that extended over her shoulder confirmed her readiness to meet any challenge with force. She wore a perpetual half-grin that mixed confidence and condescension in equal measure.

An underground gnome stood beside her. This branch of the gnome species was rarely seen and seemed darker and harder than their servant cousins. The creature spoke infrequently, but always with significant insight.

He may be the most dangerous of them all.

Finally, the witch to his right arrived to close the circle. Her magic was fearsome, and her cruel beauty mystified her opponents until the moment at which she ended their existence. Rumor painted her as everything from a power-less gold-digger running a long con to an icon of pure evil who consumed the souls of those who crossed her. Even *he* was drawn by her elegance and had to constantly remind himself that power, and *only* power, mattered to the witch. Nods of greeting were exchanged—some neutral, some almost pleasant, but all sharing the hard edge of suspicion.

He swung his wand in an arc from left to right above his head, then another from forward to back, and a pinprick of light appeared high above at the intersection of the paths. It swelled in all directions to form a transparent semicircular shield that pulsed when it reached the ground. The barrier blocked the wind and would conceal them from magical eavesdropping. It also rendered the gathering invisible by cloaking the courtyard in an illusion of normalcy.

Not that anyone would come here to find us, anyway.

With the security measures fully in place, he finally broke the silence. "Welcome, my friends." The Kilomea snorted at the designation and drew knowing smiles from the others. "It is a genuine pleasure to see you again.

Without these regular meetings, my happiness would be but a shell of its former self."

As always, sarcasm prevailed among them.

The dwarf rolled his eyes. "Oh, me as well. *True* joy." No one else added anything, so Dreven spoke again.

"Today, we must discuss plans ahead and failures behind." He paused briefly and the dwarf shook his head slightly. As the next in the circle, the Kilomea accepted her turn to speak.

"Let us begin by speaking of failure, then. You did not capture the ambassador."

The gnome added a quiet, "Indeed," and the witch nodded.

Just as I expected.

"Let us begin there, then. I have invited another to inform us on this matter." A rune sketched in the air with his wand pierced the protective shell enough to permit a portal, and a circular gesture brought it into being. His underling stepped through. Further gestures banished the rift and resealed the barrier. "My subordinate was in charge of the effort to secure the ambassador. I thought it best we heard from him directly. Do explain, Nehlan."

The elf shivered. Dreven had deliberately failed to warn his minion about the chill temperature that permeated the battle site.

Petty, perhaps, but he's earned it.

He nodded encouragement, and Nehlan suppressed his trembling to speak clearly. "The plan was a good one. It should have succeeded. However, an unexpected variable intervened."

Dreven's lips twitched at the illusory features that had

replaced the council's true faces. He hadn't concealed his own since he had nothing to fear from his subordinate. The elf thought he was clever with his bunker, his poison fruit, and his stolen power, but Dreven could and would end him at any time he felt the urge.

The dwarf's voice was low and gravelly as he spoke first. "What was this *unexpected variable?*" he asked scornfully.

Nehlan shuddered. "A group of human meddlers more powerful than most we've seen."

The Kilomea growled. "Then you should have killed them all before they had the chance to interfere with the ambassador's capture." The elf flinched reflexively from her anger.

Nehlan straightened his spine, and a look of contempt drew his lips down as he met the hulking brute's eyes. "We attempted to. The result was that one of *your* people now languishes in a human prison. Perhaps I simply trusted the wrong person. Or the wrong species."

The aggressive female moved to take a menacing step forward as a ferocious glare settled over her illusory face. "I will show you how I deal with *my* inferiors, tiny elf."

Dreven's eyes sparkled with amusement as he flicked his wand and a gentle wave of force radiated from it—not enough to be rude and only enough to draw attention. "Keep it polite, please."

The gnome declined to speak, but the witch's sultry voice asked, "What of your lieutenant, the one we gifted with the artifact? Did he perform as expected?"

Dreven turned with his servant as Nehlan turned to face her. The illusion she displayed was flat and disguised her true beauty, but his subordinate's response carried a note of respect, nonetheless. "It worked as you said it would. It made him increasingly pliable the longer he wore it. By the end, I believe he would have killed himself or anyone else at a word from me."

The witch inclined her head, and it was again his turn to speak. "Wait for me beyond the circle, Nehlan." The elf walked away, and Dreven parted the shield momentarily to allow him to exit.

The dwarf's growl was satisfied. "The alterations we have made to the artifacts are working, then."

The gnome nodded. "They certainly appear to be. It was an inspired thought." He acknowledged the witch beside him, and she grinned as her perfect red lips tilted in a smile. "My idea, but *all* of our efforts. So long as they continue to only influence willingness to serve but not thinking ability, they can only make the Remembrance more powerful."

Dreven stuck his hands in the pockets of his outer robe. The cold radiating up through the stone had become an irritant, and he tried to keep his annoyance out of his voice. "The failure to abduct the ambassador is but a minor setback. Several paths branched forward from that moment, and we have simply been redirected onto a different one. Unknown to my underlings—and something I have not yet shared with you—is that I have been aware of this new organization for a while. Our source in another of their agencies was quite irritated about them and spoke at some length." He rolled his eyes, and the others laughed. "We have interfered with their supply shipments and put plans in place for attacks on their leaders. However, it will take weeks for those to fully develop."

"And what of the new prison?" the dwarf asked.

Dreven nodded. "Yes, the new prison. It is controlled and operated by this same group. Plans are in motion for that, as well. Our minions have inflamed the city in opposition. However, it is time to make a statement, as we agreed." He stared across the circle at the Kilomea. "Are your people ready for the event?"

She bared her sharp teeth with a decisive nod. "We are. When the humans riot, we will use the chaos to launch a strike against the facility."

The witch folded her arms and shook her head. "I must reiterate that I dislike this plan. It is too conservative, doesn't address the Kemana beneath the city, and doesn't end the larger threat of this opposing group. It is a symbolic action and a waste of our time and resources."

Dreven shrugged.

We've been over this too many times already.

"Does anyone other than Iressa desire to change our direction?" The circle remained silent, and he nodded. "Then, Pesharn, I wish you greater luck than my subordinate had." The Kilomea inclined her head in acknowledgment. "Now, you all must excuse me. I need to have a serious conversation with Nehlan about his failure." The other members of the Remembrance chuckled as he turned and dropped the shield.

A very *serious conversation.*

CHAPTER TWENTY-TWO

Vincente sat behind the battered metal desk in his office and admired the objects before him. There had been unexpected treasures among the artifacts. Some were items he had yet to deduce the purpose of and others were clearly Rhazdon artifacts he would be obligated to surrender to those above. His hands itched with the desire to claim one for himself. Once he had, though, only death could steal it away. He pulled the offending member back, cognizant of the fact that those above would not hesitate to spend days killing him for being so bold as to claim one for himself.

As a distraction, he selected one of the clear crystals scattered among the other treasures and held it to the light. The most unexpected bonus was the gems used to counter magic. He would leave them unreported to those above and use them to the benefit of his own branch.

Perhaps, with a few more successes, I will be granted an artifact all my own.

As his fingers stretched toward them again, he shook

his head and covered the powerful items with a black cloth. He bound it tightly around them so they couldn't tempt him further.

The coin in his hidden pocket warmed, and he swallowed hard. Without delay, he scooped up all the items on the desk and carried them to the safe. He spun the lock quickly and yanked the handle to deposit them inside. Then, he withdrew the small figurine his superiors had provided and placed it on the desk in front of his chair, retrieved the coin, and set it on the base. He rotated it so the tiny raised bumps were in the proper position. The crystals in the artifact glowed to indicate the activation of the device, and shortly after, an image materialized above the statue.

In the foreground was his master, the wizard Dreven. Behind him, a strange elf writhed in agony under the ministrations of the rippling tentacles that held him suspended a foot off the ground. The one across his mouth muted the screams, but they still caused Vincente to cringe each time the tortured being expelled them.

The image spoke in a deep, resonant voice. "Greetings, Vincente. Allow me to introduce you to another of my most trusted people." He gestured at the being behind him. "He failed me and failed the Remembrance. Because of his previous successes, he will be allowed to live and atone for his mistakes. Possibly, anyway." The tentacles squeezed harder and drew a second round of anguished screams from the tortured elf.

Dreven shook his head as he turned back. "I share this knowledge with you because the organization that interfered with *his* success is present in your city as well. You must account for them in your planning."

"We are aware of them, master, but we'll redouble our efforts where they are concerned if that is your will."

The wizard nodded his approval. "I have the details for your next task."

Vincente suppressed the desire to stand and pace and leaned on his desk instead. Pain throbbed in the back of his skull and beat in time to the screams of the tentacled figure behind his master.

"The humans provided useful cover for your operation with their protest of the prison. Now, we must build upon that success and turn them into a mob. Others have begun this process, as you have doubtless noticed."

He nodded.

Even if I hadn't, I sure as hell wouldn't admit it.

Of course, he'd seen the lawyer speaking on television and had discerned the hand of the Remembrance pulling his strings.

The wizard continued. "Mixed with the humans, your people will break into the prison and do whatever damage you can. Sow chaos in all directions. Most of all, attempt to discover the weaknesses of the place and of the organization behind it. If it is possible to destroy it, do so, but it is our belief that this occasion will amount to only a probing attack. The information gained from the guard we took is incomplete. It seems their compartmentalization is significant."

Vincente scratched at the back of his head to sooth the banging pain. "Their defenses are sure to be impressive, master."

The wizard grinned. As usual, the elf's eyes always seemed to stab directly into Vincente's brain to probe his deepest thoughts. "Your thirst for power is a testament to your ambition. You may claim one of the Rhazdon artifacts as a reward for your efforts and as our commitment to your future successes."

Now, he grinned in return. A wave of pleasure suffused him at the thought of the strength such a boon would bestow.

"We may provide one to your second-in-command as well. However, we must…empower it additionally first."

His eyebrows drooped in confusion at his superior's words, but he quickly banished the worry. *I'll have an artifact. That's what's important here.*

"You must create a spectacle of the attack on the prison. Draw as much attention as possible."

Vincente grinned. "The man who leads the human side of my organization is *very* good with explosives. I will have him find others with similar skills. As the humans like to say, we will light up the night." He paused to consider whether asking his master for anything else would be a smart idea. To be presumptuous could leave him in a similar situation to the elf. But then again, it might be worth it, and he was still needed for this mission. Having weighed his options, he shrugged and proceeded. "We'll need inside information beyond that which we have."

Dreven waved a hand. "Magic, treasure, force—do what you must. Our time in the shadows is at an end. This action will be the true unveiling of the Remembrance. Today, the worlds will learn of us. Tomorrow, they will fear us. Soon, they will serve us."

He nodded. Chills coursed through him at the weight of the threats implicit in those words. "Yes, master." The image dissolved, and his fingers trembled in anticipation as he returned the coin to its hidden pocket. He crossed to the safe and spun the dial carefully. It took him two attempts to successfully open it.

He set the statue back in its home, then unfolded the black cloth and withdrew the artifact that had intrigued him most. The object was a piece of flat metal adorned with small jewels to represent the eyes and scales of a snake. It was a thing of beauty, as gorgeous as any artwork he had ever seen. He carried it reverently to the desk and sat, unable to pull his gaze away from the item.

"Now, where to put you for the bonding?" he muttered. Most selected arms, but Pittsburgh summers were hot and he didn't want to be restricted to long sleeves.

Unless the artifact enables me to regulate my temperature.

He chuckled at himself. There was no telling what powers might be gained, but he was fairly sure that something so mundane would not be at the top of the list. Finally, he unbuttoned his shirt and leaned back.

He placed the snake diagonally across the hard muscles of his stomach. Nothing happened, and he considered that maybe he should've asked his superior for instructions. He sent his intention to the item with a mental plea.

Come on. Whatever you require, I will provide. Together, we will show these humans what magic power truly is.

Vincente screamed as the artifact came to life and sank into his skin. He felt like his stomach had been bathed in acid. His hands clenched on the arm of the chair as he held himself rigid and struggled to control his thrashing as much as possible. The burning spread throughout his body, and he growled and hissed to vent his frustrations.

Worth it. It...will...be...worth it!

He had no idea how much time had passed. All he knew was that the pain had finally ceased. Once this fact seeped into his consciousness, he panted and stood unsteadily, then wiped the sweat from his brow. The angry red skin on his stomach faded to reveal an incredibly realistic tattoo of a snake. The head pointed directly at his heart as if reminding him of his mortality. He nodded, and his voice emerged in a hoarse whisper. "Believe me, I am well aware."

New strength surged through him with every step as he crossed to the tall windows. He stared at the broken remains of his teams and the prideful stances of his seconds as they worked with their people. The image of the battle ahead brought a grin to his face. "We'll need fresh blood."

The artifact throbbed an agreement, and a sibilant, *Yesssss,* hissed through his mind. *Time to cause some trouble.*

CHAPTER TWENTY-THREE

The narrow alley ran between the rear facades of short apartment buildings on either side. Needless to say, it wasn't a place for cars to play chicken. Diana hoped devoutly that no such traffic would arise as she moved in a crouch behind Tony to remain below the top of the four-foot-high wall that ran along the left-hand side.

Her comm came to life with Cara's voice. "In position in the front. No sign of activity."

Diana tapped her glasses to register a double-click in response. All three had assumed their bounty hunter disguises. Their official IDs had come through only days before and displayed the faces created by their illusion necklaces. They worked cover stories up that earned Cara and Diana class-three licenses and a class-four for Tony. They decided that would be a range high enough to apprehend the targets they selected but low enough to not attract unwanted attention.

The bounty was one they'd arranged based on information gleaned from the battle at the museum. SWAT had recorded the image of an enemy who fled the scene, and they tapped into the city's surveillance grid to find her. Tony stopped at the end of the wall, and Diana whispered, "Nice job getting this witch set as a bounty, Tony."

He sounded pleased but dismissive of his own success. "It's legit. She's clearly a menace. *Someone* should get paid. The police chief says it's federal dollars at this point, anyway. But it does mean we need her alive."

"Pity," Cara replied.

Diana hefted her nonlethal rifle. Its weight was annoyingly noticeable.

We'll have to make some custom lookalikes that weigh less.

"Hooray for stun guns. Final check." She looked down to ensure the AR-15 was properly strapped across her chest. The Sig-Sauer rode at her right hip. Since she'd had to leave her favorite boots behind after Cara had pointed out they were unique enough to be identifiable, the Ruger was tucked into a waistband holster at the small of her back. The others were similarly equipped. Each also wore a dark-blue button-down with the security company's logo on it—two solid circles in red and black—that mostly overlapped to cover the ARES vests underneath.

Tony had prepared the brief for the op, so it was his task to review it before they went in. "So, the expectation is that Susan Cheri—clearly an alias—is inside." Diana laughed quietly at their target's name choice, while Tony continued. "She owns the building and lives on the top floor. There are two apartments on the second level and another two on the first, plus storage in the basement."

"Residents?" Diana asked.

"The last one left about twenty minutes ago," Cara interjected. "Recon from the last couple of days puts them all at either work or school. We have about an hour before the early shift usually gets back." They'd done their homework this time and mounted cameras all around the location several nights before.

"If my contact at the PD is accurate, we have at least five on the top floor," Tony warned.

"I wish that drone was still here," Cara complained.

She could almost hear the shrug in Tony's voice. "Any longer and the deviation from its planned route would've been noticed. At least it gave us a good, if quick, look inside the windows."

"We need our own drones."

Diana sighed. "I'll add it to the list."

Tony grinned over his shoulder at her. "And someone to run them."

She shook her head. "Stop. Let's get to this, preferably before my head explodes from all your complaining. There's nothing here to change our plan, so Tony and I will go up the back to the top floor and enter that way. Cara, keep your eyes open while you clear the lower floors. There's no guarantee we have the whole picture here."

The ex-marshal's voice was all business. "Affirmative." After the museum battle, Cara and Tony had made the choice to resign from their other positions.

I couldn't have chosen better people.

Diana led the way up the rear staircase, which switched back on itself in the middle of each story. The wooden planks were old, weather-beaten, unpainted, and unstained.

Maybe we can add poor landlording to her charges.

She snorted internally as she imagined how Lisa would jump at the chance to do the same to her.

They ascended to the top of the basement level before she found the first trap—a simple tripwire attached to a collection of tin cans hanging nearby. It was more an alarm system than a death machine, but it would still cause problems if someone triggered it. She pointed it out to Tony and stepped over the wire. Her AR glasses identified the infrared beams stretched across at rib and shin height about halfway to the landing. Fortunately, they were at least able to afford the tech necessary to take care of this one. Compared to the magic deflectors, the sticky reflectors were a dime a dozen. She applied the two devices simultaneously to each side, first low, then high, to turn the beam back on itself.

The staircase connecting the second level to the third was where things became truly dangerous. She found the alarm trap easily but almost missed the next tripwire, which was attached to a grenade.

Damn. I hope the lower ones dissuade any ordinary burglar from making it this far. Getting hit with an explosive when you're simply trying to do a simple B&E could really ruin your day.

Time slowed with her next step, and she looked around carefully. Her foot froze in midair. She sensed a vibration from the stair she was about to traverse—a shimmer maybe?—and pulled her leg back.

Alert and focused, she peered at the step from every

angle she deemed safe but couldn't identify the danger. She decided avoiding it was the smart way to go, and time resumed its normal speed. "Trap on the next step. We'll jump over, then move fast in case it's bigger than we think. Stay right on my six and put your feet where I do." He nodded but looked appropriately nervous.

Cara's voice crackled over the comms. "Basement is clear. Moving up to the first floor."

Diana swung to face the proper way, took a deep breath, and jumped over the troubled stair. She pounded up the rest of the flight in a rush, then switched directions on the platform. The grip on her stun rifle was rigid and unyielding as adrenaline surged with her heartbeat. Time slowed again, and another step looked suspicious. She repeated the procedure and leapt over it and the one after that for good measure. Tony arrived safely on the top platform a moment after she did.

Identical entries stood on each side of the building's centerline, a mirror-image remnant of when the top floor was divided into two separate living spaces. It was a clever renovation that allowed for two avenues of escape. If they hadn't found the details on the construction permit for the place, they wouldn't have known, and the witch might have been able to escape. The doors looked thin and flimsy. In short, it was obvious that they were trapped.

Diana lifted a chair that rested along the wall near the left door and set it under the slightly open kitchen window at the edge of the building. She examined it quickly for traps, both magical and otherwise, saw none, and slid the opening up with a small *squeak*. After a brief pause to listen intently, she clambered in, crouched on the counter, and made sure the room was clear before she lowered herself soundlessly to the floor. Tony did the same, albeit a little more noisily, but they needn't have worried. A loud television deeper in the apartment effectively drowned out the noise of their entry. She triggered her mic. "Safe entry."

It sounded like a cooking show was playing in the next room. She pushed it from her mind.

I really don't need tips on barbecue recipes right now, thanks.

A persistent mental voice wondered where to find the best barbecue in town. An unspoken command corralled it as she focused on the mission again. They advanced cautiously with their rifles held ready for instant action. The straps provided additional stability.

She withdrew a small mirror from her pocket. It was a far cry from the fiber-optic gear ARES used, but it would suffice. She angled it to look around the corner. A large dining area stood on the right, with china cabinets and a rectangular table that could easily seat eight. It had only one visible occupant, a tough-looking man with a pistol in pieces on the surface before him.

Two men whose builds screamed muscle argued about the virtues of charcoal versus gas grills. The witch was nowhere in sight. Diana turned and pointed at Tony, slashed her hand to the right, and extended her index finger. He nodded and positioned himself for a dash into the next room. She held up three fingers, then two, then one, and the two agents moved together.

Diana fired at the goon on the couch nearest her as she rounded the corner. The discharge struck him before he had a chance to react. His head lolled back onto the cushion. The other man was quicker than she expected and had turned to face the intruders. Her rifle clicked to signal a full charge, and she pulled the trigger again. The bolt tumbled the target over the side. The whine of Tony's weapon was followed by a solid *thump*, and she turned swiftly. His opponent had apparently pushed his chair over backward to escape and cracked his head on the floor. The agent fired at the downed form to be on the safe side. The small pool of blood that seeped around the man's skull left little room for worry, however.

This was the part of the plan Diana loathed. Stunning was all well and good when the enemy didn't actively try to kill you but was far less fun when they did. Shouts and footsteps raced along the halls in their direction, and they both took cover. She fled behind the couch, while he ducked behind one of the table legs farthest from the entrance to the hallway that led deeper into the unit.

The front door slammed, and Diana said, "We may have a runner."

"On it," Cara assured her.

A woman's loud voice yelled orders and curses, which suggested that their quarry was still present. A trio of pistol-wielding troublemakers barreled into the room, two in biker jackets and the third shirtless—and *not* in possession of a physique that would call for casual nudity. Diana disabled him first for making her eyes suffer.

Tony spun out briefly from his cover, but one of the others fired in his direction and he ducked into the minimal protection the table provided once more. The other man trained a pistol on Diana.

She hurled her stun rifle up on its strap to swing it around to rest on her back. With that safely stowed, she extended both hands and yanked the firearm away from one adversary with her telekinesis, while she released a brilliant line of force out with the other to strike his partner. The weaponless man demonstrated good reflexes by charging her while the other staggered into the wall behind him.

Tony rose again and fired at the one who hurtled toward her, but his shot went wide and struck the television. The device immediately sparked and the screen shattered. The enemy leapt over the couch and hauled his arm back in readiness for a punch. Diana reacted instinctually. She swept both her hands from right to left as force and telekinesis combined to launch her opponent and keep him airborne until he slammed into the wall behind her. She turned to finish him, but a stun blast from Tony's gun beat her to it and the man went limp. Tony spun and eliminated the one in the hallway as the man struggled to regain his feet.

Laughter sounded from deeper in the apartment. "Such violence. It's so unnecessary. Why do you invade my home?"

The witch stepped into view. She was tall, almost skeletally thin, and appeared to be close to what, for a human, would be the age of retirement. Long gray hair hung in scruffy waves down to her shoulders, and she wore an ankle-length skirt and a cardigan.

She looks like somebody's grandmother.

Cara's voice came breathlessly over the comm. "The runner was easy. The reinforcements, less so. I have them bottlenecked on the first floor, but they might be able to push me back."

Damn. I need to finish this quickly.

Diana held up her empty hands. "Everything would be better if you come quietly. We merely want to ask you some questions at the office."

The woman laughed. "The signs of your power are still fading, young one. You will find that I am not so easily defeated as these fools." Tony's gun whined, and the witch summoned a circle of darkness to consume the attack. She extended her hand to reveal a wand. Ebony threads snaked from its tip in an attempt to snare the investigator. He flung himself aside to escape them, but judging by the way the magic washed over him in an oval, his deflectors had taken some of the damage he failed to evade.

She ran forward and led with a punch in the air that directed a fist of force at the witch. Her adversary merely gave a contemptuous smile as she moved her head the minimum amount required to avoid the attack, then raised her wand to counter. Diana tried to yank it from the witch's grasp with her telekinesis but couldn't dislodge it. Darkness lanced out at her, and she dropped to evade the strike. Unfortunately, the blow still landed, and she scowled at the vibration as the deflector gems crackled.

Her roll dodged the next onslaught and she lurched to her feet. Rather than attack, she gathered the energy around herself to form a barrier. The witch laughed, and the bolt of darkness ripped through the shield like it wasn't there.

Shit. That was stupid.

Diana dropped and rolled again. The strength of the impact when she struck the coffee table immediately numbed her arm. She heard gunfire, and Tony yelped. She drew her Ruger and shot at the witch from a crouch.

The woman summoned her defense again, but the bullets plowed through. One struck her in the shoulder and spilled her back against the wall.

She barked a curse, sounding angry rather than injured, and the agent squeezed the trigger twice more. The target whispered a word and flicked her wand to levitate a small desk in front of the bullets' path. It angled in mid-flight and raced toward Diana. She raised her good arm in a hasty defense, and the projectile shattered against her force shield.

Gunfire exploded from the right. Tony stood with his Sig-Sauer in his right hand and the Ruger in his left. He fired with the former at the thug who had shot him and the latter at the witch. Both struck their targets and the man careened into the hallway with a crash. The witch's condition was slightly more serious as blood welled from her side.

Diana raced forward, zip-tied their quarry, and shoved a bandanna she carried for exactly that purpose into the woman's mouth in case she had voice-activated magical items on her. Next, she confiscated the wand and slid it into the inside pocket of her coat.

I'll need to carry something to hold these wands, for real.

She triggered her mic. "Cara, status."

"They're retreating for now. I'll maintain position here, but I think they're done."

Tony tottered over and pulled his shirt apart to show the pair of bullets lodged in his vest. "So, that sucked."

Diana nodded. She extracted a roll of duct tape and

carefully folded the witch's clothes over her wounds, then bound them with the silver material. "Good shooting, Tex."

He grinned. "I'm sure you had her."

"Without question."

"Any second, right?"

Diana sighed. "An instant later, and she'd have been down."

He laughed. "Totally, boss."

She glared at him, but the way her mouth turned up at the corners probably ruined the look. "Shut up and search the place. Cara, call the PD to collect the trash."

The hasty ten-minute search before the cops arrived yielded many a positive result. They found several items that looked like they could be magical in nature and pocketed them. Also, they located the woman's cell phone and removed the gag long enough to let it recognize her face and unlock. Diana spun through the text messages and read one that gave a street address along with a date and time. She held it up to her glasses, and a map appeared, overlaid on her vision.

That's a block away from the Cube. Three days from now, eight PM. Not good.

She pocketed the device and stood. "Cara, meet me in the back. We have to get to the base. Tony, take care of the PD." She reached the landing, then remembered. "Hey, make sure they don't use the rear stairs and bring the bomb squad and a wizard in here to defuse those things." She made it safely down to ground level and met Cara, who looked sweaty and energized. She held the phone out and waited while she repeated the process of investigating the address.

The former army officer's face became an emotionless mask. "The Cube."

Diana nodded. "Yep."

Cara sighed. "Shit."

I couldn't have summed it up better myself.

CHAPTER TWENTY-FOUR

Diana raised her eyes from a display in the core as the door from the garage tunnel released and swung open. Max barked at her feet, and Rath jumped up on the table to see who it was. The first object to enter the room was a giant black case, the kind a band would take on tour for their wardrobe. Hidden behind it was the slim, blonde form of Kayleigh Dornan.

All three ran across to welcome the tech. Diana assisted in wrestling the huge box into the equipping area. Kayleigh knelt to pet Max, who immediately rolled on his back for belly rubs. Rath didn't quite do the same, but he stood close to her and grinned like a fool. The agent imagined that her own expression was similar. She'd missed the woman most among her old friends at ARES DC branch.

The tech caught her study of her boots and answered the unspoken question behind it with an amused smirk. "No, these are still the old pair. I've been busy."

Both laughed. "It's so good to see you here," Diana said.

"We'll take you out on the town tonight and show you around."

Kayleigh nodded and gave the Borzoi a final pet. "So, dogs are allowed up here?"

"Sometimes it's nice to be the boss." Diana grinned. "Besides, this is an office day. You know, though, if we simply got Max some armor, he'd probably make a great agent."

The tech laughed and shook her head. "That's not part of this shipment, I'm afraid. But would you like to see what is?"

She rolled her eyes. "I thought you'd *never* ask."

Rath echoed, "Never."

Kayleigh pressed her hand to the palm reader on top of her case and typed in a code while standing on a bench to get the correct angle. The latches disengaged and she jumped down to swing the case open. A series of vests hung on the right above a block of horizontal storage. Rows of rectangular compartments covered the left side. Diana raised an eyebrow. "That's very efficient packing you have there."

The other woman grinned. "We pride ourselves on efficiency above all things. Well, okay, that's not true. Creative and destructive are both higher on the list."

"In that order?"

"It depends on which of us you're asking and what mood we're in that day."

Diana smiled and looked at Rath, who bounced excitedly on the balls of his feet. "It's about the same around here."

Kayleigh started on the top left and opened a flap to

retrieve a cardboard box. A foam insert held fifty anti-magic bullets for either model of rifle they used. Diana whistled, and the tech answered with a nod. "And three more like it for a total of two hundred. That should give you each two magazines full."

"Do I want to know how much those cost?"

"You don't. Not only did we have to pay a premium because of the shortage, but we also had to transport them ourselves from the source to make sure the shipment wasn't intercepted on the way."

She frowned. "Is that what's been going on?"

The tech's expression matched hers. "Yep. Someone's been messing with our pipeline, although there is stress on the availability because of the folks on the West Coast. AET and the Brownstone Agency have a super-heavy demand for this over there."

"Are they dealing with the same group we are?"

"Nothing suggests that. Logically, there's sure to be more than one set of scumbags to go around."

Diana chucked. "Well, there's enough for everyone, really."

Kayleigh pulled out the box at the start of the second row and opened it to reveal more anti-magic bullets. These were sized for their revolvers. Again, the container held fifty.

"I am *truly* impressed now." She frowned. "Should I be worried that someone's after my team?"

The woman shrugged again. "Probably. It's clear that someone out there doesn't like us, and you all are the only *us* in this town. Speaking of which, how's the Kilomea?"

Diana rewarded her friend with a scowl and shook her

head. Kayleigh laughed and let the subject drop. The next box she removed was triple the width of the others and most closely resembled a shallow briefcase without a handle. She set the container on the bench and flipped it open. The agent whistled, and Rath immediately did a short run and somersault to the top of the rolling case to peer at the smaller one.

Several lines of clear gems stood on end in a protective foam casing. The rows were staggered for spatial efficiency, and her eyes widened. She'd never even imagined seeing so many magic deflector crystals at once before. "Where the *hell* did you get these?"

Kayleigh grinned. "ARES DC found a black-market dealer's warehouse. We raided it and apprehended him. These are only part of the stash of goodies we discovered inside."

She shook her head, momentarily overcome with a desire to surround herself with items of magical power.

I can see why the bad guys are so into the idea.

"How'd you find them?"

"We received a tip, actually." Kayleigh shrugged. "Someone Bryant knows put us onto the place."

"Okay," she said slowly.

I'll have to ask him about that. He's keeping secrets.

The tech had moved to the large boxes in the bottom row. She opened one to reveal grenade canisters with small chili peppers engraved on the handle. Diana grinned. "Production, then?"

Kayleigh smiled proudly. "Yep, these are standard issue now. Half the price of a sonic, and more effective when dealing with either a single target or a group of targets spread out."

"You're really good at your job. In fact, some might call you great. I happen to know of a field office that needs—"

The woman raised a hand to stop her and spoke loudly. "But you'll *love* these." She turned to the other side of the crate, where the vests waited. "We've improved the electrical absorption and added capacitors to store the charge before it can reach the resistors. The weight adjustment is negligible." She pointed to the areas inside the vest where the energy-collecting devices were clustered.

"If one of those takes a bullet, will it hurt us? I mean, extra?"

Kayleigh shook her head. "It's lined with nonconductive material. They'll simply short out forward. Worst case, they blow more resistors."

Diana nodded. "Cool, but why? Innovation for fun?"

"It started that way, but I noticed that your team tends to brawl more than most."

"Whatever it takes, right?"

"I'm not judging. Your effectiveness speaks for itself." She reached into the lower portion of the case. "But we realized we could give you an edge." She held out a glove. It appeared almost identical to the standard versions that paired with the rifles and prohibited others from using them, but each knuckle had a rounded stud on top. Diana looked up and met Kayleigh's grin with one of her own. "Silver knuckles. The better to punch you with?"

The tech retrieved a cord and connected it to the vest, then to the top of the glove. "You charge the vest before you head out. It will add a shock to several punches before depleting. If you take an electrical blast that charges the capacitors, the glove can draw power from them again. They have their own internal capacitor, but it only stores enough additional energy for one punch. The thing was too heavy when we tried to add more in there."

"Nice," Diana whispered. She examined the cord and pictured a variety of scenarios she couldn't wait to make a reality. "You know, at some point, we'll have to wear body-suits under the armor if you need to constantly connect things together."

Kayleigh grinned. "Don't tempt me. I've watched *Iron Man* something like one hundred and thirty-seven times."

The agent laughed, and Rath said, "I am Iron Troll."

The visitor turned to him. "We didn't forget about you, buddy. You get one of the new vests in your size as well, but yours powers these." She extracted a pair of batons and flicked them open. "They should have half again the number of charges as before, and that's assuming you aren't hit with something that charges up the capacitors."

Rath accepted them reverently and spun them once in his hands. "Is good. Is *very* good."

The women both grinned. Diana asked, "Is there anything for his biggest form?"

Kayleigh shook her head. "Ems and I have researched that angle for weeks, but the weight trade-off is too diffi-cult. You'd have to carry the stuff for him, and there's no way that makes sense. We're looking into using carbon fiber, but so far, we haven't managed to find a tight enough weave to avoid reducing the damage of the batons. The armor might be doable. The team is working on it."

"This is quite a haul, regardless."

"And last, but not least, the best thing of all." The tech grinned and spread her empty hands wide.

It took Diana a moment to realize what she meant, and excitement filled her reply. "Really?"

She nodded. "Yep, I'm staying for a while. It's a temporary assignment till y'all get your act together up here."

The smile that stretched Diana's face was almost painful. "You said that wrong. I'll fix it for you. *Permanent* reassignment to get our act together for us."

The other woman shook her head, but Diana saw the truth.

One of us, my pretty.

CHAPTER TWENTY-FIVE

She was tired from the late night out showing Kayleigh the sights of the city. When Bryant had called at six AM to say he was inbound, she'd forced herself to get to the office by seven. Two duplicate versions of the coffeemaker and espresso machine from the fifth floor had been set up on the bottom level, and they both dispensed the life-giving fluid. She already had a tumbler in her hand, as always, with the logo of the Coworking space on it. "It's still a stupid name for the company," she grumbled to the empty room.

Bryant arrived at eight, and the rest of the team stumbled in shortly after. He stood near the display table and flicked idly through reports from the local stations' websites. The smarmy lawyer's face appeared on many of them, with graphics heralding the "Ultramax threat." Kayleigh waved as she passed on her way to the improvised workspace on the floor above. Once they were all gathered, he said, "I have new data for you. The regional

PDA has run surveillance on this prick, and some useful information has come up."

Tony lowered his mug long enough to ask, "Legally?"

Their boss sipped his coffee before responding. "Yep. There are a few judges who give us a little leeway, but never for anything that outright crosses the line."

The investigator nodded in satisfaction.

"We piggybacked their feed and copied the raw data as it came in," Bryant continued. "Our folks managed to dig some useful nuggets out of it. There's no sign that PDA has done the same, but that's okay because this is squarely in our area of interest."

He pressed a few buttons and images of nonsensical emails popped onto the screen. "These are very heavily encrypted and required a magic computer tech to decode. They indicate that the lawyer will call for a major protest at the Cube tomorrow night, and they already have cells recruiting people to join them."

Diana shook her head. "Well, that's concerning."

"Very. Given what you found, it seems likely that this could be another cover action for the Remembrance. So, we need to figure out what they intend to do and how they'll do it." Bryant called up an aerial view of the city streets around the prison for several blocks, and they spent thirty minutes planning potential scenarios, including where they would gather and deploy to create maximum trouble for the enemy. When they finished, he checked his watch. "The warden's expecting a call from us."

Diana stepped forward and activated the controls for the side displays to bring them online. A few moments later, she booted up the ARES custom video communication program. After a few minutes of negotiation, the Cube's leader finally appeared on the screen.

Bryant greeted her with his usual smile. "Hello, Warden Murphy."

She waved grimly. "Good to see you all."

It didn't take long to fill her in on the details they had acquired of the possible attack and potential counter scenarios they had devised. "We're ready," she assured them. "This is a contingency we've planned for."

"What's the response?" Diana hoped her unease wasn't obvious.

The warden looked to the side, most likely to consult her notes or a handbook of some sort. "At the first sign of a crowd, we will abandon the upper levels and move underground. If it happens in the evening, like we expect, there won't be that many people in the building above, anyway."

Cara asked, "Won't that leave your data vulnerable? They could simply make off with the computers."

Murphy shook her head. "All the machines in the office are dummy terminals. Actually, that's all we use throughout the whole facility. They're all connected to a server or something down here. I don't understand it, and when they tried to explain, my life started to flash before my eyes so I made them stop. What I *do* know is that there's a physical switch we can throw that pulls two strips of connectors away from each other to physically disconnect the upstairs computers from the system."

"Handy," the ex-marshal said, and the rest nodded their agreement.

"The prison itself has independent everything and is

strong enough to handle the biggest earthquake that's ever hit this area, so long as we're not at the epicenter."

Tony shook his head. "Imagine if there were a magical who could cause earthquakes. That would suck hard."

It was a sobering thought, and the warden resumed her explanation with a frown. "Anyway, we'll have all our drones out, but if there truly are civilians involved, we won't be able to risk using the weapons."

"How can we assist?" Diana asked.

Murphy shrugged. "Our plan is to turtle up. There's no way they'll get in here, so we're good. But anything that gets the job finished quickly is worth doing."

They said their goodbyes, and Diana exhaled slowly. "This could get really ugly."

Tony nodded. "The Police Department and SWAT will be on scene or nearby. They'll call everyone in once the announcement goes out, so they don't bust our insider knowledge. But since the lawyer will claim it's a peaceful protest, they can't do much beyond basic crowd control. If something *does* break out, they face the same problem as the Cube's drones."

Cara asked, "So, what's our role in all of this?"

Diana checked with Bryant, but he deferred to her. "We'll be there in case the real bad guys show up. We'll hole up in the office building and try to surprise them if they come inside. Even though there's only one entrance, it probably makes sense to split up." Everyone nodded agreement. "So, I'll stick with Rath. Tony and Cara will pair together, and Bryant can be a free agent."

He managed a half-smile. "Why is it that nobody wants to work with me?"

"You're funny looking," she answered promptly,

Cara added, "You have taco breath entirely too often."

"Your raw attractiveness makes me look ugly by comparison," Tony finished.

They all turned to stare at him, and he shrugged. "What? I'm sensitive."

The stress diminished in a round of laughter. Once they recovered, Diana said, "We have an advantage. We know where they'll be, and we know when they'll be there. Between now and then, we get some rest, run some scenarios at the agency, and see if we can figure out what they might be going for." She tapped a fist into the opposite palm. "After that, we'll lie in wait. If all goes well, we can surprise these bastards and show them how we deal with assholes who make trouble in our town."

CHAPTER TWENTY-SIX

Four PM

The rally was at eight, and for safety's sake, they added a substantial cushion. The equipping area at the ARES facility was quiet as the teammates focused on internal preparations. Even Rath was abnormally subdued as he donned his equipment. They had each retrieved their gear from the cabinets before they retreated to their own places on the bench to get ready. Bryant was near Diana and hauled his gear from a tall rolling case.

She sat to don her own items. Kayleigh's boots weren't practical for the evening's activities, so she abandoned them in favor of lace-up combat boots that rose to mid-shin. Tactical pants and a black high-collared shirt completed the base layer. She strapped on a set of shin guards, tightened them over her pant leg and boot, then did the same with the Kevlar thigh protection.

That part of her ritual completed, she stood, stomped around to ensure her heels were set in the footwear, and added her heavy fabric top. It was also an unadorned black and somewhat blade resistant. She lowered her vest over her shoulders and pulled the straps tight before she twisted left and right to make sure it was seated properly.

The utility belt wrapped around the bottom of her tunic and held it in place. She slipped her Ruger into the holster beside her spine and touched the grip of the Bowie knife that hung in the center. A cylinder was attached on the left of the pistol, appropriately sized for captured wands. Zip ties and a medpack completed the items on her belt. She holstered the Glock on her right hip and slotted two additional mags for it in the pouch on her vest. The rifle came next, and its replacement magazines went into her chest pouches as well. She stowed an extra spare for the carbine in a pouch on her left thigh-guard. She smiled as she stashed the tiny canister of pepper spray that Kayleigh had given her a long time before into the matching container on the other leg.

She stood and slung her rifle over it all and checked to make sure the strap positioned it exactly where she wanted it. There were two locations for grenades on a short line that dangled where her holster would have been if she were left-handed. She slotted in a sonic and a flash-bang. They'd all agreed incendiaries were a bad choice to use in their own facility.

Diana rolled her neck and glanced around surreptitiously. Bryant was pulling his vest on. Tony sat fully equipped and stared at the lockers. Cara tested the draw of her revolver. Rath twirled his batons in circles and lazy figure-eights in the space between the equipping area and the core. She reviewed her placements to be sure her hands knew where the two anti-magic magazines for her rifle and pistol were and where the spare standard carbine mag was, so she could find them by touch.

Rath had two grenade holders on the bandoliers across his chest. Pepper grenades occupied both slots. The rest of the team had selected their additional devices and ammunition according to their own preferences.

She drew the shock gloves on and flexed her hands to adjust the fit before she plugged the cables in. With deft movements, she twisted the connectors to lock them in place. She threaded them back along her arms to the vest's connection points under her armpits. They had tested the new toys and found the cable distracting, so she wound a Velcro loop around each arm above the elbow to keep the line from moving.

Bodysuits really aren't a bad idea.

Now that she'd finished suiting up, she turned to check on her team. They stood in a small circle with her at the center and waited for their glorious leader to direct them. She spoke quietly, since she was fearful of breaking the thick layer of confidence, real or projected, that they displayed. "Let's go."

The agents and the troll filed out in a line to a pair of SUVs in the garage. They locked their carbines in the holders in the rear. Diana slid behind the wheel and Bryant took shotgun. Rath rode in the back and gripped the seatbelt where it cut across his chest.

Booster seat. Right. I need to make it standard.

She took the lead and led the other car from the parking garage to navigate the streets toward the north side and the Cube's secret access. It was located along the river as part of a securely locked former manufacturing complex. The gate swung wide at a signal from Bryant's watch and closed itself after they passed through.

There was a total of five buildings, and they drove to the one nearest the water. The huge double door in the front was already in motion, and they pulled in without stopping. The cars swung in opposite curves to park facing the exit before the motors cut out.

They piled out and retrieved their weapons from the rear of the vehicles, then crossed to the guard who stood nearby. He wore the Cube's standard uniform with riot gear over it, minus the shield and helmet, and had a stun rifle strapped across his chest.

If they get past us, you will all need a lot more than stunners.

Diana didn't speak. She only followed as he led them silently into the tunnel.

The corridor was secured by heavy metal doors every ten yards or so and ran for almost a mile, according to the display on Diana's glasses. The warden hadn't been kidding when she'd told them during their tour that the exit was secured and could only be accessed as an entry if their route was enabled by someone from within the Cube.

Finally, they entered on level three, which they hadn't yet seen. The Warden had been truthful, as it was a carbon copy of the level above and the emergency exit was the only variation. The final barrier clanged shut behind them, as had each previous one as they passed it. A green light appeared above the door, and the guard raised the walkie-talkie attached to his vest. "Exit three, secure."

"Exit three secure, confirmed," squawked the comm almost immediately.

He led them to the elevators, and they rose to the ground level of the facility. Murphy waited at the top to wish them luck, and they exchanged a few words. The team crossed into the office building through the same security gauntlet they'd experienced during the tour, only in the opposite direction, and peered out the glass doors. There was nothing to see. Yet. Diana checked her watch.

Three hours to go.

She toggled the switch to temporarily isolate their comms from the channel they shared with the personnel in the Cube. She could still listen to them, but they wouldn't hear her or her team. "Kayleigh, what's your status?"

The blonde's energetic voice answered a moment later. "All good here, boss. I'm set up in the core. I have taps on the Pittsburgh Police surveillance grid, plus their comms and drones, which are *ancient.*"

Diana shook her head and smiled. The tech took the use of non-cutting-edge technology as a personal affront.

Kayleigh continued. "We're in on the Cube's sources, too. Drones and area cameras both, but nothing on the inside." The Warden had only been willing to share so much, and Diana couldn't blame her. The wider the band-width, the more likely the enemy would notice it. She made a mental note to have a hardwire established between the two facilities. "I have feeds from each of your glasses, and also our own drones."

Tony blinked in surprise. "We have drones?"

Her voice was tinged with scorn. "Of course we do. I brought them with me. It's stupid not to have them in the first place."

Diana shook her head again. "Well, I guess you'd better

plan to stay awhile and get things set up right for us, then, right?"

Kayleigh ignored the comment. "One of *my* drones is circling at a two-block radius. The other is holding position over you. They're each good for hours of flight time, and I have a spare ready to go up if it's needed."

Cara asked, "Are they armed?"

"Nope. Too dangerous."

"What if we put stun guns on them?"

The tech sighed. "We're not really into the whole urban pacification thing at ARES."

Tony weighed in with an audible grin. "What's a little stun between friends?"

She didn't reply directly and instead, said, "Boss?"

"Yes?"

"You'd better add getting a lawyer to your to-do list with these folks around."

They all chuckled, and Bryant added, "No lawyer. Too expensive. You all need to behave."

Diana killed her mic. "It seems our original plan is still a good one. Bryant, Rath, and I will blunt the initial attack on the ground floor. If we're lucky, they'll split their force and try to get into the underground levels of the Cube, which won't work out so well for them. If we're pressed, we'll fall back to the stairwell and hold them on it for as long as we can. When forced to retreat, we'll head up to C."

She pointed two fingers at the remaining team members. "Tony and Cara, you be ready to ambush them if they make it to B. Otherwise, we can nail them from two sides between the levels. If they do engage and you feel the need to retreat, throw the grenades and get up to D. We'll pop in and try to block them after you leave. And if they ignore levels B and C and go directly to D for some ungodly reason, we'll attack from the rear."

They nodded, and she gave them a confident smile. "Ideally, we'll kick their asses and saunter out the front door in an abundance of glory. Worst case, we go out the windows." She toggled her mic. "Kayleigh, status of the helicopter?"

"Standing by for liftoff at the air reserve base. It'll take off the moment you say go and will be ready to evacuate you if needed."

Diana nodded and muted her comm. "Questions, anyone?"

Tony raised a hand, and she gave him a withering look. "Yes, Detective Ryan."

"Ma'am? I was wondering what these assholes are actually after here, ma'am."

She laughed. "We're simply taking our best guess here, Tony. It stands to reason that if their goal is to make a statement, which it seems to be, their best choice is to get into the Cube itself. But we know that won't happen, barring something incredibly unexpected that we'll have to find a way to deal with if it happens. That leaves them the option to cause trouble in here. They don't know it contains nothing useful, so we'll turn that to our advantage and eliminate those we can. If we can manage prisoners, that would be nice, but not at the cost of harm to the team."

Everyone nodded, and she checked her watch again. "Two and a half hours. Let's get into position, just in case, and then we do the hardest part of the job—wait for the action to start."

CHAPTER TWENTY-SEVEN

As they waited for the evening's adventure to begin, Diana, Rath, and Bryant sat in a circle, talking easily over the comm with Cara and Tony. After the fear of the unknown had faded into the exhaustion of waiting, Diana made up an excuse and sent Rath up to check on the other two, which left her and Bryant alone.

He wasn't fooled. As soon as the troll was out of earshot, he gave her a searching look. "What's up? Are you okay?"

She nodded.

Except for the incredible awkwardness of this moment, I'm great. Thanks.

A part of her wished there would be a sneak attack to forestall the next few minutes, but it didn't come. "So, I know."

He frowned. "What do you know?"

"What you are."

"Handsome? Charming? Smarter than average? A real prize, like my mom always said?"

Classic. Humor to deflect pain.

"A wizard."

He blinked, seemed about to speak, then blinked some more. Finally, he said, "Samuels." She nodded. "Did he tell you all about it?"

Diana shook her head. "Nope. He only said that you had chosen a different path than most."

"Well, that's true enough." He laughed. "Although technically, I'm descended from wizards, not an actual wizard."

She waved her hand. "Semantics. Is the different path the whole no-wand thing?"

"That's one way to put it."

"Well, I've been collecting these when I can in case they're useful." She extended the canister she'd used to store the wands she'd taken.

He opened it and grinned. "There may be one in here that would fit the bill. But, generally, I prefer guns."

"Why?"

His grin stretched wider. "Any fool can throw people around with telekinesis. Bullets take skill."

She flicked the container with a bolt of power, tumbled its contents into his lap, and stood. "Now you have something to entertain you, skill-boy," she snarked and stalked off in a dramatic huff.

Rath chose that moment to return, stared at them both, and shook his head in the same manner as a despairing parent would. Humans would never, ever, make total sense to him.

The crowds began to gather a half hour before the listed protest time. Kayleigh fed images from their own sources and local news to the team's glasses. They showed a diverse number of people carrying a wide variety of signs. As the group had managed to put a name—Stuart Young—to the lawyer's face behind the fearmongering, it was merely a matter of weeding out the Remembrance plants from the concerned citizens.

The next twenty minutes were more of the same, albeit with larger crowds as the people closed on the Cube from all directions. A street-level shot from the facility's cameras showed the office building illuminated by decorative floodlights, the epitome of corporate America. Unfortunately, it hadn't managed to hide the prison beneath for nearly as long as they'd intended.

Kayleigh's voice was energized, and Diana pictured her striding around the core, reviewing data sources, and interacting with several computers at a time. The thought brought a smile to her face despite the gravity of the situation. "All right. I see patterns in the crowd's movement. Most notable are two suspicious groups incoming from north and west. I can't get close enough for facial recognition for fear of spooking the crowd, but they seem to be traveling together and in larger numbers than any other group on my scans."

"Got it," Diana replied.

Bryant added, "Essentially what we expected." She looked at him and had to admit it was strange having him along. There was a certain out of sight, out of mind advantage at work. Switching back and forth between regional SAC and BAM field agent didn't seem to be a problem for him, though. His fingers drummed on the trigger guard of his carbine as he waited and scanned the data in his lenses.

Kayleigh's voice took on a note of concern. "The bigger worry looks like it's coming from the east." The feed shifted to a drone in motion, presumably under the tech's control. It rocketed forward, then paused and hovered with its camera centered on a pack of Kilomea moving from rooftop to rooftop. Diana counted eight in total as they crossed hand-over-hand on a line strung from one tall building to the next.

"You know, if that drone had a gun, you could probably shoot that rope right out from under them," Tony said matter-of-factly.

"I wasn't lying when I said they weren't armed, detective."

Cara added, "Maybe the warden's drones?"

"I don't have control over them, and her people made it clear that they were needed for their own protection." Another window opened, and they could see the scene from the Cube's hardware, which hovered high above the main routes. The feed homed in on three smaller drones that flew lower and seemed to prefer stealth rather than overt action.

"Okay, so they belong to either the Remembrance or the protestors," Dianna said. "What are they doing with them?"

"My best guess is data collection for possible prosecutions if things go bad. Since they're located on the way in, rather than around the facility itself, they can fly a little lower."

Diana barked a laugh. "So, what, it's okay to get the

crowd riled up before they're all gathered together, but not when they are?"

"Apparently," Bryant replied.

She refocused on the feed. One of the Kilomea had noticed the drone and held a knife in his hand. Her mind corrected—*huge knife*—when she remembered that although they looked normal size in the drone's view, they were far from it. The image the feed caught before it went black was that of the blade spinning toward the drone with wicked accuracy.

Kayleigh was irate. "Shit. I do *not* have an endless supply of drones. You make sure to smack that guy at least once for me."

They laughed, and the overhead drone camera replaced the lost one. Diana asked, "What's the timing?"

"The big guys will arrive immediately before the others. My estimation is less than a minute's difference."

Diana shook her head. "No coincidences. Alert SWAT and the PD about the ones to the north and west. They'll want to be ready in case they do something crazy like threaten the crowd. They should try to funnel them toward the office building where we can deal with them." She looked at Bryant and saw her own worries on his face. "In fact, Kayleigh, tell them they should consider pushing the protestors back while they can. That's a lot of potential firepower coming in."

Diana, Bryant, and Rath moved into position. The floor was essentially a wide central area with five offices along each side. Diana had chosen an office on the left as she faced the lobby, and Bryant had chosen the same office on the right. Rath had stationed himself one room back from her in a good position for a surprise attack if she were forced to retreat. She lowered to one knee and aimed her rifle at the entrance. Bryant would do the same on the other side. She triggered her mic. "Floor B, what's your status?"

Tony replied immediately. "We're hiding out in cubicle land, with overwatch on the stairwell."

"Waiting is boring," Cara whined dramatically.

Diana laughed. "It's too late to switch, I'm afraid. If it's any consolation, if they do make it to you, they'll be fired up."

The data feeds in her glasses disappeared to avoid distraction. Kayleigh had promised eventual upgrades that would let them see heat signatures, but for now, a clear view was a better view. A single loud crash was rapidly followed by several more in the lobby, and she tensed. The doors banged wide, but no one came through. She whispered, "Contact," and received a click from Bryant followed by a quiet, "Acknowledged," from Cara and Tony.

A single Kilomea entered. She ducked into the office as he checked the first one on her side. She delayed, hoping to hear another enter before she revealed herself. Another *click* sounded over the comms that she took as Bryant's signal that the intruder was about to step out of the second office. She waited a moment longer, then leaned around the corner at knee height. Diana pulled the trigger in two sets of three and allowed the recoil to lift the barrel, and the hulking brute fell as blood spurted from his wounds. His dying shriek shattered the stillness, and more creatures burst through the doorway.

Rifle fire roared from her right as she rose to add her

carbine to the assault. In a sight that had to be seen to be believed, the Kilomea intercepted the bullets with improvised shields. It looked like they had broken the heavy guard desk apart and carried large sections of it in front of them. Most of the agents' barrage was deflected, and what did manage to penetrate didn't stop the enemy's progress. The ones with the barriers angled toward the BAM team. Both humans backpedaled ahead of the advance.

Diana shifted her aim to their feet, but the two closest managed to bring the furniture down hastily to deflect. Bryant tried firing across at those nearest her, but the one near him interposed his shield to protect them. They were both forced to evade when the advance guard hurled the pitted chunks of desk at them. Bryant ducked back into an office, while she rolled into the center. True, it made her an easier target, but she didn't want them too close to Rath.

She thrust up from her roll and fired into the kneecap of the lead Kilomea on her side, but the second one was on her almost immediately. Normal-sized beings flooded through the entrance behind the brutes, some with rifles and others without.

"Watch the door," she shouted as she ducked a horizontal slash from a giant sword the brute had drawn from over his shoulder. He chopped it down at her, and she spun away. She flicked his leg with her telekinesis like she'd done to Rath in practice, but the Kilomea didn't budge. A force blast provided a follow-up to her attack and spun the blade from his grasp to fling it across the room and embed it into the wall.

Rath careened into view and landed on the Kilomea's shoulders to stab at the beast's neck with both his batons.

They sizzled, and he held them there until the monster dropped to his knees. The hulking brute's eyes rolled back in his head, and he fell onto his face as the troll pushed clear.

Diana dove, too, as a direct line of sight to her opened for a rifleman and he sprayed bullets at her. She finished her roll and brought up her own weapon to return fire, but her target was now blocked by another Kilomea, this one with long knives in each hand. *Long* long knives. She'd barely registered his presence when his giant foot delivered a kick that launched her through the open doorway of the next office to land on the desk. The Kevlar at her back took the brunt of the impact, but she sighed inwardly as she thought of the bruises that waited in her future and staggered to her feet.

Bryant drew his pistol and fired anti-magic rounds at the wizard and witch on his side of the room as a Kilomea closed. He holstered the weapon as the giant kicked at him, stepped nimbly aside, and ducked to avoid the follow-up jab. The agent grabbed its outstretched arm and delivered an uppercut to its elbow. The silver studs on his glove crackled on impact. The Kilomea looked confused as his limb numbed, and Bryant used the moment of distraction to draw his Glock again and deliver two shots into the creature's face at close range.

The body collapsed, but the man was now the focal point of three rifles. He hissed, "Scield," and his shield materialized. The bullets and magic failed to penetrate it, and he grinned as he counted down the remaining time. He repositioned, grabbed a sonic grenade, and primed it. His protection dropped as he hurled it and he raised his rifle. When it detonated, one rifleman went down, but the other two reacted in almost the worst way possible. Their fingers tightened on their triggers to spray the room on full auto.

Bryant fell to his stomach and sighted along the floor to fire his M4 at the aggressors. Two collapsed with wounded legs, and the third staggered into a nearby office. A shimmer surrounded the witch and wizard, and his bullets bounced off. He scampered for cover as a wash of flame filled his half of the room.

The sprinklers activated, and he had to grin as Diana shouted, "Again? *Damn* these people!" He ejected his rifle magazine and slapped in one loaded with anti-magic rounds.

Cautiously, he crawled forward and aimed at a wizard's torso. The mage grunted and staggered back, then straightened and released a focused cone of fire at him, which forced him to duck into the cover of an office. He triggered his mic. "Some of them are wearing Kevlar."

Curses filled the channel. Diana grumbled. "We need to find dumber enemies."

When he stuck his head out to review the situation, he had to agree. The force now advanced in an inverted V, with the riflemen in front on the outside, the wizard and witch a couple of steps back toward the middle, and a giant Kilomea in the center. The massive creature had retrieved a desk from one of the offices and carried it before him like a riot shield. Bryant wasn't sure if he intended to block with it or use it as a projectile, but both options were troubling. His eyes widened when he saw more reinforcements enter the room behind them. "Kayleigh, have they abandoned trying to break into the Cube?"

Kayleigh was slow to answer. "Affirmative."

"That's bad."

Diana had to agree with Bryant's assessment. It was time to get serious about delaying the bastards. She tripped her mic. "Five seconds, Bryant. I'll distract them while you retreat to the stairwell. You too, Rath." The troll had hidden in the office nearest the stairs after his first attack since a direct charge against the enemy wasn't a viable option. She raced from her hiding place, summoned a force shield before her, and flicked the right-hand wizard's wand away with her telekinesis. The rifles tracked her, but their fire couldn't penetrate her shield.

So this is how that feels. No wonder they like it.

She swerved to the right and felt the presence of her comrade fleeing behind her. The angles were perfect. She dropped her shield and directed a wave of force forward in a semicircle. The wizard closest to her managed to call his own shield to insulate against the attack. Beside him, the rifleman was thrown into a nearby wall that separated the room from the lobby. The other three were hurled through the windows to land in the streets outside. Panicked screams echoed as a flaming bottle sailed in to burst on the floor. She rolled into cover, away from the remaining enemy, and shoved a wet strand of hair out of her face after the sprinklers activated for a second time. "Kayleigh, trigger lockdown."

"On it," the tech replied. An instant later, heavy metal covers descended over the windows, and a massive door slammed down to block the lobby off. Heavy fists battered against the barrier with no success. The wizard hid in an office now that the odds were no longer in his favor. Diana and Bryant took the opportunity to relocate and she raced up the staircase to bypass the second level and climb to the third.

She took the moment of reprieve for the short respite it offered and breathed heavily. "Status outside?"

"It's a little rough out there," Kayleigh reported. "More stuff is being thrown at the building, some fistfights, and general pushing and shoving. The local PD has set an airspace perimeter. They're afraid any helicopters might cause panic. I think they're mainly scared of the TV ones riling the crowd. Your chopper is hovering just outside it, two minutes, plus or minus fifteen seconds, away."

"We can work with that." Bryant pounded up the stairs with a grin.

"Where were you?" Diana asked suspiciously.

He shrugged. "I left them a present." The nature of the gift became clear when an explosion roared from the bottom of the stairwell. He shook his head. "It's like rule number one. Gotta watch for traps, right?"

"Okay," Kayleigh said, "I have a large group of signatures heading onto the second floor—about two-thirds of the entire group. The rest are coming to you."

Diana sighed. Break time was over. "I guess we all get to play, then."

CHAPTER TWENTY-EIGHT

Cara inched her eyes the side of the cubicle she hid in, enough to see the stairwell through which trouble would come.

The second floor of the office building was full of squat, gray interlocking cubicles and only four actual offices, one at each corner. They had decided that the enemy would most likely expect them to take position in the small rooms, so they crouched in the central area, instead. It felt terribly exposed.

A series of explosions had rebounded from the stairs a short time before, and Cara's fingers itched for action. The metal support splint that encircled her forearm irritated her, and she tapped it absently against the desk. Finally, the time had come for action. The enemy crept in from the staircase—a mixture of humans, wizards, witches, and two giant Kilomea. That was all she was able to identify before she ducked to avoid detection.

She whispered into her comm, "There's a bunch of them, Tony."

"The plan's still good."

They'd agreed to wait until their opposition exited the stairwell, then would aim the rifles over the barriers and spray on full auto. It was a sound strategy for an opening salvo. Several more seconds passed before he said, "In three, two, one."

She extended her rifle over the cubicle wall with the trigger depressed and swept it from left and right as the magazine emptied, prompting roars of outrage and pain from the invaders. She popped the mag and replaced it with anti-magic rounds to deal with those who'd blocked her first salvo. Somewhere across the room, she knew Tony would be doing the same.

Cara remained low but repositioned and moved to a cubicle several back from where she had been. Several shouts indicated that the enemy had spread out in search of them.

This is about to get seriously messy.

She stood, assessed the scene, and targeted the witch nearest her. A triple burst dropped the woman, but the ex-marshal was forced to duck and scramble away from the electrical blast discharged by the wizard beside the fallen opponent. She leaned out and fired low, but the wall of the cubicle between them somehow interposed itself and it's metal frame deflected the bullets. The entire section of cubicles tilted and skewed, and she raced around to the far side. She crouched and caught her breath for a moment and grinned at an angry shout from near the stairwell. "There's nothing here, boss. No computers. Nothing worth taking."

A deep male voice answered, "All right. Half of you stay

with me. The rest head up to the next floor. We'll terminate these people and join you shortly."

Cara risked a look and saw the Kilomea and several others advancing on the staircase. A tall man dressed in black gestured to organize the remaining enemies in a search pattern.

Not good.

"They'll find us, Tony. Time to move to Plan B."

That involved doing something unexpected—charging the enemy. He responded with a grim, "Affirmative. On your lead."

She took a deep breath and bolted into the corridor between the cubicles and the shuttered windows on her side of the room. Without slowing, she raised her carbine and squeezed off two rounds at the person in front of her to catch him in the shoulder. His rifle barked at the same time that hers did, and three bullets burrowed into her Kevlar vest like a heavy punch. The force unbalanced her, and a wizard appeared behind the rifleman with his hands already in motion. She stumbled into a dive around the back of the cubicles as lightning seared toward her. Unfortunately, she didn't make it all the way, and one of her deflectors popped with a loud *bang*.

Dammit.

———

Tony thrust from hiding at the first sound of gunfire from across the room. A wizard directly ahead was escorted by a man with a rifle. The investigator raised his carbine, but before he could fire, a cone of flame emerged like a beam and intercepted the gun. Tony panicked, pushed the magazine release, and threw the weapon away before it could explode. He drew his pistol in a move long engrained through training in the MPs and as a patrol officer. A furious burst delivered its entire load of anti-magic bullets. The wizard ducked behind a cubicle wall, and the rifleman apparently thought it was his lucky day. He pulled his own trigger rather than make any attempt to evade. The rounds struck the enemy in the chest, three dead center, and he fell with a gasp.

Ahead, a pair of portals appeared, and a flood of the simian creatures Diana and Cara had described from the museum barreled into the area, already running. He slotted a normal magazine into the pistol and drew the Ruger with his left hand. A little calmer than he'd been before, he measured his shots carefully, one for each of the approaching monkeys as he walked slowly backward. In the MPs, offhand shooting had been a contest and he'd kept up the practice as a way to preserve the memory of that time in his life.

It served him well now, as each weapon tracked and dispatched the small creatures. After his weapon ran out of bullets and he'd reached the back wall, he cut to his right as Cara dodged in front of him and raised her rifle to finish the monkeys with precise double taps.

Tony quipped, "It's like discount-bad-guy warehouse in here." He paused to stow his Ruger and switched magazines on his Glock, as he'd opted for the anti-magic rounds again.

His partner growled her disdain as she replaced the

magazine in her carbine. "The two wizards on the left are yours. That punk from the museum is here. He's mine."

———

Cara fired a stream of bullets at the second-in-command she'd seen at the museum. He smirked when he recognized her and shouted, "The bitch is mine. Get the other one," and returned fire. She ducked into the corner office and went to ground until the hail of metal stopped. Tentatively, she stuck her head around to see him sling the weapon over his back. He grinned as he drew a pair of long knives and advanced. "How's the arm? It looks like my buddy hurt it in your last skirmish. Maybe I can finish the job for him."

She drew her pistol and stepped out, and he scampered away to hide amongst the wreckage of the cubicles in the center of the room. "Why don't you come out and play? Afraid?" she called as she stalked forward, leading with her weapon as she cleared each pile one by one.

He surprised her with a leap over a cubicle divider and used his momentum to hurl her into the steel window on the opposite wall. Her gun clattered across the floor, but she paid it no mind as she threw a kick at his knee. He flicked his left knife low in a counteraction, and she intercepted it and allowed her shin guard to take the impact without a problem. She struck with a backfist that caught his cheek. His head snapped back, but he managed to evade enough that the silver contacts didn't touch him.

Cara pursued and threw punches at his chest, but they were thwarted by the Kevlar. Her gloves sparked but failed to affect him.

Okay, nonconductive fabric. That makes sense.

The blade in his right hand licked at her and sliced a thin line along her left ear. A stray piece of her hair drifted slowly downward. She snarled and kicked at his groin, forcing him to block low, then launched a better punch at his face. This one connected cleanly, and a satisfying snap echoed as the shock gloves did their work. He staggered back and seemed dazed, and she thrust into a kick. Her adversary did the only thing he could and stepped in to catch her mid-leap, then used her own momentum to redirect her into the wall.

Cara impacted hard but landed with her balance still intact. She kicked him in the side of his knee. It buckled, and she hammered another fist at his face. He rolled away, and metal glinted as he dropped the knife and drew a backup gun that looked more homespun than factory grade. The holdout pistol fired two rounds before it jammed and burned his hand with a small explosion on the next trigger pull.

Seriously? A big, bad professional wizard like you relies on crap-cobbled shit as backup?

The first round battered her vest hard enough to shock her, and the other furrowed the flesh on the upper portion of her right arm. She steeled herself against the pain and finished her attack, stamping down on the limb that had held the pistol. The bone cracked, and the burned hand flopped limply.

"Serves you right, jerk," Cara said. She pressed the silver studs on her glove into the side of his neck. He spasmed, and his eyes rolled back in his head. She forced herself to her feet and did her best to ignore the pain in her arm.

There was no time for recovery. She had to find her partner.

———

Tony launched himself into the aisle on Cara's signal and eliminated one of the wizards with his first triple burst.

You'd think they'd have realized that the shield thing isn't reliable by now.

The other struck him with a force bolt that knocked him against the wall. The agent had barely enough presence of mind to drop and roll to evade the one that followed. Plastic, microchips, and ink spattered the air as the blow pulverized the computer monitor in the office behind him. One device in the whole damn place, and it was turned into a weapon of destruction.

He climbed to his feet, took two steps forward, and threw himself to the side to avoid the next blast.

The idiot thinks he's fancy with the extra flourishes before he shoots. All he's doing is telegraphing.

Tony wove to dodge the attacks, but his progress was slow. He snatched up a picture frame from a desk nearby. Deftly, he flicked it like a Frisbee at the wizard, who hesitated in a moment of shock before he knocked it away with a swing of his wand. The agent holstered his pistol, then stole two more projectiles from the desk and hurled them at the mage. The enemy redirected them with a contemptuous grin.

Idiot.

While the chucklehead was distracted playing tennis, Tony had made it one cubicle closer.

He swept his arm across the next desk to capture the things strewn there and threw them in series. All the while, the gap shrank more and more. His adversary finally seemed to realize what was happening and allowed a pencil cup to hit him in the head while he thrust his wand forward, his eyes wide.

The agent dropped and rolled again to avoid the force beam that disintegrated the cubicle behind him. This time, he was close enough to be able to act. He rocketed at the mage, hoping the man wasn't fast enough to track him with the wand.

When he collided with the wizard's legs and looked up into that grinning face, he smiled in response. He punched the wizard's thigh. It wasn't nearly hard enough to disable him, but the shock studs on the glove made the bastard dance as the impulses triggered his nerves. The man fell and Tony snagged his wand. Without that, his opponent seemed powerless. He added an extra kick to the side of the man's head to be safe, then resumed his search for Cara.

When the two finally located one another, she pointed at the staircase, and he nodded. She seemed to be struggling to get there, so he abandoned any thought of taking the wizard prisoner and hurried around the cubicles toward her.

It soon became clear why she had difficulty. Cara dragged an enemy along beside her with the arm that had been wounded at the Museum. His eyebrows furrowed in a question, but he noticed the blood that seeped out of her other arm. He rushed forward to offer aid, but she shook her head.

"Flesh wound. It's no biggie. Take this guy." He obeyed and she pulled a compression patch from her belt pouch. She bound it around the wound and used her teeth to pull the first tie closed while he shook his head in bewilderment.

"You're an idiot, you know that?" He threaded the other fastener and stretched it tight. She nodded and seemed about to thank him when her eyes widened. He spun to look behind him, certain that he was about to be attacked, but no enemy loomed anywhere near them. His gaze settled instead on a device that hadn't been there when they'd entered. It looked very much like a timer attached to explosive charges and stuck on the wall. Several more were affixed in a similar fashion around the room. He imagined there would be some among the cubicles, too. They all counted down with the same number and ticked past the eight-minute threshold.

Tony triggered his mic. "Boss?"

Diana's voice was soft, almost a whisper. "Go."

"It looks like they've set bombs on this level. They're not familiar enough that I'm confident I can disarm them. Plus, there's no way to know where they've put all of them. Timers on the ones I see read seven minutes and forty seconds."

Her voice was much calmer than the investigator felt. "Okay, time to put an end to this party. Meet us on four. We'll clear the way for you."

CHAPTER TWENTY-NINE

Diana watched the stairwell from the fourth floor. Her carbine was loaded with anti-magic bullets and trained on the entry as she waited for her team to push through. Bryant was ready with their remaining grenades to throw down after them to delay the enemy.

She toggled her mic. "Kayleigh, have SWAT clear the area. Warn them that the building will explode and get that chopper in here. If anyone complains, tell them they can take it up with me later. Also, release the windows." Bryant grinned at her. "Being in charge suits your tyrannical streak."

She rolled her eyes. "Quiet, you."

Kayleigh replied, "Affirmative on SWAT. They're moving, but I read a malfunction on the lockdown. Did anything happen?"

Diana looked at the steel barriers that blocked their exit. "No."

"That's not good."

"No, it isn't." Tony and Cara turned the corner of the

landing below and struggled with the body they dragged between them. Diana used her telekinesis to take some of the weight and allow the pair to move faster. Shouts echoed through the stairwell, and Bryant threw a flash-bang. It detonated and generated more shouts, and they heard what sounded like every adversary in the tri-state area pounding up the stairs.

Diana pointed Cara and Tony to the far side of the room. "Get one of those covers off. We need a window to go out." They dragged their prisoner to the wall with Rath's help and set to work. Bryant waved at her, and she looked down the staircase. He held up their last two grenades, and she nodded. He primed and threw them, but no sooner were they out of sight than they boomeranged back. She swatted them away with her telekinesis, and they detonated before they could reach the enemy.

Bryant frowned as he moved away from the stairwell. "Well, that sucked." She nodded her head in agreement and joined him in a dash to a defensive position. The floor was a giant open workspace, with tables and chairs scattered in clusters throughout and the familiar and seemingly mandatory corner offices. They managed to rearrange some of the furniture into makeshift barriers, and each crouched behind a different one.

She called, "Incoming," and Tony huddled into the protection of his own collection of junk and raised his pistol. The first wave was mundane. The troops carried rifles and fired at random to keep them pinned so the reinforcements could enter. Diana leveled her rifle barrel over the top of the bulwark, exposed as little of her head as was necessary to see the enemy, and took single shots aimed at the magic users behind them. Tony fired at the mundanes in the lead, and Bryant divided his fire between the two groups.

Their foes continued as a mixed force, which meant the team wasted anti-magic bullets on those who didn't require them. Diana's magazine clicked empty, and she rammed in her last set of the expensive rounds and fired at anyone holding a wand. She eliminated a couple, but the remainder summoned tables, chairs, and filing cabinets and used them to block her fire.

By the time the rounds were depleted, the enemy had filled a third of the room and now spread in all directions.

Kayleigh's voice was annoyingly calm. "Ninety seconds on the chopper."

Diana dashed from her cover a scant second before an enemy mage ripped it apart with a force blast. She charged the rifle-carrying woman nearest her, made sure to use her as a shield against the line of sight from the others, and snatched her weapon. Before her opponent could wrestle it back, Diana kicked her hard below the edge of her vest. The blow to the stomach jerked her back, while the rifle Diana held kept her close. She yanked down on the weapon and drove the woman's face into her rising knee, then dropped both her and the rifle to dive to the side as a blast of lightning struck the wall where she'd stood.

Bryant thrust from cover and attacked the wizards with a pistol in one hand. He whipped his offhand forward and yelled, "Get over here!" One of them unexpectedly complied, fell on his back, and slid across the room with his leg outstretched. The agent timed his play and vaulted up to land on the wizard with bone-breaking force. He kicked the wand away for good measure.

Tony was surgical with his shots. He squeezed off single rounds and exposed as little of himself as possible. Despite the other battles that raged around him, he confined his fire to those who might threaten Cara, who had opened the electrical panel for the metal window covers with her multi-tool and now hastily rewired it.

When the leader they'd last seen ducking cowardly into the vault appeared, the battle frenzy increased as if his very presence inspired involuntary violence. The riflemen renewed their relentless barrage, and Cara had to stop her work to assist their team. Diana had lost count of the bullets in her pistol, which she'd drawn after the fight with the riflewoman since she was out of anti-magic rifle rounds. She was shocked when it locked open but shoved it into its holster and sent a force blast at a distracted witch to dislodge her wand. With her other hand, she summoned a table and hurled it at an enemy who had drawn too close to Cara for comfort.

Diana growled. "Cara, get back to the window. Tony, your only job is to protect her. We'll deal with this asshole."

She noticed the detective handing Cara his backup gun but ran out of time to wonder why when Kayleigh said, "Sixty seconds to the chopper, five minutes on timers." The battle paused for a moment as the riflemen retreated to the stairs, taking only enough shots to keep the BAM agents at bay. The leader smiled his superior smile, stared Diana in the eye, and intoned, "I'm so glad it's you again." He raised his hands, and a whirlwind of furniture took flight to circle at random and hinder their ability to shoot. The bastard was delaying them. *Again.*

Bryant confirmed it. "If he stalls long enough, boom."

"Yeah, not gonna happen." Diana attacked without preamble. She used her telekinesis to subtly redirect anything aimed toward her, and every time an enemy appeared in a gap, she shoved them aside with a force blast. Still, it was slow going, and each delay made her angrier, which caused the power to build inside her. She finally reached the eye of the storm and found the leader, his right-hand witch, and another pair of magicals with wands pointed directly at her.

The shadow bolt struck her first and it was so fierce that all her deflectors shattered at once. The witch's ice blasts sought her next, but she had already rolled away by that point. Lightning crackled as she continued into the position she wanted, and her vest absorbed the spell with the staccato music of popping resistors. Once in place, she marshaled the power within, threw her hands up, and propelled a wave of force outward in all directions with a defiant yell. The leader staggered back, and his lieutenant was hurled into the wall nearest the stairs. The other two wizards tumbled in different directions, one toward Bryant and the other toward Tony, exactly as she'd intended.

I love it when a plan comes together. Heh.

Bryant only had time to shove his empty pistol into his holster before the wizard's involuntary flight brought him close. The enemy had recovered well and wrapped himself in an electrical shield of some kind that protected his landing. He whipped his wand, and the agent raced toward him. Even after his deflectors and resistors did their work, the force of the enemy's magic was still powerful enough to make him stagger, and he dropped to one knee.

He threw his magical line out and snagged his foe's feet, but the mage fired a blast of electricity, and the powers canceled where they met. As Bryant rose, another electrical attack reached him to raise a wicked burn on the side of his neck. His vision blurred. He stepped closer, and the wizard released another blast. He dropped to one knee as his grasp on consciousness faded. "Aspida. Sanitatem," he whispered, and two charms burned into his chest as they were consumed.

The first summoned his backup shield, which would protect him against anything physical and most things magical for a shorter time than the other. The second was a healing charm, which flooded his body with the magical equivalent of painkillers and kicked his systems into overdrive. He hadn't had the opportunity to secure an energy charm, so he felt depleted once the healing had done its work but was undamaged. Kienka had told him the magic could rescue him from death's door, but he'd hoped to never have to test her word.

He lunged and timed his punch to land at the same moment that his shield dropped. The studs on his gloves struck the mage's cheek, and the shock knocked his target back. He cursed and raised his wand, but Bryant didn't hesitate. The next blow struck the man in the stomach and he folded. The final delivery crashed into his temple to sweep the last semblances of consciousness away.

Bryant straightened to go to Tony's aid, but the man already had his opponent well in hand. The wizard threw shadow magic at the detective, and his suit shrugged it off. Tony responded with his gunslinger routine. He held his Glock and Ruger at the same time and fired each calmly at the mage. Then the enemy did something truly unexpected. He summoned a portal and sidestepped into it to avoid the attacks, then immediately emerged again to launch his own assault.

I have to remember that one, Bryant thought.

The distraction allowed the wizard to send in a shadow bolt that dislodged the Glock and shoved Tony's arm back. He turned the involuntary move into a quick draw and hurled the Bowie knife he snatched from the small of his back at his adversary. The wizard reacted in what seemed like slow motion and a curl of his wand summoned an oval of darkness to deflect the blade. The shield wasn't positioned right to do anything about the anti-magic rounds that pierced his thigh, chest, and shoulder, though. He collapsed to his knees, and Tony stepped forward to kick the wand out of his hand.

Rath had waited near the ceiling, crouched like Spiderman atop one of the cameras that jutted from the wall at intervals throughout the room. When the witch was hurled back, he dropped to the attack. He missed her shoulders as she toppled and growled in frustration. The troll landed cleanly and spun, drew his weapons, and swept them in an X before him. They crackled as they scraped across her chest and she shouted in pain and anger.

He brought them back and stabbed forward. The witch responded by whipping her head to the side to avoid the batons. She kicked out at him, and he swiveled so her heel caught his thigh, rather than his knee. He turned the motion into a spinning hook kick but was intercepted by a blade of ice that extended from the top of his adversary's wand. Fortunately, the sharp edge faced away from his skin, but the impact still hurt. He rolled into a backward somersault as she swiped the magical weapon at waist level. She used the delay in his attacks to scramble to her feet.

Rath sensed the enemy leader behind him and circled toward the inside of the room to avoid any surprise attacks. The witch fired a cloud of icy needles at him, and he fled, using his acrobatic tricks to spin, tumble, and otherwise evade them.

He considered growing bigger, but the moment seemed to call for agility over power. At the thought of power, he pushed the button to retract his left baton and slid it into his right holster before he retrieved, primed, and threw a pepper grenade in a continuous swing. The woman waited until it landed at her feet, then created a canopy of ice over it with a wave of her wand. It exploded, but a second gesture sealed the cracks in the cover and no damage was done.

He changed direction to careen toward her and hurled the flash-bang. He'd hoped that it would at least give him time to get close, but his canny opponent intercepted it with a ball of ice and it ricocheted to where Cara knelt by the windows. Rath sighed in relief as Tony smacked it with the butt of his pistol and forwarded it to Bryant. It detonated, but the troll looked away and his headphones protected him. The woman gestured with her wand again, and the floor became slick with a coat of ice. By now, his momentum had become too great to halt. He slipped and slid inevitably toward the witch.

Uh-oh.

Diana narrowed her focus on the enemy leader. Her fingers flexed with the desire to punch his arrogant expression down his throat. She advanced cautiously, as he seemed content to wait until the last possible second before engaging. No words were exchanged, but his eyes conveyed his lack of respect for her in particular, and for all humans in general.

I fucking hate bullies.

She threw both her fists forward and used her telekinesis to deliver a blow to his left leg and her force blast to his left shoulder. He absorbed the strikes, then twitched his wand and a nearby table hurtled at her head. She slashed with her right hand, and the projectile split down the middle as if chopped by an ax.

I'm getting better at this force thing.

He gestured to launch more items in her direction. She picked them off smoothly—redirected some, blocked others, and destroyed the rest. Her anger surged again when she reminded herself that he was toying with her. A ball of shadow formed in her hand, and she lobbed it at his face. He looked shocked for a moment, then slipped to the side and used yet another table to deflect the attack.

This stupid room has way too much furniture in it.

She used the distraction to dart in, only to circle out again as he raised his hand and eight wickedly barbed tentacles spiraled to swipe at her from all directions. Her survival reflex kicked in and she threw herself prone and summoned her force shield to hold them at bay as her mind spun through the appropriate denials.

He's a wizard. He can't do that! What the hell? That didn't come out of his wand.

Diana indulged the protest for only an instant before she resumed the battle. She waved her arm in a circle and imagined a line following it, then yanked hard. A rope of force materialized around the tentacles and drew them together.

The enemy nodded as if to congratulate her on her innovation. He banished the appendages only to call them again immediately. She deflected or avoided seven, but the eighth caught her calf and hauled her to the floor. His superior grin became more smug and she fumbled for her final grenade and threw it at him. He circled the wand to create a portal unlike any she'd ever seen. The gateway opened to a barren world and tortured screams and cries emanated from within. He flicked it into the grenade's path, and the explosive detonated in whatever world or place lay beyond the rift in reality.

He barked a command to his left, and Diana turned her head quickly. Rath slid along a sheet of ice toward the witch they'd faced before. An identical swath appeared beneath her as the tentacle yanked her harder toward the portal. Her mind gabbled briefly to remind her she did *not* want to go to wherever *that* was. She drew her Ruger with an awkward twist and aimed it at the leader, but he twitched the tentacles and one grasped her hand to make all but the last round miss. That scraped his leg and dropped him to a knee, but his magic did not fail.

Diana had nothing left and no way to eliminate him before he pushed her into the rift. She did the only thing she could think of, which was to roll and fire a blast of force in front of Rath. He made it look like that had been his plan all along when he used the barrier to stop his slide and hurl himself upward to twist in midair, strike the wall with both feet, and launch himself at the witch.

The troll grew as he powered downward and collided with her halfway to his largest size. She stumbled toward Diana. It was like watching Bryant's game of pool with Gillians. She saw the opportunity and threw all her remaining power into a force bolt directed at the woman's chest. Physics took its course, and she screamed as she was thrust into the rift. She conjured a frost rope in a last frantic attempt to save herself and tried to lasso the nearest object. The rope missed its target and glanced off her leader, instead. This distracted him enough that the tentacles vanished and the portal collapsed.

Diana slid on until she careened hard into Rath, who had met the wall and sank to the floor an instant before. The wizard turned in a fury, but at that moment, the steel barriers over the windows opened.

Kayleigh shouted, "Everyone down!" over the comm. Tony was the only one still standing, but he dropped prone as minigun rounds from the weapon mounted on the side of the Air Force chopper chattered and swept over the area as the airman sought her target.

The wizard reacted swiftly, created a different portal, and stepped through it to evade the bullets.

"Ceasefire," Diana yelled and lurched to her feet. She hobbled toward the window, followed by a somewhat dazed Rath. Black knotted lines unspooled from the chopper as Kayleigh reported, "Two minutes on the timers. Areas are clear. The warden assures me they'll be fine."

Diana grabbed Cara, helped her to the line, and threaded it around her thighs and waist in a hasty tie. "Use another one to climb up. This is your backup. Maybe you could consider not getting hit in the arm every time we go into the field."

The ex-marshal raised a single finger in salute and swung out to follow the directions. Diana helped Tony next, and he began his climb. Then, she stared at the prisoner. For a moment, she considered throwing him out the window, since it would offer a better chance at survival than remaining in an exploding building, but Rath solved her problem. He lifted the enemy onto his giant shoulder and gave her a serious nod before he broke into a huge grin.

"Get to the Choppa."

She groaned at the joke. "I'll be up right after you, big guy. Good work." He nodded and climbed easily. The additional weight was no concern at all in that form. She turned to locate Bryant, who examined one of the bombs on the far wall. "Bryant, get over here. We've gotta go."

He nodded and began to cross the room toward her

when the bomb nearest the stairwell detonated. Later, they would sift through the evidence and conclude that the battle had shorted something inside it, which caused it to detonate ahead of time. Her eyes widened in horror as the next one closer to Bryant exploded. He was out of range of the initial blast, but not far enough away to escape the debris and shrapnel launched by the massive force. She was powerless to help, and he screamed, "Go!" as his side of the building began to collapse.

Bryant gestured with his arms to create a portal as the floor buckled. She leapt out the window and summoned her telekinesis to bring two lines toward her. Once she'd seized them, the helicopter veered away from the building. The shockwave from the explosion rocked her. She held tightly to the lines, closed her eyes, and hoped they had gained enough distance that the debris wouldn't catch her.

CHAPTER THIRTY

It had been a week since the protest at the Cube and the ensuing destruction of the office building above it. The lawyer blamed it on the police, the police blamed it on terrorism, and no one had the real story—except for ARES and the PDA, who both received missives from the Remembrance claiming responsibility and a promise that it had only begun.

Bryant, miraculously, sported only severe bruising and minor injuries from shrapnel that had reached him before he managed to seal his escape portal. He left town less than twelve hours after the event to assess the other startups. Cara spent a day in the hospital for treatment for her injured arms. Even with a healing potion, it would take a little time. Tony held down the fort in Pittsburgh, and Diana and Rath split their time between their home base and DC. She'd met with Senator Finley to brief him personally with SAC Carson Taggart at her side. If either had noticed her stiff movements, they had not remarked upon them.

She felt battered and bruised in body and spirit for several days, then finally rallied. Setbacks happened, but there was no need to let them define her. By the end of the week, she was back to normal, ready to take on the next challenge. It came in the form of another anonymous text from a familiar number that simply read:

Two hours.

She called her team and arranged to meet at the exit of their tunnel to the Kemana. The three agents made their way to the palace without incident and were ushered into the presence of the lady at the appointed time. Diana detected a warmth in the emissary's tone and expression that reassured her about the meeting to come.

Lady Alayne was in her customary place on the dais in the throne room. She inquired about their health and about the events of the week before. Diana, Cara, and Tony related them as well as they could. When all had been recounted, the leader of the Kemana said, "We have heard from our sources that the Remembrance has emerged from the shadows."

Diana nodded. "They took responsibility for the attack. It's merely a matter of time before the press hears about them. *That* should be a mess."

The elf laughed. "What is it the computer people say? Information wants to be free?" She shook her head. "They have one thing right, though. It is difficult to keep secrets these days."

"Very true. Have you had any problems with them down here?"

The emissary leaned over to whisper in her ear, and Lady Alayne nodded. "No events, but a definite increase in conversation. We are always watching and listening to what goes on in Stonesreach, and their message does resonate with some of our citizens."

"Many?"

The elf shrugged. "More, perhaps, than any of us would like. Of course, talk is fine. Only actions are an issue."

Cara spoke up. "But the one often leads to the other, does it not?"

"It does, indeed, Cara Binot." Alayne nodded. "We will remain vigilant."

Diana hesitated, then ventured, "Lady Alayne, should something occur here, would you be comfortable calling upon us for aid? Because we most certainly offer it."

Again, the emissary leaned in to speak into her ear. She frowned but the expression seemed a little regretful. "At this time, we prefer to handle our own affairs. Rest assured, though. Should that change, we will let you know."

She nodded outwardly but sighed internally.

Dammit. There goes asking them for help with our problems. Still, it was worth a try. "May we be of assistance in any other way?"

The elf shrugged. "No, but thank you. We merely wished to meet to ensure that we share what knowledge we could with one another. As always, please do not feel the need to await an invitation. If you are in the city, you may contact my emissary, and he will arrange a meeting if the matter requires it."

Diana thanked her, and the older elf escorted them from the throne room. Before she let him push them out the doors, however, she stopped and turned to him. "One of my colleagues told me I needed to get in touch with Nylotte. Could you tell me where to find him?"

The emissary tilted his head. "Interesting." He didn't explain what he meant, only provided them directions, and they left the palace.

His instructions led them onto the side street they had found during their previous visit, and a creeping dread began to build in her stomach. It grew as they counted the number of shops, then fully materialized as they stopped outside the one owned by the Drow who had intercepted them the previous time. Diana groaned.

"You should probably stay out here." They didn't argue, only took up positions to watch in both directions. She shook her head and muttered, "Bryant, you're a dead man," as she swung the door open and stepped inside.

The shop was filled with surfaces made of polished wood that reflected the lights above. The items on them seemed to glow from an inner source that wasn't quite obvious. She had been in the room for less than ten seconds when Nylotte—very definitely a her rather than a him—swept in from the back. Her voice was syrupy. "Diana, *so* nice to see you again."

She pushed down the flippant reply the woman's words summoned. "You as well. You were recommended by Kienka, through an intermediary, as a source of equipment for my team."

The elf smiled and gestured for her to sit across a low table, then took the other seat. "Yes, Kienka. We were close once and came to Earth at the same time. She has chosen to be a greater part of your world. I have no interest in that and prefer to live here among my own kind."

There aren't really many of your particular kind around, though, are there?

"Why did you leave Oriceran?"

Her laugh emerged from deep in her throat, and Diana imagined that it too, like her looks, would turn heads. "A brazen question. Let's simply say it was an opportune time for a change, and leave it at that, shall we?"

Diana nodded, unfolded the paper she'd brought, and slid it across the table. The Drow reviewed it with an experienced eye. "Most of these items can be procured easily. Others, I already have. A few will be difficult, and thus expensive." She looked up expectantly.

"Give me prices, and we'll work from there."

The woman smiled. "In some cases, I may request items in barter rather than currency. I believe that Kienka also operates in this way. Hopefully, that is acceptable."

Diana had the distinct impression that if it wasn't, they wouldn't do any business at all, so she nodded.

I'll figure that out when we get there.

The Drow leaned back, folded her arms, and gave her a knowing look. "But that is not the only reason you are here, is it? Even without this list, you would have found your way to my door."

The agent sighed. It was true. She had discussed it with Bryant, and he had worked his contacts only to discover that she was the best option. "Yes, Nylotte. I would like you to train me in magic."

The Dark Elf straightened with a nod. "Before I will even consider it, I must test you."

She forced her voice to remain calm, even as her body tensed instinctively. "How?"

Nylotte waved an arm. "Simply a game we play with our children on Oriceran, Diana. I give you my word that you shall come to no permanent harm. If you will not take mine, remember that you are under the protection of the lady while inside Stonesreach."

The woman had a point. Diana nodded, at least partially reassured. "Okay, what do you need me to do?"

The Drow held up her palms. "You have heard of pushing hands, I'm sure?"

Diana was aware of the game where two partners placed palms together and attempted to flow with the other player's actions. She held her hands up, and the elf placed her elegant fingers a centimeter away. The woman began with a push—either force or telekinesis, but Diana couldn't be sure. It was easy enough to resist with her left hand and press with her right.

Nylotte nodded, then switched magics. Shadows coalesced around the elf's hands and stretched to encompass hers. Diana reached for the feeling she'd had the other times she'd controlled shadow and drew power from the Drow to reflect it back to her. The next change was to fire, and she yanked her hands back with a screech of pain. "Ouch! Damn, what the hell?"

The elf stood and looked at her with something between mockery and disappointment. "Don't be a child." She opened a nearby drawer and pulled out a vial filled with red fluid. "Drink this."

The agent looked doubtfully at her, and Nylotte made a gesture toward the palace that lay beyond the walls of the room. She drank, and the liquid flowed through her in a cool surge to heal her burned skin and banish the pain. It

AGENTS OF MAYHEM

cost her to ask, but she did it anyway. "Will you accept me as a student?"

Nylotte nodded. A serious expression graced her visage for the first time since Diana had known her. "Yes. I understand your schedule is challenging, but you must commit to both training with me and on your own if you wish to succeed—*especially* given what you face."

Diana tilted her head. "What do you mean?"

The elf laughed and tossed her head-turning long hair. "Events are in motion, Special Agent in Charge Diana Sheen. You are well known among a certain set of individuals in the community. Individuals you might prefer did *not* know you so well. As I said, the sooner we begin, the better."

"I'll do whatever it takes. Tomorrow?"

The elf nodded. "Noon."

"How long?"

"Until you can no longer go on, of course." She shrugged. "That is how it has always been, and that is how it always will be."

She escorted Diana outside and closed the door behind her. They had not discussed a fee for the training, but she was sure it would be high in both treasure and effort.

And likely blood, based on the little I've seen of her.

To the others, she said, "We have ourselves a supplier. On to the next to-do item."

CHAPTER THIRTY-ONE

T he team had survived the long walk back from the
Kemana to the base and collapsed in the fifth-floor
conference room to enjoy the day's fading light. They were
all seated around the big oval table, Diana on one side,
Cara and Tony on the other, and Kayleigh and Rath on the
ends. Max stretched out under Rath's chair. Each had
coffee, except the troll, who had a pineapple juice box.
They had finished sharing information about the visit to
the underground city with the two who hadn't accompanied them.

"Okay, let's look at the to-do list." Diana turned to face
the tech. "Item one, force our newest member to stay,
whether she wants to or not." Sounds of agreement came
from the other side of the table, and Rath declared, "No
leaving. I am the law."

Kayleigh grinned. "I told you, I'll be here until you get
your act together. Right now, it's anything but. You don't
even have a proper lab, for heaven's sake." They nodded,
having agreed not to pressure her in any *serious* way.

Cara said, "I withdraw my suggestion that we need a med tech right off the bat. Recent events have demonstrated that there are enough hospitals around that are well-equipped to handle trauma. Healing potions can only go so far. Unless we can find someone to specifically assist with injuries from magic, it's probably not worth making it a priority."

"Does everyone agree?" They nodded. Diana looked at Rath and thought again that they needed to learn more about how to take care of him.

Maybe Nylotte will tell me. She snorted inwardly. *At the cost of one arm and half a leg, no doubt.*

She crossed the med tech off the list. "So, what do we need next?" She wanted to let her team weigh in on the important decisions, even though she had the final call. "DC has a couple of long gunners and a number of general agents, plus a face." She grinned as she remembered Trent's first attempt to weasel his way in with her and Lisa at the bar.

Cara and Tony frowned. The detective asked, "A face?"

Diana nodded. "Someone who's good at infiltration and who can slip in and out of a wide variety of situations to get information. And, of course, they need to be able to kick ass."

Nods and murmurs of agreement passed all around the table. The ex-marshal tapped a finger against her teeth. "I wouldn't have thought of this before our last adventure, but it might be good to have someone proficient in explosives."

She hadn't considered it either, but it suddenly made a

lot of sense. "For offense, or defense? Like, demolitions expert, or bomb squad?"

Cara nodded. "Yes."

They all laughed, and Rath interjected, "You don't mess with the demolition man."

Diana turned toward Kayleigh. "Thoughts?"

She shrugged. "It's not a bad idea, and you're under no pressure to copy DC exactly. The needs are different here. At home, we have to assume the need to lock down areas, like at the hotel. There's not quite so much of that here since it's not the center of government."

The others nodded, and Diana said, "Any counterarguments, speak now. Otherwise, we'll look for experts in infiltration and making things go boom."

None were forthcoming. "I'll do some searches and find you some names. They'll be ready tomorrow," Kayleigh promised.

Diana smiled at her people. "Okay, everyone, get some rest." She pointed at Tony and Cara. "Soak those legs. Who knows when we'll be called back to see Lady Alayne?"

They groaned loudly at the thought of another trip to the Kemana.

Ninety minutes later, she steered the Fastback through the curves that climbed Mount Washington, possibly faster than strictly necessary. She hadn't eaten at any of the restaurants that dotted its crest and looked forward to the new opportunity. The car slipped cleanly into a parallel parking space on a side street, and she walked down the sidewalk. Diana smoothed the constricting black V-neck dress that extended to mid-thigh, where her matching pants showed over her knees before meeting the high black boots that zippered closed below them.

Her hair was piled on top of her head in a messy bun, and she wore a silver necklace that matched the shining illusion detector on her wrist. The ARES smartwatch was hidden under her long sleeve, and she carried a sparkly clutch a little bigger than the Glock resting inside it. She laughed to herself.

I should look into a thigh holster for some flat knives or something. Having only one weapon makes me feel unarmed.

Bryant stood outside the restaurant and grinned at her approach. He was dressed in gray—another tailored suit with a black pattern flowing through the fabric. This one had no tie but a mock turtleneck that looked very attractive on him. He held the door for her, and she entered. The lobby was a reminder of times past. The elegant chandelier and wood accents painted a picture that would've been perfectly modern fifty years before. Windows covered the entire length of the far wall to reveal the cityscape sprawled below them. She turned and smiled. "Nice place."

The host intervened and took them to their table, and Bryant sat with his back to the view so she could enjoy it. He grinned at her again. "You did say I owed you."

"I had thought of a beer and a burger, not this."

He raised an eyebrow. "Beauty deserves beauty. That's a pretty dress, by the way."

She laughed. "Did you have a good week out of town?"

"Not too bad." He shrugged. "Things are moving ahead. We'll be ready to put people on the ground in Buffalo next week, and the others are coming along."

"It seems they picked the right person for the job."

"ARES is good at that, based on how well the bureau is working here. But how are *you* doing?"

She sighed. "Honestly, I knew I'd miss DC, but it's harder than I expected. I recognized that Lisa was an important part of my life, but I didn't realize quite how much I depended on her for relaxing downtime. It feels like this place is always hopping. Hopefully, things will settle down soon."

Bryant shook his head. "That's not likely. After all, you've been adopted by a troll."

They laughed and chatted about non-work stuff over a good meal and a bottle of wine. Once they had shared a dessert, they stopped in the bar for a nightcap. Bryant raised his scotch and clinked her glass of bourbon with it. "To the successful launch of ARES Pittsburgh."

"BAM Pittsburgh," she clarified as she tapped his glass in return. He laughed.

He has a nice laugh.

She set her tumbler down. "Oh, before I forget." She opened her clutch and scrabbled through the few items in it to find the folded sheet of paper. She slid it across the bar to him. "My team's needs. Read away, moneyman."

He unfolded it and groaned. "Okay, a lot of this makes sense. But you do *not* need a semi-trailer."

Diana grinned. "Oh, yes we do. And here's why."

The story doesn't end here. Diana and FAM's adventures continue in <u>Counter Ops</u>.

The story doesn't end here. Diana and FAM's adventures continue in Counter Ops.

AVAILABLE FOR PURCHASE HERE

CONNECT WITH TR CAMERON

Stay up to date on new releases and fan pricing by signing up for my newsletter. CLICK HERE TO JOIN.

Or visit: www.trcameron.com/Oriceran to sign up.

If you enjoyed this book, please consider leaving a review. Thanks!

AUTHOR NOTES - TR CAMERON

MARCH 28, 2019

Again, thank you.

Thank you for reading the second book in the Magic Ops series, and for continuing on to the author notes! I hope you had as much fun reading the story as I had writing it.

The response to the first book has been fantastic, and thank you especially to everyone who has left a review! Those are beyond helpful.

But I have a confession to make.

It's difficult to admit.

It's about Rath.

I mentioned in the notes at the end of Magic Ops that this series is my first author collaboration. I had the core of an idea, and then Martha and Michael got into the mix and made it so much better.

They added the troll. I would never have been so bold, after the abundant love for YTT. They also suggested he should be an action movie fan. I thought it was a great idea, of course.

What I didn't realize was how much fun he was going to be to write.

Because, seriously, Rath is a hoot.

He's more or less taken on a life of his own, and I don't know ahead of time what adventures he's going to get up to with his faithful steed, Max. I only know that he'll find a way to win, because, as Thor has wisely shared, "That's what heroes do."

I'd like to be serious for a moment, if you'll indulge me. Another truth is that I am incredibly lucky to have the opportunity to partner with such a creative bunch. The positivity they share is always amazing and occasionally overwhelming, and it's all because of the attitude that underpins everything they do: we can all rise together.

I've always been a team player, and I believe in this principle right down to the core of my being, deep in the tasty marrow of my bones.

Wait. Ignore that last part. I've said too much.

So, Anyway...

The BAM team is coming together nicely. Book three will add a couple more agents and really dive into the trouble that awaits them all. I hope you'll join me for that adventure!

Quick media notes: Captain Marvel, saw it with my daughter and we both loved it; Spiderverse, loved it; and Avengers: Endgame, am actively fearing the heartbreak that's on its way. Oh, and Netflix folks, watch Love, Death, and Robots, "Three Robots." You'll be happy you did.

You know, maybe Rath should start asking Diana for a cat, too.

Until next time, Joys upon joys to you and yours – so may it be.

AUTHOR NOTES - MARTHA CARR

APRIL 8, 2019

I played my first game of Dungeons and Dragons this past Saturday night with a few author friends (and one civilian). Right up front I have to thank author pal, Charley Case for being the very patient Dungeon Master to so many newbies.

"Okay, tell me again, what's this for?" And then about five more questions... He answered them all like a champ and without the slightest sign of irritation. He should have ten kids, at least, with a patience streak like that.

A few important things I learned about playing D&D...
1. If you're 59 years old don't start at 8 pm because it won't end till 1 am at the earliest. Somewhere around midnight I realized I could fall asleep in my chair against my will. And my only narrative became, who can I kill to get out of this place. Although what other people started shouting when it was their turn was super amusing. Exhaustion and enthusiasm will do that to you.

2. A Ranger is a cool character to have unless you never leave the bar. Most of my skill set was for tracking or

seeing in the dark. Not much to track in one room (where the game was set this time) and author pal, Claire Taylor kept setting things on fire, so that ruled out that dim light skill I had.

Despite any of that I had a blast! Can't wait to do it again. It was like an urban fantasy novel brought to life and I wondered what took me so long to get there.

3. When I first bought this dream house, I thought it got that title because of its size and a lot of cool features. Turns out I was wrong. Sitting there, bleary eyed around the table, I realized it was a dream house because it easily holds so many people having so much fun, all the time.

Stay tuned – I'm determined to get out and do more things too since I retired from the day job. Next up, found an adult Easter egg hunt at night with flashlights. The Offspring is going, per usual, along with a few others. I'm also signed up on another day to make my own medieval sword. Seems I've found my inner nerdette and she's alive and kicking.

More adventures to follow.

AUTHOR NOTES - MICHAEL ANDERLE

APRIL 17, 2019

THANK YOU for not only reading this story but these *Author Notes* as well.

(I think I've been good with always opening with "thank you." If not, I need to edit the other *Author Notes*!)

Thank you to you guys for making this series such a phenomenal success. ;-)

FAN'S NOTES - Where a fan helps me out with THEIR love of reading and we learn a bit more about our fellow readers out here!

Fan Name / Pen Name and Location

Kurik from Darlington England

About how many books do you read a year, or total in your lifetime?

200ish a year. (ok, that's more than I did when I read a lot - Mike)

Name your favorite LMBPN Series or Character(s) and what you like about them.

Barnabas, the quiet and satirical yet wholesomely violent one.

(Mike: BWAHAHAHAHA! "Wholesomely Violent One" - That needs a t-shirt ;-))

If you made up an LMBPN Character, what would be three attributes you would use? (For Example, Bethany Anne is Justice, Family (including friends), and Coca Cola. Brownstone is Keeping it Simple - Respect - and BBQ)

Honesty, fidelity and gin.

Tell us a few short sentences about yourself, and your reading hobby (When did you start reading, why, how much do you read and preferred genre's etc. (as ideas)):

Started in the school library at 7 and have not stopped. Fantasy was first then scfi and military stuff. I read when I can to relax. It's good if the book is informative and uses good English as I can learn as I enjoy! (Mike: Hats off, my cursing must make you crazy to figure out WTF I am saying.)

You can have my <what?> before you can have my reading time.

Food. (Mike: That's hard core.)

Place you have loved to read the most in your life - best memories (mine was as a teenager at my grandparents house under the feather bed on cold days.)

On the Yorkshire Moors, in the sun listening to Sky larks, curlews and cuckoos whilst tucking in to a good tale. (Mike: I thought for a minute I was going to have to edit this one :-o)

AROUND THE WORLD IN 80 DAYS

One of the interesting (at least to me) aspects of my life is the ability to work from anywhere and at any time. In the future, I hope to re-read my own *Author Notes* and remember my life as a diary entry.

Five50 - Pizza Bar in Aria Hotel, Las Vegas

I just had to review hundreds of hot female warrior images from Google and Pinterest to find a pose for a new series… A bit embarrassing since I'm at the bar where all of the servers walk by and some of these images were NSFW.

Geez, my cheeks are red.

FAN PRICING

$0.99 Saturdays (new LMBPN stuff) and $0.99 Wednesday (both LMBPN books and friends of LMBPN books.) Get great stuff from us and others at tantalizing prices.

Go ahead, I bet you can't read just one.

Sign up here: http://lmbpn.com/email/.

HOW TO MARKET FOR BOOKS YOU LOVE

Review them so others have your thoughts, tell friends and the dogs of your enemies (because who wants to talk with enemies?)… *Enough said ;-)*

Ad Aeternitatem,

Michael Anderle

**JOIN THE ORICERAN UNIVERSE FAN GROUP ON
FACEBOOK!**

BOOKS BY MICHAEL ANDERLE

For a complete list of books by Michael Anderle, please visit

www.lmbpn.com/ma-books/

All LMBPN Audiobooks are Available at Audible.com and
iTunes. For a complete list of audiobooks visit:

www.lmbpn.com/audible

Made in the USA
Monee, IL
01 August 2020

37399467R00194